KINO

A Novel

Jürgen Fauth

An Atticus Trade Paperback Original

Atticus Books LLC
3766 Howard Avenue, Suite 202
Kensington MD 20895
http://atticusbooksonline.com

ISBN-13: 978-0-9832080-7-5
ISBN-10: 0-9832080-7-7

Typeset in Palantino
Cover design by Jamie Keenan

"Art is free. However, it must conform to certain norms."

Joseph Goebbels
Hotel Kaiserhof, Berlin
March 28, 1933

Chapter 1

Mina stumbled and fell headlong into her apartment, smacking her knees and the palms of her hands on the hardwood floor. She bit her lip, cursed, resisted the temptation to cry. Rubbing her bruised joints, she turned to see what had tripped her.

Just inside the door sat a pair of metal cases, knee-high, hexagonal, green-grey, a sticker centered on each with Mina's name, unabbreviated, the way nobody ever used it. The label was handwritten in blocky capitals, with a peculiar choice of preposition that made the canisters seem more like presents than parcels: FOR WILHELMINA KOBLITZ.

Mina sighed. She reached for the keys and mail she'd dropped and picked herself up. She had spent the entire day at NYU hospital, where her husband Sam was ill with dengue fever. He'd caught the tropical disease on their honeymoon, which they'd cut short immediately after the resort doctor in Punta Cana diagnosed him. "Bad luck," the doctor had said. The disease wasn't exactly rare, but there also hadn't been an outbreak in years.

They'd been back for three days now and the marriage was off to a rocky start. The reception had been a disaster, the honeymoon was ruined, and Mina was beginning to resent the long hours at the hospital. This was not how she had envisioned her new life. She spent as much time with Sam as she could, reading in the uncomfortable plastic chair under the glare of the fluorescent lights while her new husband tossed and turned, his eyes glassy, moaning and sweating through his pajamas. In his brief lucid moments Sam complained about the pain in his limbs, the heat, the all-too-real nightmares. Even when he slept, the moaning didn't stop.

Dengue fever could be fatal, but the smug New York doctor had assured Mina that Sam would be fine. He told her to go home. It could be another week before the fever subsided, and she should take care of herself, rest. Mina thought the doctor was too eager to touch her arm. She was attractive, a little short but busty. Men tended to under-estimate her.

The Greenpoint one-bedroom seemed smaller to Mina than ever. They had lived together for almost a year before getting married, and now the apartment was a mess, every open space crowded with wedding gifts–blenders, toasters, sheets, and silverware. The kitchen counter was covered with unopened mail. She hadn't unpacked their suitcases yet.

FOR WILHELMINA KOBLITZ.

Belated wedding presents from a distant relative? The last time she'd heard her full name had been at her college graduation, almost four years ago.

Mina pushed aside a stack of magazines and lifted the canisters onto the kitchen counter. Picking one at random, she popped its twin latches and opened the lid. Inside were four reels of film.

She opened the second container. Three more reels, kept in place by a jammed-in Styrofoam wedge. Sturdy plastic held black celluloid wrapped around the center. Wasn't this stuff flammable? Mina pulled a reel out of the case. She set it on the counter and wheeled it around until she found the end of the film strip, locked down with a pin that held the sprocket holes in place. She carefully unwound it, thinking how odd it was that even though her grandfather had been a filmmaker, she'd never held celluloid before.

Oh, she thought.

Did this have anything to do with her grandfather?

Mina had never known the old man, a German director who had emigrated to America during the Second World War. He'd made one big flop in Hollywood that still showed sometimes on late-night cable. All his German movies had been lost, and he'd killed himself before Mina was born. Her father refused to talk about him.

The celluloid in her hands was entirely black, and Mina kept unrolling it, unable to stop. She tried to wrap it around the fingers of one hand and turn the reel with the other, but the film kept slipping off. She let it stack up on the counter into a loose loop that curled on its own. After two more revolutions she hit a logo, something like a coat of arms. Then, white words on black: the credits. She held the film up to the neon kitchen light, but the letters were too small to read. She kept unwinding it further, and some of the celluloid slipped off the counter and onto the Swiss espresso machine they'd gotten from Sam's boss. The words grew bigger until there were only two lines, and now she could make out letters, repeated on every advancing frame:

EIN FILM VON

KLAUS KOBLITZ

Into the empty apartment's silence, Mina made a surprised noise not unlike her husband's feverish moans. She was holding in her hands one of her grandfather's lost films.

Chapter 2

Subject: Please Don't Hate Me
From: mina.koblitz@gmail.com
To: samiam@eclecticarts.com
Date: Saturday, May 10, 2003

Oh baby. I want you to know how horrible it felt leaving you in that hospital bed this morning. Your doctor assured me that the worst was behind you, and I'll be back in three days. I promise. We set up a screening for Sunday, and then I'm flying right back to you. I tried to explain, but you seemed pretty far gone and I don't know if you caught any of it.

I came home last night to what looks like one of the movies my grandfather made in Germany before the war. There were no stamps and when I asked Mr. Palomino who'd brought it, he shrugged. A "messenger boy" who'd made sure he put them inside the apartment. I talked to somebody at the Museum of the Moving Image, and she gave me a number at UCLA and I ended up talking to a guy at the Kinemathek in Berlin, Dr. Hanno something-or-other. He had the worst accent and he was rude, too. I'd forgotten about the time difference and woke him up. But you should have heard him when I mentioned my grandfather's name. Suddenly I was royalty. He asked me all kinds of questions about the film, the condition it's in, the reels, the cans–apparently they're called "cans"–and he asked me to measure the width of the celluloid, and how far from one sprocket hole to the next. He got really worked up. He thinks it's *The Tulip Thief*, my grandfather's first film, made in 1927.

That's a big deal if it's true, Sam. All of his German movies were lost, or at least that's what we thought, and suddenly, there's one sitting in the hallway of our apartment in Greenpoint. I asked how much it'd be worth, but he didn't want to say.

Now here's the thing: it's an old kind of negative, and it's in a weird format, something called *Doppelnockenverfahren*. It's like the Betamax of film. You need special equipment to show it, and the only remaining projector that can handle it is in Berlin at this film museum.

You see? I feel like shit for leaving you and coming over here, but I hope you understand. If this is for real, it's worth a *lot* of money. Maybe enough for a brownstone with a little garden where we can drink our coffee outside. I could pay off my student loans. Lucy and Josh promised they'd come and visit you every day. I haven't told my parents–my Dad's probably still mad about the wedding, and grandfather is a touchy subject with him anyway. Well, I guess everything's a touchy subject with him.

I left in such a hurry this morning, Sam, I simply grabbed my suitcase from the trip. I hadn't unpacked yet, so why not just take it, right? Wrong. It's fucking *cold* here and I don't even have a coat or a pair of warm shoes. Instead, I have three bathing suits, my mask and snorkel, and a pair of fucking flippers. I'm such an idiot. I guess it's all been a little much. I don't even speak German. Getting here was awful, too: they made me take off my shoes again at security, and there were five babies on the plane. I counted. Five. I took a Xanax and drank some wine but there was no way I could sleep. My mind kept spinning. Now I'm completely whacked and it's not even noon. Technically, we're still on our honeymoon. We should be making love in the honeymoon suite, drinking piña coladas, and snorkeling in the clear blue water.

Get better quick. Call me.
I love you,
Mina

Chapter 3

The man from the film museum, Dr. Hanno, walked into the hotel lobby at precisely 5 p.m. Seventeen o'clock, he had called it on the phone. He was younger than Mina had expected, handsome, barely thirty. He had short blond hair, wore rimless glasses, and carried a leather backpack over one shoulder. His last name was Broddenbuck, and when he said it he eyed Mina conspicuously as if he expected her to make a joke. She didn't know what was funny and just looked back at him blankly.

Mina was wearing a cotton skirt, T-shirt and a denim jacket, and right away, she went into a monologue to explain her unseasonable outfit–the aborted honeymoon, the dengue fever, her cluttered apartment, the reels, and the suitcase–the stupid suitcase she didn't think to repack.

"Until I can shop for warmer clothes," she said, suddenly worried that she was speaking too fast for the German. His expression was blank. "Is it okay if we stay here? If this lobby's no good, we could go up to my room?"

Dr. Hanno lowered his eyes and fidgeted with the car keys in his hands. He was flustered.

"Oh, I am sorry," Mina said. "No funny business—I'm happily married." She wiggled the fingers of her newly-ringed left hand at him, but that only made matters worse. "Frau Koblitz," he said with a stilted German accent. "I made reservations at a restaurant. We were going to have dinner and talk about your grandfather, no?" Mina sighed. Flexible this guy wasn't. There was a cool draft and she was getting impatient. In fact, she was freezing cold standing in the damn hotel lobby. Outside, Germany seemed impossibly cold and gray. She didn't know what she was doing here, when she was supposed to be with Sam. "Isn't there anything we can order in? If you come upstairs, you can take a look at the movie."

Dr. Hanno's confidence returned at the mention of the movie. "Yes," he said. "With pleasure. Do you like Turkish food? I could pick up something and return?" Mina grinned her best grin. She could take control of the situation. "Meet me upstairs," she said and gave him the room number.

He came knocking on her door with food, two fat triangular sandwiches wrapped in aluminum foil that reeked of garlic.

"I've never eaten one of these before." Mina sat on the edge of her double bed, unmade and still warm from her jetlagged afternoon nap. Dr. Hanno sat in the narrow chair by the coffee table next to the window. Mina was hungry. The shredded lamb was delicious.

"My mother doesn't approve, but I live on *Döner*," he said, watching her eat. She had not waited for him. "Don't you have Turks in New York?"

"I grew up in Connecticut."

Dr. Hanno gave her a blank look. He cleared his throat. "So you brought..." *Döner* in hand, he eyed the room. On the floor by the bed, next to the opened suitcase spilling T-shirts, beach towels, and a pair of flip-flops, sat the two metal containers. "Ah!" he said. "*Jawoll!* May I?"

Mina nodded, wiping a smear of yogurt sauce from her face. Dr. Hanno, who was already hoisting the cans onto the table, amused her. With quick, familiar movements, he unlatched them and removed the first reel. He threaded the celluloid through his fingers with studied precision and held it up against the light.

Mina had no patience. "Is it real?"

Without taking his eyes off the film, Dr. Hanno slowly nodded. "Naturally, we'd have to run some tests in the lab, but just from looking at it, I can tell you that film in this format hasn't been produced in over sixty years. It's a nitrate print that shows clear signs of advanced age. We won't be able to know about wear and tear, possible damage, missing parts, and so on, until we've looked at it more thoroughly. From what I can tell, it's astoundingly well preserved. Dirt, dust, scratches, and tears seem to be minimal, and it doesn't look like there has been much shrinkage or fade."

Now he took his eyes off the film to look at her. "Do you understand what this means? The value is incalculable."

"I like the sound of that," Mina said. "I've got staggering student loans to pay off." The truth was she thought that she'd exaggerated the worth of the movie in her email to Sam. How many people were really buying DVDs of 75-year-old silent films? Sam had a high-paying job as a game designer and insisted that he didn't mind paying off her debt—but she felt like an idiot for ever starting law school in the first place. She had been trying, she figured out only after dropping out, to please her father.

Dr. Hanno looked at her as if she were speaking a language he didn't understand. "I wasn't talking about money. I am talking about cinema. Preservation, the cultural heritage of the tenth art! I am not talking about money. I am talking about Kino!"

Dr. Hanno kept surprising Mina. She understood he loved movies, but this sudden fervor was intimidating. Clearly, he was a man who wouldn't have hesitated for a second before leaving a feverish lover behind in a hospital room in order to watch a movie. What was her excuse?

"Kino," Mina repeated.

Dr. Hanno smiled. "It was your grandfather's nickname, before the war. The *Wunderkind* of Neubabelsberg. Everybody called him Kino."

"Oh. It means the movies, right?"

"Yes, from *Kinematographie*. You didn't know?"

Mina felt herself getting defensive. "My father doesn't talk about him."

"You know about his suicide, and that he made films for the Nazis, and about his leg, yes?" He had cooled down again and carefully rewound the reel and closed the can's latches.

"His what?"

Dr. Hanno held his head sideways. "His peg leg. He was missing a leg, below the knee. A childhood accident. Surely you must know this?"

Mina thought of photographs she'd seen, but she couldn't remember any of them showing her grandfather below the belt. Was it possible? What else didn't she know? Mina felt something like vertigo.

"Please, tell me," Dr. Hanno asked, "What *do* you know?"

Mina shrugged. "It's not like he was really famous. He made a pirate movie in Hollywood and it flopped. All his old movies were lost. He killed himself before I was born. My father thinks he's an embarrassment."

"Well," Dr. Hanno said. "In film histories, he is usually considered a 'minor émigré filmmaker,' but he was a real *auteur, avant le mot*. An encyclopedia entry will tell you that he was born in Königstein near Frankfurt in 1903 as the son of an industrialist, and that his 1927 debut *Tulpendiebe* made him the youngest writer and director in the history of Ufa studios. Marriage the same year, eight more movies in Germany, five of them during the Third Reich."

"So he really did work for the Nazis."

"Well," Dr. Hanno said. "Ufa was brought under the control of the propaganda ministry – technically, he was still working for the studio, not the party. There really wasn't a choice if you were going to make films. Unless you left."

"Which he did."

"Right, but he didn't emigrate until 1943, which brought significant problems entering the U.S. He settled in Santa Monica and worked as a screenwriter. Bouts with depression, public drunkenness, run-ins with the law, drug addiction. Throughout the 1950s, occasional work in television commercials. He made one last movie in 1963, *The Pirates of Mulberry Island*, his only American film. It opened on September 10, 1963. The next morning, he was found dead 'by self-inflicted gunshot wound.' Survived by his wife Penny and son Detlef."

"My father."

"Yes, of course." Dr. Hanno was watching her. "And what about your grandmother?"

Mina shrugged. "You know more about my family than I do. She's batty. Father can't stand her. We went to visit her once for Christmas, and it was a nightmare. She threw things at me. I was frightened."

Dr. Hanno studied Mina carefully. She wiped a smear of garlic sauce from her chin.

"None of Kino's German work survived. No screenplays, no work prints, no set design sketches, nothing. All we have are contemporary sources—newspaper notices, advertising, press releases, and reviews—to give us an idea of what his movies were like. Even from the scant evidence, it is clear that your grandfather was a polarizing figure. The reviews of his early films, especially *Tulpendiebe*, were either terrible or over-the-moon raves. Later, this changed." He pointed to his backpack. "I brought a few—maybe I can translate for you?"

"Of course."

Dr. Hanno pulled out a folder and rifled through a stack of papers. "From what we know, *Tulpendiebe* is a love story set during the tulipomania, in the seventeenth century."

"The what?"

"The tulip craze. In those days, Holland was a major economic power, and people were speculating on tulip bulbs. It was the original bubble, and your grandfather used it as the backdrop for a romantic love story. As a trend, expressionism had largely run its course by 1927, and there was a new taste for realism called '*neue Sachlichkeit*.' But from what we know, *Tulpendiebe* is more of a fable, shot entirely in the studio, and Kino was accused of relying on outmoded tricks. *Film-Welt* called it 'worthless escapism.' 'Cloudcocooland,' one headline said. *Filmkurier* attacked it for getting historical details completely wrong and even pointed out that the film was 'questionable, botanically speaking.' Worse, in the politically charged atmosphere of the time, nobody agreed on what it meant. There seemed to be a message to it, but none of the extremists liked it: the Freikorps paper *Deutscher Sturm* noted that it was done in the 'American style' and called it a 'shameful call for class warfare.' The communist *Rote Fahne* said it was 'bourgeois' and 'likely to distract from the true struggle.' Moderates and socialists worried that it was reactionary and anti-democratic. Here's *Licht-Bild-Bühne* from August 6, 1927: 'With his first cinematic feature *Tulpendiebe*, young director Klaus Koblitz has given us a cheerful fairy tale that is certain to please nobody but children, dimwits, and certain French Dadaists. The plot is hair-raisingly absurd and ludicrous. Next to the profound artistic works of talents such as Carl Meyer and Fritz Lang, it appears like an infantile prank.'"

"Ouch," Mina said. It pleased her, though, to know that here was a scholar, this Dr. Hanno, who knew so much about her grandfather. What if, instead of the drunken loser her father made him out to be, her grandfather had been an important artist after all? Someone to be proud of? Dr. Hanno seemed to think so.

"We also know that the film was a success. 'A poetic dream of a movie, lucid and full of meaning,' *Berliner Zeitung* wrote, and there were many more reviews like it. Later, people would call him a visionary and, briefly, here and there, a genius. The public liked it, too—*Tulpendiebe* did well enough financially, and your grandfather continued to make movies until he left the country."

There was a pause. Their eyes met, and Mina knew they were both thinking the same thing: did the other films survive, too? Somebody had kept this one all these years— why not the others? Mina shook the idea off, exasperated. "Why was I sent this? Who wanted me to have it? What am I supposed to do with it?"

Dr. Hanno leaned forward and spread his hands over the cans like a magician casting a spell. "Have you told anyone else?"

Mina shook her head. "Just you, somebody at the film museum in New York, and a professor at UCLA film school.

And of course Sam, my husband, but I don't think he really understood. His fever is so high. Too high."

"So you'd say word got out?"

It hadn't occurred to Mina to keep the film a secret. She shrugged. She did not want to feel guilty for one more thing.

"I suppose word got out."

"Your husband is ill," Dr. Hanno said. It wasn't a question. He was prompting Mina. She told him the name of the disease but he looked at her blankly.

"Our honeymoon was ruined. We should be on the beach right now."

Mina was tired. She wondered why she was telling this stranger so much. She felt an overwhelming need to brush her teeth, wash the garlic taste from her mouth. She wanted this conversation to be over. Sam's fever wasn't any of Dr. Hanno's business. Though she had just told him about it, hadn't she? She needed to sleep.

"You came here to screen the movie without your sick husband," Dr. Hanno said, explaining it to himself. He looked up at her. "Congratulations."

Mina nodded, not sure what he was congratulating her for. Her marriage, or her dedication to Kino? All she wanted was for him to leave, but Dr. Hanno had one more thing on his mind.

"I have arranged a projectionist for tomorrow morning at the museum. Would it be okay if I watch with you? I would very much like to see the film."

"Of course," Mina said, irritated by his good manners. "Why do you think I called you?"

After Dr. Hanno left, Mina cleaned up the remains of the Döner dinner. She wanted to call Sam at the hospital, but it was the middle of the night in New York. She took a small bottle of vodka from the mini bar, poured it over ice into a plastic cup, and drank it quickly. She lay on her unmade hotel bed and missed Sam. He'd always been the one who had gotten sick, from the time they'd met in Mr. Domino's art history class. Sam was a digital artist, and she had already been skipping out of the law curriculum. Their first winter together, he spent weeks in bed with the flu, and when Mina came to visit they had sex between his damp sheets while he sniffled and blew his nose. It hadn't bothered Mina then.

But the dengue fever was the sickest she had ever seen anybody. It scared her, seeing Sam delirious, out of his mind with an overheated brain, and if she was honest with herself, she was glad she didn't have to be in that room with him anymore. In sickness and in health, those had been the words during the ceremony. Mina hadn't paid much attention at the time.

She felt the vodka work on her head, her muscles. *"Kino!"* Dr. Hanno had said, holding the brittle celluloid between his fingers, as if that explained anything. She wanted to laugh at his enthusiasm, but his passion for the movies made her feel better about her own curiosity.

Mina wanted to go home, to be there when Sam's fever broke, but first she needed to see her grandfather's silent movie. Somebody had picked her, had decided that she, Wilhelmina Koblitz, should have it, and now she had to see for herself if it was any good.

Chapter 4

Subject: Jesus Fuck Piss
From: mina.koblitz@gmail.com
To: samiam@eclecticarts.com
Date: Monday, May 12, 2003

I'm cold, confused, and wide-awake, and I can't fucking believe what happened.

Don't even bother reading this email whenever you get it – stop reading and call me. You still haven't called me. The nurse refused to wake you even though it's a reasonable hour where you are. She said your fever is unchanged. Jesus Christ. Shouldn't you be better?

Since I can't talk to you, typing to you is the next best thing, and explaining things might help me figure them out, anyway. And there's nothing much I can do until the sun comes up.

This day's been awful from the start. First thing this morning, I went downstairs to find something to wear, and the smug receptionist tells me, "*Fräulein*, it is Sunday, and according to the law, stores are closed today all over Germany." As if I am stupid. So I'm still wearing my skirt, and it's even colder today.

Back up in the room, there's a message on my phone. I'm hoping it's you but instead I get "Mina, this is your father. Call me as soon as possible. It's urgent." And then he gives his damn phone number like he does every time. A minute later, he called again, so I picked up, feeling sheepish because I hadn't talked to him since the disaster at the reception. Dad knew something was up, and when I told him I was in Berlin he suspected it had to do with grandfather right away. He might be a class A prick, but my father's not an idiot. He kept dropping pregnant pauses, so I told him the whole story. Stupid and I knew it, but I am a terrible liar.

He immediately started yelling about lawyers and copyright and protecting the family's interests. "Don't let anybody near the film, don't let anybody see it, don't let anybody handle it, and definitely don't screen it!" For a second he sounded like he was getting on the Concorde, but then he must've remembered some important business meeting, and he was like "you come home this very minute."

I haven't taken orders from my father in years, but he tries. I told him I'd stick to the plan and come home on Monday. I had to hang up because he wouldn't stop shouting. He called back but I didn't answer.

Dr. Hanno sent the projectionist to pick me up, an ugly man called Frank who didn't offer to help with the cans. His little eyes darted every which way, and all he said was "*Guten Morgen.*" The streets were wide, with tall old buildings and the occasional bombed-out church. Construction everywhere you look, and graffiti like before Giuliani. Dr. Hanno was waiting for me at Potsdamer Platz–picture downtown Hartford, all glitzy boring skyscrapers and a ridiculous glassed-in courtyard. He had three guys in suits with him.

"Frau Koblitz," he said, sheepish, "the gentlemen from the museum board respectfully ask to see the movie."

They had short white hair, square European executive glasses, leather suitcases. Given the right circumstances, they probably projected power and wealth; to me they looked like pathetic corporate functionaries. I can't remember their faces.

"You've got to understand, young lady," they said, "we simply couldn't miss the opportunity."

I had just hung up on my father and I definitely wasn't going to get bullied by a bunch of old Germans. I told them no. "Out of the question."

"We are sorry?" they said. One of them was playing uncomfortably with his tie, another had a cell phone call on hold.

I said, "I need to protect the interests of my family."

Dr. Hanno appeared flustered. "These gentlemen are members of the board," he repeated, like that was going to make a difference to me. I told them I could just pack up and go back home, no problem. Dad would have been proud of me. They were angry, clearly, but they decided to play nice. They smiled and mumbled something about understanding perfectly and shuffled off.

But Dr. Hanno was worried. "It's always better to accommodate the gentlemen from the board," he said.

I'm sure that kind of thinking is how he got to be director of the Kinemathek at his age.

"How did they know about *Tulpendiebe?*" I asked.

"I had to file a special request for using the facilities on a Sunday."

"So you'd say word got out?"

Dr. Hanno looked ashamed, and he didn't speak while we rode a glass elevator up to the screening room. We sat in the back row, leaving one empty seat between us. Dr. Hanno gave a signal to the projectionist, who peeked out of the booth with his beady eyes, the lights went down, and the movie started. The only sound was the hum of the *Doppelnocken* projector and Dr. Hanno's breath – there was no score and no piano player. It was just us and the images.

Between Dad's call and the old men from the board, my mood was shot. Before, it had almost been a fun quest, you know, finding a special projector back in the old country, talking to important professors, the mystery of it all. But Dad really upset me, and those men in suits pissed me off. It was cold in the screening room, and I could feel a headache coming on. *Young lady,* that's what they had called me, and I already wished that I'd been more rude.

Anyway, the movie.

I don't know what I expected, honestly. Something ponderous and silent, German expressionism or whatever. It started with the logo I'd already sort of seen in our apartment, holding the film up to the kitchen lights. Then, a pair of huge eyes: a close-up of a little girl, staring straight into the camera. Her father, whose face we don't see, Peanuts-style, is reading her a bedtime story. The cover of the book he's reading from supplies the title credit: *Tulpendiebe.*

Right away, Dr. Hanno started to whisper to me like a real-life DVD commentary track. How back in the twenties, framing devices were all the rage, *Dr. Caligari* being the most obvious example. He translated all the intertitles, even the one that said "Holland, Anno 1636."

The main part of the movie is set in a picturesque Dutch seaside town, canals and fields and windmills and so on, but it's all done in the studio with painted backdrops, making it look stylized, like a kid's book, with extras in clogs and bonnets and pantaloons. Fake, but sort of charming. Would have been better in color.

The story is about an acrobatic young sailor, a strapping fellow from out of town who is arrested because he mistakes a precious tulip bulb for an onion and eats it for lunch, along with his herring. You see, there's this tulip craze in Holland and people are speculating on them for ridiculous amounts of money. The sailor is brought before the Duke, who is losing his grip because he is worried about his sick daughter. A villainous merchant known as the tulip notary is really in charge and advises the Duke to send the sailor to prison.

There's a big trial scene with a lot of speechifying that was especially annoying because there was a triple delay: first, the actors mime talking on screen, then the words are displayed in German, then Dr. Hanno translates for me, and that's when I can finally put it all together. They say stuff like, "He is the one who stole the tulip!" I repeated that one out loud because it was so absurd: "He is the one who stole the tulip!"

Get this: Dr. Hanno shushed me.

Somewhere around here I'm starting to wonder. Guy gets arrested for eating a flower? This is what I came to Germany for? The best thing about the movie was the Duke's beautiful daughter, Lilly: wispy blonde hair, porcelain skin, giant saucer eyes, kissable lips. She's suffering from a mysterious wasting disease. Naturally, the sailor falls in love with her on first sight, and I kind of did, too. I feel like I've seen the actress before. She looks out of place, almost like nobility, like Cate Blanchett or Katherine Hepburn maybe.

In jail, the sailor meets an Englishman who is also locked up for stealing a tulip–he dissected it out of scientific curiosity. They escape and go to the tulip exchange together, which is this place where people are speculating in flowers like it's the stock market. Among the crowd on the trading floor, they meet the Widow Gustafson, an old woman who is trying to convince people not to trade everything they own for a tulip bulb. She shouts, "Your prosperity is based on an illusion!" but nobody listens. As it turns out, she is the widow of the explorer who first imported the flowers from Constantinople, and hidden away back at her house, she has actual tulips in bloom. There was an elaborate montage of close-ups showing the flowers from every possible angle. I have to admit, they looked pretty good, even in black and white. So, the widow, the sailor, and the Englishman conspire to end the tulip craze. The sailor's in love with the Duke's daughter, Lilly, and somehow he figures out that he can heal her with the tulips. He rips them up and eats the petals and it makes her laugh.

It's possible that I napped for a little while at this point. I remember a lot of sneaking around and subterfuge and intrigue, and somehow the sailor, the widow, and the Englishman cause a run on the tulip exchange. Everybody is trying to sell their worthless tulips. The tulip notary deploys soldiers to keep order, there's rioting, and he flees with all this gold to a windmill. Of course there had to be a windmill, right?

The sailor and the tulip notary fight, somehow the windmill catches fire, and there's a big conflagration. At one point, the sailor is hanging from the burning, spinning blades. The people who have lost everything in the tulip crash come marching up, the windmill collapses, and the sailor jumps to safety while the tulip notary gets crushed under the flaming ruins. The townspeople just stand and watch as he dies, screaming. It's a really graphic moment, the guy pinned under the burning piece of wood, twisting and turning in agony as he dies.

The sailor, the Englishman and the widow distribute the tulip notary's gold to the townsfolk and order all the tulip bulbs to be planted. In the end, the windmill is rebuilt in a big field of blooming tulips, and everybody lives happily ever after. Then you see that the man reading the book to the little girl in the framing story is the sailor–he's married to Lilly, they've got a daughter, and they live in the windmill. The end. That's it.

When the lights came up, Dr. Hanno was euphoric, his face and neck covered in red splotches. He was gushing: "Incredible, just incredible. The visual storytelling anticipates Cocteau and Welles. For 1927, for a man of his age, your grandfather's grasp of the possibilities of cinema was astounding. History books will have to be rewritten. If we can show that DeMille and Abel Gance saw this movie, we will have to reevaluate their innovations." And so forth.

Had we watched the same movie? I told him that I didn't like how Lilly didn't get to do anything whatsoever. First she was sick and then she had a baby. Not much of a feminist role model. I'd seen grandfather's pirate movie, so I suppose I had no right to be disappointed. I could see that Dr. Hanno wanted to talk more, defend the film and make me understand its brilliance and so forth, but I felt pissy and deflated. This is what I left you for? I grabbed my canisters from the projectionist and told him I'd be in touch.

Dr. Hanno turned all serious and official, standing between me and the door: "*Frau* Koblitz, I have a serious request to make. In the name of the institute, and in the interest of film history, I would like to ask you to leave the reels with me. *Tulpendiebe* casts the entire pre-war history of German film in a new light. It anticipates some of the most daring motion pictures ever made. Careers will be built and dissertations written on what is in those cans. If anything happened to this print, the loss would be inconceivable."

I told him it couldn't be so bad since he thought the film had been lost all along. Somebody had sent it to me, and I wasn't about to leave it with anybody else for any reason. Besides, my father would definitely kill me. I took my cans, pushed past him, and said *"Auf Wiedersehen"* to Dr. Hanno Broddenbuck.

Back in my room, I tried to sleep but no luck. I'd made such a mistake coming to Berlin. *Tulpendiebe* won't make us rich, and instead I've blown a bunch of money on airfare. Who had sent it to me, and what was I supposed to do with it? I closed the curtains and lay in the darkened room and thought about the fate of the tulip notary, trapped under the burning log. What a horrible way to die. It had looked so real, completely out of place with the rest of the movie. Hours later, it still gave me the chills.

I shouldn't have left you alone in that hospital bed.

Eventually, I fell asleep with the TV on CNN Europe. In the middle of the night, I was suddenly wide awake again. I called the hospital, but the nurse said you were getting more tests. She said you were worse.

Worse???

I went to the mini bar for another drink when I noticed the sliver of light by the door: it wasn't properly closed. I distinctly remembered locking it. Right away I knew. I had left the canisters on the table where Dr. Hanno had eaten his Döner Kebab the night before, and now they were gone. They are gone. The cans are gone. The movie, it's gone. Somebody came into my room and stole it.

So I figured I might as well write down everything while it's still fresh in my memory. It's 6 a.m. now, and I should probably call the *Polizei*. I dread it. I don't speak the language and everybody in this country looks at me like I'm a freak. Please please please call me as soon as possible. I'll send this epic email now. It felt good writing it. Once I hit send, I'll be alone again.

The motherfucking cans are gone, and I miss you like hell. I will make this up to you.

All my love,
Mina

Chapter 5

In Sam's fever dream, he was clutching a machine gun on the bridge of a metal-plated steamboat, squinting into the thick, humid Caribbean fog, listening for the sounds of Korean gunboats. Sam recognized the ship; he'd spent the weeks leading up to his wedding designing it. As a 3D artist for Eclectic Arts, the radical computer gaming outfit, he was part of the team that created the environments for an action-adventure game set in a post-apocalyptic world ravaged by environmental catastrophes. Players had to survive torna-does and mutants, searching for a safe haven to begin a new life. Ever since he'd gotten sick with the dengue fever, Sam's dreams had been set in the artificial universe he'd helped construct. The goal of this part of the game was to cross the Gulf of Mexico, which was infested with sharks and pirates, on a retrofitted, rechristened riverboat known as the Snatch. In Sam's dream, it looked even more realistic than in the next-gen console versions of the game.

In fact, his dreams were much too realistic–the sweat, the burn of the cheap gin the survivors drank once they ran out of molten Key West hail, the stench of the rotting shark sashimi they were forced to eat. But even when the ship's doctor threatened to amputate his gangrenous foot, Sam preferred these dreams to the dreary reality of the hospital room. Here, he knew what came next: the Snatch was about to be attacked by solar-powered pirates. He reloaded, held his breath, and waited for the voice from the fog bank: "Prepare to be boarded." There was the pop-pop-pop of machine gun fire, and his face slammed into the deck.

Sam opened his eyes to a close-up of his father-in-law, Detlef Koblitz, leaning over him close enough to smell the musk of his aftershave. It took Sam a moment to readjust to this reality. He had been losing track of time, spending longer in his dreams than in the hospital room where his tortured body tossed and turned. His skin had broken out into a rash, a "classic symptom," as the doctor had noted with a certain degree of satisfaction. He had sweated through his hospital gown. His throat was parched, his heart was beating hard, and an IV drip itched in his wrist. The hail storms and armored riverboats seemed no worse than this.

Detlef was shaking him by his arm.

"Sam, can you hear me? Sam. We need to talk."

For a moment, Sam wondered if he could simply pretend to be too sick to talk. Detlef Koblitz was a stickler for manners, and his relationship with Sam was based on a carefully adjusted display of camaraderie. Mina's parents liked Sam because he earned a real income and they thought he had a "stabilizing effect" on their daughter. Detlef wouldn't be shaking his sick son-in-law if he wasn't seriously upset. Sam eyed him. The last time Sam had seen Detlef was at the wedding reception.

"I was sleeping," he said. "I'm not feeling so good." He reached for a glass of water from his bedside table. Detlef didn't notice and didn't hand it to him.

"How is the fever?" Detlef asked. "I'm sorry to say it, but you look terrible."

"If this is about the wedding—" Sam said.

"Oh no," Detlef shook his head, too far, as if he'd been waiting for this cue. "Don't worry—everything is forgiven."

That's rich, Sam thought. After all, it had been Detlef who had first brought up Iraq, even though he knew how passionately Mina and Sam were against the war. In fact, that must have been exactly why he did start talking about it: the day before the wedding, President Bush had landed on a battleship and given a victory speech, and Detlef couldn't keep himself from mentioning this "triumph." Mina had laughed a very unbridelike laugh and said something rude about the President's tight flight suit. Then one of Sam's hillbilly uncles chimed in about "those idiots on the left" and how they never knew when they'd lost. The war was a success, freedom was on the march, and everybody who refused to see that hated America. "Present company excluded," the uncle said with a grin that made Sam's skin crawl with anger. Sam and Mina had attended peace rallies and marches even before the invasion, and they had kept up with arguments against the government's shifting rationales. They knew not to trust Colin Powell and the *New York Times*. The night the bombing started, Sam had come home to find Mina crying in front of the TV, where Shock and Awe glared in the night sky over Baghdad. At the reception, Sam tried to laugh it off, but he couldn't help getting upset. Why were these people, his family, gloating about this transparent political theater? Voting for Bush was insult enough—they didn't have to rub their faces in it. Not at their wedding.

"Mission Accomplished, my ass," Sam had said, and it escalated from there. Sam was laid-back and forgiving, but once the tipping point was reached, his anger was formidable. He washed down the rest of his champagne, reached for another glass, and launched into a rant about international law, Scott Ritter, the looting of the museum, Halliburton's no bid contracts, the Supreme Court's blatant partisan intervention in the Florida recount, and the lunacy of waging war on an abstract noun. Detlef said something about results speaking for themselves, and then it got personal.

"You and your kind," "Red-state half-wits," "Good thing it doesn't matter what any of you kids think in Brooklyn."

There was out-and-out yelling, one of the bridesmaids actually spit at Mina's father, and when the hillbilly uncle got the band to play the Star-Spangled Banner, Mina lost it for good. She climbed up on stage and went punk-rock on the lead singer's guitar, breaking the neck and kicking in one of the stage monitors.

Sam hoped they'd laugh about it in time, but it was much too soon for that. When the feedback noise abated, the guests found themselves standing around in an embarrassed silence. Everybody had said something they regretted. Sam and Mina, who were packed to leave directly for their honeymoon, got their ride to the airport early. Over a round of stiff drinks at the bar at the gate, they agreed that they'd done the right thing: nobody was allowed to spout offensive bullshit at their wedding. They had done their duty for peace, love, and democracy.

Mina lifted her martini. "Osama bin Laden ruined our wedding!"

Sam shook his head. "I blame Bush."

Mina was determined to ask her father for the money the band wanted for the destroyed equipment, but Sam knew better than to bring it up with his brand new father-in-law. Instead he just nodded. Everything was forgiven.

Detlef was still holding Sam's arm. "Have you heard from Mina? Have you spoken to her? She's in Berlin. I have left her a number of messages but she hasn't called me back. Do you know what's going on? Have you heard from her?"

So that was it. Detlef had gotten wind of Mina's blitz trip to Germany. Sam wasn't up for this, didn't have the strength to defend her. He sighed. "I don't know. The nurse told me I slept through a couple of calls yesterday. I might have an email from her, I don't know." The game was behind schedule and he was supposed to stay in touch with Eclectic Arts over the honeymoon, but the idea of an inbox full of desperate business emails about textures and polygon counts horrified him.

"Would you mind checking?"

"Fine," Sam said and reached for his silver notebook computer. "It'll take a minute to boot. Why? Is something the matter?"

"I know all about the mysterious reels and her rushing off to Berlin. She left her husband in the hospital. Her curiosity got the better of her. She was always a spontaneous girl. Unpredictable. Don't you feel terrible that she just left you here?"

"No," Sam said, trying to sit straight so he'd be eye level with Detlef. "What is she supposed to do here? It's just as well she doesn't have to see me like this."

It was true: Sam didn't blame Mina for going. He'd always thought that it was cool that Mina had a grandfather who had been a filmmaker. Not too long ago, he'd watched *The Pirates of Mulberry Island* on AMC while Mina slept. In a way, having her leave on a harmless adventure was a relief. He'd felt guilty for ruining their honeymoon, for his part in the fight at the wedding, for making her sit in the hospital chair while he thrashed around in this fucking bed with this fucking fever.

But that didn't mean Sam would have done the same thing. He'd always suspected that he loved Mina more than she loved him—or at least that's what he thought until he asked her if she'd marry him and she said yes. Regardless, it had been her independence, her energy that had attracted him to her in the first place. Mina wasn't afraid to act on her instincts, and he admired her for it.

His head hurt. It felt as if his brain was inflamed. What could he say to make Detlef leave? "She's talking to experts, and she's flying back today. I'm not worried."

Detlef Koblitz pulled up his chair and leaned in even closer. He angled his head conspiratorially. "Sam. I don't understand what she's trying to accomplish over there. Everything she wants to know about her grandfather, I can tell her. Anything at all. It's not a pleasant story. My father, the great director, was a complete failure, in every conceivable way: as a filmmaker, father, husband, and as a human being. He worked for the Nazis, he failed his family, and finally, he shot himself in the head. He snuck out like a coward. What else does she need to know?"

Detlef Koblitz was getting agitated. In his sticky bed, Sam squirmed, trying to find a less awkward position. He had not known Mina's grandfather had been a Nazi. Had she?

"When Mina's grandparents brought me into the world, they were already broken. They wanted me to fix something in their lives, and when I couldn't do that, they made me suffer. The great misunderstood genius withdrew, hiding behind projects that never materialized. Whenever I saw him, he was ranting about the *Scheissdreck* they were calling cinema nowadays. I hated the old man for acting that way and I hated my mother for letting him. You should have seen the fights. You can't live like that, pretending pipe dreams can keep you afloat. 'Art,' they called it, but that was just a disguise for their self-absorption. I was thirteen when his big pirate movie flopped. The one that was going to change everything. It was pathetic. Mina has to forget that movie and come home. Nothing good can come from digging around old tragedies."

Sam didn't know what to say. He had a high fever. He was sick. He had never seen his father-in-law this worked up. He wished Mina were there, just to keep Detlef away from him. "Don't you want your wife?" Detlef asked. "You're sick and alone. I hate seeing you like this."

Sam pointed at his laptop. "There are two emails from her."

"Read the last one first," Detlef said, leaning forward. He rested his elbows on the bed. Sam resented this intrusion into his space.

"Ah, it's the feverish groom!" A booming voice came from the door: the doctor, horn-rimmed glasses impossibly low on his nose. "And you must be the father?"

Detlef wasn't getting up. He nodded at the doctor and angled the computer his way. "If you don't mind," he said, tapping the mouse pad.

Oh, I mind, Sam thought, but the doctor was reading his temperature chart. "We're entering the last bump in the biphasic pattern. You're getting a little worse before you'll get better, but you're on track. We'll have you back home with your lovely wife by the end of the week." He glanced around at Detlef in the guest chair. "Where is she, anyway?"

"On her way home!" Detlef said, triumphantly. "Without the goddamn movie!"

Sam nodded to himself. Mina was coming home.

Chapter 6

Mina raced through concourse B of Berlin-Tegel on the back of an electric cart, about to miss her flight. The cops had driven her crazy with their forms and TV show English and in the end, they had promised her nothing. Hotel robberies were not uncommon, they said, and really, *Fräulein*, they had to be honest: stolen items were rarely recovered. One of them had mumbled something about Turkish immigrants that Mina didn't even want to understand. Dr. Hanno had been answering questions in the next room, and he looked terribly upset. He just waved at her weakly; there was no hint of smugness in his demeanor. She had expected just a little bit of *Schadenfreude*, a little bit of "I told you so," but the film historian was clearly grief-stricken about the loss of *Tulpendiebe*. Behind his glasses, his eyes were red, as if he'd been crying. Dr. Hanno had been on Mina's list of suspects—after all, he knew exactly where she kept the canisters, and he seemed desperate to get his hands on them—but now there was no doubt in her mind. He was heartbroken.

A Mercedes cab had taken her to Tegel at breakneck speed. Her flight was only minutes away from takeoff. Cruising down the airport corridor on the cart, Mina seethed with anger.

She was angry at the German police who didn't care that she might miss her flight, angry at the check-in woman who had forsaken any pretense of friendliness and actually rolled her eyes before calling the gate and commandeering the cart. She was angry at the hospital nurses for not letting her talk to Sam, angry at Sam for being sick and getting worse. She was angry at her father for thinking he had any right to tell her what to do with the movie, the movie that had been sent to *her* and which was *hers* to lose. The movie she had promptly gone and lost. Most of all, Mina was angry at herself for bringing the wrong clothes, for coming to Berlin for a shitty silent movie, for not leaving the film with Dr. Hanno. She was angry at Dr. Hanno for being so fucking heartbroken.

The airline employee by the gate motioned for Mina to run down the connecting tube. The airplane door closed with a hiss as soon as she boarded. The other passengers shot her dirty looks. The plane pushed off from the terminal before Mina managed to grab a *Herald Tribune* and settle into her seat next to a man reading *The DaVinci Code*. She wasn't looking forward to another nine hour flight, the second one in three days, but at least she was going to be home again, reunited with her husband, her apartment, and her clothes. She dug in her bag for a Xanax and bit it down dry, the bitter chemical taste filling her mouth. Distractedly, she glanced over the headlines—"In Baghdad's Anarchy, the Insane Went Free"—put the paper down, and leafed through the airline magazine to see what the in-flight movie would be.

Then she realized that the plane had turned around and was docking at the gate again. People were craning their necks to see what was wrong. The announcement came in German. Mina watched as people sighed and began to close their books and magazines.

"English, please," she said out loud, unable to contain her frustration. "For God's sake." Mina was angry at the Germans for speaking German. "Folks," the captain's voice crackled over the intercom, this time in English. "I am terribly sorry, but federal regulations require that at this time, we deboard the plane for a routine check. Please stay calm, and we'll be in the air in no time. Thank you for flying Lufthansa."

"Deboard?" Mina said to the man seated next to her. "Federal regulations? What's that supposed to mean?"

The man closed his book and shrugged. "You can't be careful enough these days."

Once all the passengers were back at the gate, a man in airline uniform made another announcement: there had been an anonymous bomb threat and the plane would have to be combed. This would take several hours, and unfortunately there were no available flights to New York today. Everybody was welcome to rebook for the next day. Business class upgrades were available at a discount.

Through the terminal glass, Mina took a good look at the plane. Was there really a bomb on it? She couldn't help but wonder if the anonymous threat had something to do with her, with her grandfather, with *Tulpendiebe*. *Oh shit*, she thought. *I'm getting paranoid. There's a war going on in the Middle East and I am wondering if the terrorists are after me.*

Through the cotton calm of the Xanax, she felt a kind of weight come down on her. Mina sank into one of the plastic seats and put her head into her hands. It was all too much, too fast, too close. She had no comfort zone left and she was all alone.

On that crisp September morning, Mina had slept late and woken up with a hangover when Sam called her. He worked on 23rd Street, in an office overlooking lower Manhattan. "Look out the kitchen window," he said, but it faced another apartment building and she didn't know what he was talking about. "Look up," he said, and that's when she noticed the plume of smoke rising above the roofs.

After the second plane hit, Sam's building was evacuated, and when the subways were shut down and the towers vanished into white clouds that seemed to cover the lower part of the island, Mina feared for Sam's life. She was so afraid for him that it wasn't until hours later, after he'd called from the Brooklyn side of the Williamsburg bridge, which he'd crossed on foot, after she'd spoken to her parents, afraid for her, that it began to finally dawn on Mina that the buildings she had watched collapse had been full of people.

Six months later, Mina had dropped out of law school and was engaged. She didn't know what mattered anymore. She just stopped going to school one day, just couldn't get herself to get out of bed, and it didn't seem to change a thing. When Sam asked her to get married, she had surprised herself by saying yes right away, almost before he could finish his proposal. Her parents, who had barely spoken to her since she'd dropped out of school, seemed genuinely happy. It had made her happy, too, made her feel as if she had a future and a purpose. It all seemed connected somehow.

But now she was alone and afraid, an ocean away from Sam.

Mina took a coupon for the Tegel Ramada and added her name to the waiting list for the first flight the next morning. Then she found a payphone and called the only person she knew in Berlin.

"You do sound a little paranoid," Dr. Hanno said.

Mina couldn't stop glancing over her shoulders. "I'd like to get out of here. Can you pick me up? I don't feel safe." "Why don't you want to go to the police?" "They're useless. They told me there was nothing they could do about the movie getting stolen, so what are they going to do about a bomb?" Mina bit her lip, wishing she'd whispered. Was that man in the long red leather jacket by the Mövenpick counter watching her?

"The police merely informed you of the statistics," Dr. Hanno said. "Burglarized property is rarely retrieved, that's a fact. You should have left the film with me."

Finally, Mina thought. A little resentment. Sooner or later, everybody got irritated with her; she was used to it. Nobody put up with her better than Sam. Sam would already be on his way. He would hold her tight and she would calm down. Wasn't that why she had gotten married in the first place?

"Please," she said. "You have to come and get me. Somebody doesn't want me to leave Berlin. What else do they want from me? They've already stolen the movie."

"You must refuse to let yourself be terrorized," Dr. Hanno said. "That's just what they want. Follow the advice of your President Bush."

Mina sighed. Was he serious?

"And what's that?"

"Go shopping. I will take you to the finest department stores in Berlin, and we will buy new clothes for you to stay warm in. I'll be outside the baggage claim area as soon as I can get there."

Relieved, Mina hung up. Maybe Dr. Hanno was right and none of this had anything to do with her. The man in the red leather jacket was gone.

Dr. Hanno drove a black Mini Cooper with a white racing stripe, and they headed straight to Friedrichstrasse, where a series of large department stores had recently opened. "Berlin is doomed to always become but never to be," Dr. Hanno said as they entered Galleries Lafayette. "Karl Scheffler said that, when the twentieth century had barely begun." He pointed. "If you follow this street down, you get to Checkpoint Charlie. Fifteen years ago, I couldn't get across. Just imagine, a whole country, like a prison!"

"You were born in the East?"

"I grew up on Karl-Marx-Allee," Dr. Hanno said. "You want to guess which part of the city that was in?"

Mina stopped to look at Dr. Hanno. He was attractive but not her type. Also, Mina was married. She did not want to know about his life, where he grew up, if he had brothers or sisters. Nor did she want a German history lesson.

Shopping, at least, took Mina's mind off things, and for a while she stopped looking over her shoulder. She picked out a pair of jeans, boots, a purple sweater and a bulky parka. A black velvet scarf. Like the plane tickets, the hotel room, and everything else, she charged the clothes to the joint account. Mina had assumed they would keep separate bank accounts, but Sam had insisted—and since he made all the money, it was hard to argue against it.

"Much better," Mina said, dressed in her new things. It was good to be warm, finally. She thought about calling the hospital and remembered the nurse, chastising her. It seemed like it was only ever the middle of the night in New York. "Now show me around this ever-becoming city of yours."

They walked down Unter den Linden, a wide boulevard lined with postcard shops that led to the Brandenburg Gate. "The wall ran right across there," Dr. Hanno said, chopping his hand like a hatchet. Mina nodded. She hadn't realized how much time she'd spent cooped up, in the hospital, in planes, in hotel rooms, and there was a normalcy to walking with this man, in new, warm clothes, that soothed her. It began to feel like the burglary and the bomb threat had happened to someone else. She almost liked Dr. Hanno.

"I still can't believe it's gone," Dr. Hanno said.

"The wall? Wasn't that over a decade ago?"

"The film."

Mina shrugged in her new parka and stroked the new scarf with her fingers. She wondered if Sam would like it. He noticed every new thing she bought. "I thought it was kind of ridiculous."

Dr. Hanno looked at her, his disappointment obvious.

"Perhaps that's true by contemporary standards, but it is nonetheless a fascinating work from a historic perspective." He made a gesture that he probably thought of as academic, like a professor at a lectern. "The film uses the tulip craze as a metaphor for the inflation, as a way to talk about the situation in Germany, which was suffering under the lost World War and the Treaty of Versailles. *Tulpendiebe* is about a group of outsiders who interfere with an unjust, doomed system. In the end, the sailor, the Englishman, and the widow restore order, but they do it through anarchy. Politically, it's a paradox: authority has gone insane and the revolutionaries want things to return to normal. The film seems almost deliberately constructed to be at cross-purposes with itself. Does the tulip notary represent the abuses of the Weimar Republic, corrupt capitalism, or the Kaiser, who was forced into exile? In current terms, *Tulpendiebe* is about a gang of terrorists who bring about democracy. No wonder reactionaries hated it as much as the communists. It's utopian without buying into any of the prevailing ideologies. It anticipates the stock market crash of 1929, but despite of all contradictions, it is optimistic and humane. Kracauer just lost the last shred of credibility."

Mina stared at Dr. Hanno, amazed that he had gotten all of that out of the same movie she had seen. "And that's in addition to 'Eisenstein and Dreyer need to be reevaluated' or whatever you said yesterday?" Mina said, smirking. "Aren't you exaggerating? In the end, the townspeople get rewarded for their idiocy. They traded everything they had for tulips, but then they get it all back, plus a bunch of gold. I don't see how they deserved that."

They had reached the Brandenburg Gate. Mina thought the iconic structure was disappointingly small. She stopped underneath the arches.

"Who do you think stole the movie?"

Dr. Hanno turned to face her. It was possible he blushed.

"You don't suspect me?"

Mina shook her head. "You're a scholar, not a criminal. But what about your projectionist? Could he have been paid off? Who would even want that movie?"

"Well," Dr. Hanno said. "There *was* some interest."

"The gentlemen from the board?"

But Dr. Hanno would say nothing else. Mina had forgotten about them, had been too frazzled to mention them to the police. Should she have? It upset her that the movie was gone without a trace, and no matter how little she cared for it or believed it could change her fortune, she wanted to know why it had appeared on her door step.

On the far side of the gate, Dr. Hanno pointed out the Reichstag, a bulky square building topped by a futuristic glass dome. "Our government moved back here recently. It is a more flexible democracy than the older American model. We have four parties in parliament, not just two, and we don't start pre-emptive wars anymore, either."

Mina bristled. Was this German lecturing her about democracy? Did he think she supported Bush? He was the one whose grandparents had allowed Hitler to come to power–but then she remembered that her grandfather had been German too, that he had made movies for the Nazis, and then she didn't know what to think anymore at all.

Dr. Hanno said he needed to pick something up at the museum, so they walked south toward Potsdamer Platz. Mina didn't care where they went, as long as they kept moving. They came across a large field of square pillars, roughly the size of a Manhattan city block. The pillars, which were made from glossy, dark grey stone, marble perhaps, began ankle high and then grew higher and higher, forming a kind of maze.

"The new Holocaust memorial," Dr. Hanno said. "The reviews were mixed. It's a colossal failure, in my opinion. It doesn't make you remember anything. Look, they're playing hide and seek." He was right–a group of kids were darting in and out between the pillars, giggling and screaming. It looked like fun.

"Let's go in," Mina said and started down a narrow path that descended into the maze. She took a few random turns, and already, she had lost Dr. Hanno.

She was surrounded by pillars in every direction. There were slight variations not only in their height but also in their angles, so that the view always shifted. There weren't any dead ends–although she was deep within the memorial's labyrinth, there were always multiple choices for an exit. She could hear children laughing. An American was taking photos of a woman posing next to a pillar. "Smile," he said.

Mina took another turn and found herself face to face with a man blocking her way. He was wearing a red leather jacket; it was the man who'd been watching her at the airport. He looked like he was in his sixties, not unkind, but intent. Too intent. Fear shot up through Mina's spine as he put a finger to his lips and lifted the collar of his jacket to reveal some sort of official symbol. "Inspector Tobias Schnark," he said. "*Bundeskriminalamt*, Division of International Cultural Crime. I'm sorry I have to contact you like this, but there's no other way." He held out a manila envelope, and when she reached for it, he took her hand and stuffed the envelope into the roomy pocket of her brand-new parka.

"This is Kino's *Tagebuch*–your grandfather's journal. Read it and wait for me to contact you again. It is important that you do not show it to anybody–not to local law enforcement, not your father, and definitely not that–" he tilted his head in a direction that presumably indicated Dr. Hanno, "–film scholar." He said it as if it were an insult. "Do not trust that man, do you understand? Do not repeat your mistakes!"

Then he was gone. Mina felt the envelope in her pocket. She tried to remember the name he'd given her, the department he'd said he was with, the government symbol he'd flashed at her, but all she could recall was his leather jacket and the piercing earnestness in his eyes.

"There you are," Dr. Hanno said, coming up from behind, a little out of breath. "Well, what do you think of this place– does it make you feel the weight of history, or is it more like a playground?"

Chapter 7

Es war einmal vor langer, langer Zeit.
Do you know what that means, Herr Dokter? It's how all the fairy tales start, the Grimm ones and the not-so-grim ones, and mine, too. That's what you want, isn't it, a fairy tale? That's why you gave me this cheap notebook and pathetic ball point pen. As if writing ever solved anything. Dr. Freud would have given me a fountain pen, something with style-he was a man of impeccable taste. His cocaine tin was exquisite, oriental, encrusted with gold like a Fabergé egg. You shuffle in here with your prescription glasses, coffee-stained frock and rubber slippers, and I want to scream.

Dokters, that's what my mother used to call the lot of you, in her thick Hessian accent. I hate you and your kind, Herr Dokter, your patronizing nods and absent eyes, always trying to remember where you read something, already thinking about the next patient. You're pathetic and deluded, *ein armseliges Würstchen*. You cannot save a soul.

But of course, you must think the same of me—*eine arme Sau*, a curiosity, a miserable one-legged has-been drunk committed into psychiatric care by his own wife. Let me assure you, Herr Dokter: I wasn't always a pathetic old doped-up cripple. Once upon a time, in another country, I was a young and hopeful cripple. I was a prodigy, the youngest filmmaker in Ufa's history, the toast of Berlin. I still dream of champagne picnics on the *Pfaueninsel*, the Zoo-Palast filled with an ocean of flowers, just for me. I dream of Studio B and the sets we built for *Jagd zu den Sternen*.

But all of that has been lost, destroyed, buried, bombed, and burnt. I lived my life for light and love, and now the bean counters and brain shrinkers want to break me. I've been held captive by men in uniforms before. My adversaries conspired with history. Men like you, they come and go. World Wars drove me out of my home and took my limbs. Hollywood chewed me up and spit me out. I have been *verraten und verkauft*, locked up, ruined, rejected. My own wife dumped me here like a mangy dog at the pound. The days are getting shorter and there is no way back. *Gottverdammt nochmal*, it's ugly here at the ass end of my life.

Fine. *Abgemacht*. Why the hell not? Keep the pills coming, and I'll write in your dime-store notebook. You'll get your fairy tale. Words are a poor substitute for a camera and an editing table, the might of a studio at my disposal, but words are all I have left now.

This is the simple truth: my wife, that gorgon, that lying two-faced monster, has become my worst enemy. It was she who ruined everything we had and could have had again. For decades, she has turned every triumph into a wound and every opportunity into a disaster. I have not made a movie in twenty years! She ruined my life and my career. Penny cost me everything, and you, Herr Dokter, are just another one of her pawns. Your kind is legion, following orders and taking instructions, always on the wrong side of art and truth. She knew exactly which lies to tell, what to put on the forms when she signed me over into your questionable care—a danger to myself and others and that was good enough for you, wasn't it? You are compliant, like the bastard cops who brought me here, my worthless son, and everybody who ever called himself my friend and then abandoned me when the time came.

But it's darkest before the dawn, *nicht wahr*, and none of you can keep me from my destiny. I have a talent and people have misunderstood me all my life. There are things that are impossible for a man with a prosthetic leg, but if you give me a cast and a crew, I have no limits. I came from nothing, I scaled the Olymp, and I can do it again. Even when the Nazis burned my movies, I clung to hope. You have marked me crazy and yet you ask me to explain myself. Art will prevail! I'll make another movie yet. Cinema cannot be detained! Nothing can stop me, for I am Kino.

Well then. *Es war einmal vor langer, langer Zeit*, my father owned a paint and dye factory on the Main: Koblitz & Söhne Farben AG. As soon as my brothers and I were old enough to hold a pen, we worked at the factory to learn our trade "from the bottom up." Father was a stern son-of-a-bitch; mother was thin-lipped and distant. They had no imagination, and we were forced to spend endless days in dusty rooms, stooped over balance sheets and quarterly earnings reports. It was slavery.

When the Great War began, Heinz, Jupp, and I were too young and too rich to march off to Flanders, and so we remained sheltered behind a five-meter brick wall and the rows of gnarly oak trees my great-grandfather had planted. Once father learned that the *Kriegsministerium* was paying handsomely for chlorine, a byproduct of dye production, his nationalism reached new heights. He spoke of the tremendous honor of serving the Vaterland in its hour of need, and we sold them our toxic waste as a weapon for the trenches. The margins were phenomenal and he transformed the B plant in Hoechst to produce mustard gas.

My parents and the *Bonzen* who came for *Skat* and mother's garden parties pretended that nothing was wrong at all. I never once went hungry while boys just a few years older got mowed down, bayoneted, bombed, gassed, and ground up by the thousands, *fleissig*, *fleissig*, feeding our prosperity with their industrious killing and dying. In the winter of nineteen-sixteen, women came begging for food and my father chased them away with his hunting rifle. In the streets of Frankfurt, people recognized our Daimler and spit when we passed by.

On one particularly cold night, the tanks of chlorine father had installed in the moldy overflow warehouse caught on fire and exploded in a magnificent green flame. An infernal blaze of superheated acid gas raged through both wings of the house, a blinding blast that set the curtains and furniture on fire, followed by the hissing and fizzing of the chlorine. I was in bed, and I remember the sudden smell that turned into burning pain in the throat, nose and lungs, the scalding bite of the chemical digging into the flesh of my leg, fire. My younger brother Jupp was thrown from his bed and landed face-down in a puddle of acid. Heinz led us through the window onto the lawn before our room caught fire. Flames claimed the house, the stables, the maids quarters, even great-grandfather's gnarly oak trees burned down in a hellish conflagration so bright, one could see the blaze light up the night sky from the Römer, over ten kilometers away, or so the *Frankfurter Rundschau* reported the next day. My parents' charred bodies weren't recovered from the ruins until the next morning.

It was justice—not the human kind, bought and sold, but some sort of cosmic justice, God's will, what the Oriental religions call karma. Along with the poison gas, my father had let the war into our home, and we all paid the price. I came to in a hospital bed next to Jupp's, in a room filled with every available quack who wasn't at the front, a whole flock of *Dokters*, hovering over us, shrugging impotently.

Dokters. The smell of disinfectant, the snap of rubber gloves. Useless at best, clueless most of the time, always dangerous. When your kind runs out of answers, you call for pills and electroshock. That night after the explosion, they ordered up morphine, and nuns brought wet towels to wipe down our sweat-covered bodies. My leg was disintegrating from the acid, and the infection progressed quickly, threatening to kill me. I watched Jupp struggle in the bed next to mine, trying to draw breath with his decomposing lungs. He was the youngest and liveliest of us, and it took him hours to die. Finally, the *dokters* had to capitulate before the chemical, and soon, they shrugged some more, folded their hands. They called a preacher for Jupp.

For me, the saw.

It was *dokters* who pinned me down, applied ligatures to prevent hemorrhaging, pulled up my skin below the knee cap, and divided it with one quick stroke of the double-edged knife, leaving the flexor tendons intact so the stump would retain the power of motion. With the practiced ease of men who had performed hundreds of these procedures during the war, they transected the muscles. They had a special piece of linen with three tails ready that was threaded through the space between the shin and calf bones and tied together to hold the muscles and skin back. The *dokter* with the oscillating saw stood between my legs and worked quickly, to keep the calf bone from splintering.

And that's it. The leg's detached, a separate thing. You can't feel it yet because everything is pain, but you can see the assistant who takes it away swiftly, to be burnt unceremoniously in the hospital's ovens. Skin and muscle flaps are folded over the stump, and before the wound is dressed, they insert studs for screwing on a peg leg.

Knock on wood.

That was nearly fifty years ago. I still remember every second of the procedure, and to this day, I feel the pain in the absent limb. But I can't for the life of me remember what it was like to have two feet.

Dokters did that to me. I doubt you ever had occasion to perform an amputation, and for that reason alone, you're even more dangerous than those who took my leg. You are worse than useless. I despise you, and I am frightened of the moment you run out of ideas.

I am the only one who sees these pages half-filled, and I am terrified. One must be fearless to plow through sentences and paragraphs to unknown conclusions. Do you understand what I am trying to tell you? Heinz and I were the only survivors. We inherited the firm, the land, the money. I didn't want any of it–it was blood money, and I had paid for father's greed with my leg. But the fire hadn't lessened the hatred of our family. Disgusted, I gave my inheritance to charity and left Koblitz & Söhne to Heinz. I kept just enough to get by and went to Berlin to live among the common people: workers, shopkeepers, butchers, tram drivers, waiters. I was free of the pretensions of the rich. Nobody knew me as the son of a *Kriegsgewinnler*, a war profiteer. Berlin, seething capitol of a brand-new democracy that no one wanted. The city promised all I longed for: depravity, chaos, revolution, everything my sheltered upbringing had denied me. I enrolled at Friedrich Wilhelm University and rented a shabby room that smelled of beer and herring in a second *Hinterhaus* on Rosenthaler Platz, from a family of *waschechte* Berliners too polite to ask about my leg. They assumed I was a veteran, like everyone else, not a one-legged shut-in apprentice accountant from the provinces who'd grown up sheltered by five-meter walls, a *Landei* determined to join the twentieth century.

For the first few weeks, I dutifully took the tram to Unter den Linden to attend lectures. At the gymnasium in Frankfurt, our tutors had been stern and humorless Wilhelmine men with moustaches and starched collars who taught the same way other men lay brick or shovel graves: a solemn, joyless duty. Listening to lectures about Greek literature and natural science in Berlin revealed to me that learning was a pleasure.

After classes, I headed west to the shops and restaurants of Friedrichstadt. I'd stop at my bank to furtively withdraw a few marks at a time, just enough to afford a pastry at Rumpelmeyer's or coffee and a soft-boiled egg at a Ku'damm Café, where I sat for the entire afternoon. Soon, I took out more money and went for dinner, or to the *Tingeltangel.* I discovered the Wintergarten, just south of Friedrichstrasse station, an opulent world made for pleasure, a temple of delights, a palace of sparkling crowds and thrilling acts. I drank champagne between artificial fountains and grottoes filled with exotic plants, and no matter what happened on the stage–dancing girls in leather and fur, trapeze artists, a woman from Spandau getting hypnotized by a Mexican magician–you could always see the stars through the enormous vaulted glass roof. It was like Walt Disney's theme park–but with tits. Wonderful, classy tits!

To a *Landei* like me, the crowd at the Wintergarten was as thrilling as the stage, so different from the plump industrialists who visited in Königstein or the rough-hewn working men who ate *Knackwurst* at the Gipsverein, where Herr Oberlin tended bar. At the Wintergarten, each person was fascinating, sophisticated, cosmopolitan, witty, and most of all, sexy. I laughed at the men's one-liners and desperately wanted to touch the women's silken dresses. I wanted to know them all, but even more than that, I wanted them to know me. After a couple of beers, I allowed myself to imagine that the applause was meant for me.

It was there at the Wintergarten I met Steffen. He approached from across the terrace with that graceful gliding gait of his, a smile so magnificent there was no way not to return it. By the time I noticed him, he'd already extended his hand, and before I could get up to take it, he'd introduced himself and taken the seat across from me. His cheeks were flushed–his cheeks were always flushed; it gave him a healthy complexion, even though I soon learned the real reasons were not of a healthy nature. His wild eyes were focused on me, and he talked quickly. He did not want to be forward, but he had a proposition. Here was the attention I craved! Steffen's charisma made me feel blessed every moment his eyes were on me. Later, I knew movie stars like that, but unlike them, Steffen saw you when he looked. He smoked a cigarillo and talked fast, with so many clauses, interjections, and Scheunenviertel slang that was a mixture of *Boxverein* gangster jargon and the quasi-German the Romanian gypsies used. I learned later that he affected this accent when he wanted to impress. I didn't understand half of it, and the other half was unclear, but apparently, he was looking to play a prank on his friends—here he waved at a table across the terrace and rattled off names: Lady Miss Fear, Babsie, Kuno Kartoffel, Ute the Mole Girl, two more I didn't catch, and Anita Berber's sister Katja—and he needed my help. My help!

Why me? What kind of prank? I wanted him to slow down but I couldn't help smiling. He said he thought I had a mysterious air about me—he was talking about my leg—and he imagined that his friends would simply adore it if I robbed them. Furtively, he unbuttoned his jacket to show me the handle of a revolver. "It's not loaded." He winked.

I looked back at his friends. One of the girls blew me a kiss. I still didn't understand.

"You want me to rob you? Do I get to keep the loot?"

Delighted, Steffen clapped his hands. "Adorable!'Do I get to keep the loot?' Please, you must indulge us. Wait for us in the alley behind Dorotheenstrasse. I swear the loot will be to your liking."

Now, I was not a complete innocent. Heinz and I both had favorite girls at a bordello in Frankfurt, and I knew how to use a prostitute. I thought of Steffen Kung as a playful dilettante, clearly drunk, looking for a way to spice up his Saturday night with a harmless prank. I wasn't entirely wrong, but I had missed the point.

So I agreed. Why not? I had a surplus of optimism and no fear. Under the table, Steffen handed me the revolver. As instructed, I laid in wait for him and his friends in the alley, held them up–"*Geld oder Leben!*"–but instead of offering up their money, they turned and ran. This wasn't part of the plan! Dragging my wooden leg, I chased after them across the street, and for good measure, I fired the gun into the air. Bang! It was loaded after all, and the shot echoed down the street. Roaring with laughter, Steffen and his friends disappeared into one of the apartment buildings. I followed, climbing the stairs with my leg thumping on the wood steps until I reached the apartment under the roof, a wide-open space that was hung with Indian tapestries and cluttered with divans, mirrors, pillows.

"Now I have you!" I shouted, out of breath, heart beating with excitement. I fired another shot into the ceiling. Plaster fell in a cloud of dust.

Their arms went up.

"Oh my," said a girl with a monstrous mole on her cheek. "Please don't kill us! We'll do anything you want!" To make her point, she wiggled out of her skirt. One of Steffen's friends, his arms still in the air, produced a silver tin of cocaine. *Zement*, they called it.

This was the night I learned there was a real upside to my "predicament," as my brother Heinz liked to call it. You'd be surprised how excited a certain kind of girl–or guy–can get over a missing limb. I started off with Ute the mole girl straddling me, delicious, her blouse still on, but then I felt a hand on my thigh, and somebody was removing the strap that kept the artificial leg in place. I turned and Steffen kissed

me and I returned the kiss and Ute was fucking me hard
while someone else was fondling my stump. When the sun
came up, we were all sitting at Aschingers, spent and eating
pea soup, which was, as Steffen grandly announced, based
on a recipe created by a Nobel Prize winning chemist. I used
part of this story in *Meine wilden Wanderjahre*, but of course
that doesn't mean anything to you.

There's a rush when you encounter something fresh,
something that floors you, a great thing you didn't know
existed – a kind of opening in the world, a precipitous
teetering on the edge of possibility that's thrilling beyond
belief. With age, these moments become more rare, until all
that's left is a distant intimation one April day when the
wind is just right. By the time you're as old as me, you barely
remember they existed at all, unless they come to haunt you
in your dreams.

Gottverfluchte Scheisse.

I get flowery when I'm sad.

Do you see what you're putting me through?

The stars above the Wintergarten are still there, but the
building was ruined in a bombing raid in forty-four. I saw
photos of it, in the newspaper. They made me wish I could
have been there for the last show. It must have been
tremendous when the roof burst.

Steffen and his friends roamed the cafes, lounges, cabarets,
bars, dance halls, and back alleys of Berlin every night of the
week. He was always flushed, all hugs and love and drive,
his restless eyes darting while his mouth chattered on, fueled
by the company and the cocaine. He knew everyone:
dancers, musicians, retired Dadaists, free thinkers, anarchist

lesbians, drunken Russian émigrés, actors, nudists. He was reckless and infectious and he became my teacher in depravity. As long as there was one *Tingeltangel* or revue, just one jazz orchestra playing anywhere in Berlin, Steffen would be there, up front, hollering and doing his own inimitable dance, throwing his limbs every which way and waving a bottle of champagne.

He had picked me out of the crowd at the Wintergarten as a kind of mascot, a handsome, crippled freak with a Rheinland accent and a fabulous peg leg. I was young and I learned quick. Drugs let my mind, liberated from my lurching body, soar. Under the Japanese-themed ballroom ceiling of the Residenz-Casino, where the tables had telephones and pneumatic tubes, the kaleidoscopic lights of the whirling mirrored globes and colored water displays sent me on dizzying flights of fancy while go-go dancers shook their tits and stretched their boot-clad legs, whipping the wild and drunken crowd into a frenzy.

And there was sex. There were always girls who didn't mind trying it with a guy like me. Something about the leg's absence made fucking more immediate; at least that's my theory. You probably have a name for this, Herr Dokter, but I assure you, reading about it in a book is nothing. A thing like that has to be experienced. Berlin was a school in bodies, desires, horrors, lust, jealousy, fantasy, and pain. I don't mind telling you that I've tried it all: girls, boys, three, five, ten, every which hole. Does that shock you?

It didn't take me long to understand that Steffen provided cocaine and girls for the countless friends he seemed to have in every section of Berlin. Most nights, our rounds–from the Vaterland to Café Braun, from the Stork's Nest to the Cosy-Corner–were on a schedule. The outrageous crowd that followed Steffen knew they wouldn't have to pay cover fees or champagne tabs. There was always enough *Zement* for everyone. In return or perhaps for fun, they might go to bed with people Steffen introduced them to. It was Steffen's particular genius to mix business and pleasure in a way that made everyone happy. From Steffen I learned to seek pleasure in everything I do. If it's not fun, why bother? That was his motto, and I came to see the wisdom of it. In those days, Steffen meant everything to me.

Steffen had a new prosthesis handcrafted for me by the capital's best manufacturer, with real hair and a flexible ankle, and my limp practically disappeared. He took me shopping for smart clothes, and when I began to dabble in writing, he bought me notebooks, leather-bound beauties from Italy, much better than this *Ramschladenscheissdreck* you have me write in.

As a joke, Steffen introduced me as whomever occurred to him at the moment. I was an orphaned painter, an undercover Spartakist, a science protégé on scholarship. Steffen introduced me, and then I had to keep up the lies—that was the game. I was a saxophone player in Bix Beiderbecke's band. I was a Swedish mesmerist. When I was asked about the leg, I talked about dogfights high above the Somme; when they wanted to hear my award-winning poetry, I said the poems were so Futuristic they hadn't been written yet. All it took was a straight face.

There was one lie that made me seem more interesting than all the others. Everyone wanted to drink with me, get high with me, and sleep with me when we told them I was a movie director. It was the lie that turned me into the center of attention and opened the tightest twat. One night over dinner, Joachim Ringelnatz–the whimsical poet who wore a sailor's uniform wherever he went–eyed me funny and asked if I wasn't a bit young to be working for the cinema, "*für's Kino.*"

I had my mouth full of lamb stew, so Steffen came to my defense. "Don't you read the papers? Klaus is a prodigy! The youngest director in Neubabelsberg!"

I put down my fork, swallowed, and pointed a finger. "Joachim," I said. "I don't work für's Kino. I *am* Kino!"

And that's how I gave myself my own nickname. At the time I didn't have the faintest idea about the true potential of cinema. To be honest–and I know this will sound incredible to someone of your generation–I had, in the summer of nineteen twenty-four, never seen a feature film.

Of course, I'd been to the *Kino* in Frankfurt, but father always made us leave the Film-Palast after the Pathé newsreel, before the movie proper. All I ever saw was the Kaiser giving speeches, columns of soldiers leaving for the front, generals being decorated. Afterwards, father tortured us with questions about what we had learned, and Heinz always knew all the answers. I begged my father to let me stay, but he said there was no point, that movies were a waste of time.

I was twenty-two and I had never seen a movie. When Steffen found out, he laughed his red-faced out-of-control-laugh and announced, still out of breath, that we would remedy the situation immediately–after a quick stop at Ronja's basement in the Scheunenviertel, where an ancient Russian woman with long white hair kept hammocks and served pipes of sweet opium. We arrived at Ufa-Palast am Zoo in a dreamy state to see Murnau's vampire movie.

How can I describe it to someone whose eyes have been sullied by decades of trivial images dancing by on TV screens? You'll never understand the rapture, the horror, the euphoric bliss I felt at the sheer visual surprise. With each passing moment, with every new shot on the screen, waves of pleasure rolled through me.

During my miserable childhood, I had been a relentless day dreamer, spinning tales from books into wild fantasies that helped me through endless days of drudgery. I dreamed of the heroes and villains of the books my mother called *Schundromane*, the adventures of Alain Quartermain, Phineas Fogg, and Hadschi Halef-Omar. After I met Steffen, I barely slept at all, and my nights were occupied with drinking and fucking and dancing. When sleep came, unconsciousness would have been a better name for it. Dreams had vanished from my life until the opium, until the movies, until *Nosferatu* brought it all flooding back.

I had read Bram Stoker's *Dracula*, and I had seen those images before–but not out in the open, outside of my head, projected against a wall for everyone to share. At once fascinating and terrifying, Count Orlok, the death bird, was a wicked apparition with a skull-like, elongated face and pale wide haunting eyes. Killing for blood was his nature, and he could not escape it. I loved the ghastly shadows of overgrown nails, the meat-eating plants, the sleepwalking bride, the caskets filled with plague-bearing rats. This was the opposite of father's newsreels, this was the technology of the night, modernity pressed in the service of poetry, culling images from dreams and rendering them visible as if by the light of the moon, for all to see.

It was magic.

To Steffen, it was just one more outrageous night in Berlin, but I went back again and again. I must have seen *Nosferatu* twenty times. "Why do you hurry, my young friend?" an old man asks at the beginning of the film. "No one can escape his destiny." Like Count Orlok, these magical moving pictures would never let go.

Three years later, I was in charge of my own set in Neubabelsberg, the largest studio in Europe, making a movie that I had written. The producers, the stars, the cameramen and the newspapers all called me Kino, the name I had given myself over Horcher's lamb stew. I was a prodigy, the youngest director in Ufa's history. The lie had become truth.

Herr Dokter: what do you call the power to turn your imagination into reality?

Steffen's reckless exuberance had one drawback: his joy never lasted past morning light, and the come-downs could be terrible. He was prone to melancholy, bitter bouts of disappointment and suspicion, and during those moments, everything he said was critical and cruel—until day turned into night and the next thrill came along. Like him, I spent my days cranky and irritable, cursing the sun and wishing it was show time at the Eldorado.

It was on one of those mornings that I took the tram out all the way to the Ufa studios and got myself a job. I liked the girls and the parties, but I was after something else. My father had been a bare-knuckles capitalist, and I had grown up rejecting everything he stood for. Now, all these years later, I can see how much I took after him. I did not judge the world by money, I never calculated human worth by mark or dollar, but his self-reliance and ambition lived in me. And thus began my illustrious career in the Weimar film industry. I got myself hired as an extra, at the bottom of the ladder. Historical epics were all the rage, and Ufa was desperate for people to fill the frame. It was a miserable job that paid *ein Appel und ein Ei*; day workers doing manual labor on the sets were making twice as much. But I wanted to be close to the camera, so I grinned and followed orders and kept my wild dreams to myself. Rags to riches! I know you Americans gobble this stuff up like chocolate pudding. I walked through two or three Lubitsch pageants, and then every available man was assigned to Fritz Lang's *Die Nibelungen.*

While Ufa geared up for the biggest production in its history, the situation in Germany was deteriorating. In June, a gang of assassins shot the foreign minister on his way to the chancellery, and just to be sure, they lobbed a hand grenade into his car, too. All confidence in the new republic went to hell, and the mark began falling against the dollar. What little money I had left was quickly becoming worthless. Instead of waiting for bankruptcy, I decided to celebrate. I spent everything I had on one raucous night: lobster dinner, dancing, *alles drum und dran*, and when the sun came up, I was sitting in the Lustgarten with Steffen and Ute the Mole

Girl, blissed out on opium tea, and–for the first time in my life–broke. A few hours later, my landlord's daughter, little Susi Oberlin, found me passed out on the Hinterhaus staircase. I was still wearing my tux, a shiny *chapeau-claque*, and a white shirt smeared with vomit. I clutched the neck of an almost-empty bottle of champagne.

"*Guten Morgen*," Susi said, ponytail wagging.

In the early morning light that was falling through the building's stained glass front door, I could see a wet trickle of urine running from my leg onto the linoleum floor. The opium had worn off, and I desperately wanted to be back in my room with the covers over my head. My mouth was dry. I took a swig of champagne. Without thinking, I offered the bottle to the little girl, who sat down next to me and lifted it to her lips, drinking until it was gone. "Nice bubbly for a lowly student," she said. She let go of a monstrous burp and handed the empty bottle back to me.

My embarrassment gave way to something else–the sense that in this city, not even the school children could be counted on to do what they were supposed to. I was broke and wasted, and I wouldn't be able to pay the rent. I'd given my inheritance away but it was just as well; by November, all of it would have been barely enough to afford a turnip, anyway.

Susi said, "You should probably go to bed now," and I was grateful for her small gesture of kindness. For the first time in my life, I felt that the travails of the time were also mine. I was a true Berliner.

"They call me Kino," I said, and Susi Oberlin burped again.

The government ordered the newspaper presses to print more money in ever higher denominations. Workers got paid at noon and ran out to spend it before it became worthless. Though I had nothing left, I never went hungry–I was Steffen's friend, and Steffen knew people with dollars, first among them his latest benefactor, Ray, an American art dealer who hosted a never-ending party at the Belvedere, a fantasy castle on the western shore of the Grosse Wannsee looking out across the sailboat-studded bay to the Lido. Ray proclaimed that he'd fallen madly in love with Steffen. Magnus Hirschfeld and some of his students were hanging out naked by the pier, there was dancing on the terrace, and in the west wing, somebody read aloud from a dirty novel they had smuggled in from France, "the most modern book ever written!" There was always enough to eat and drink and snort at the Belvedere.

Demand for drugs was on the rise, and there was more pussy to be had than ever. Can you blame me, Herr Dokter, for helping to move a little bit of both? A few deliveries here and there, the exchange of a package at Zoo station, selecting a few Tauenziengirls and boys to join us out at the Belvedere? Jawoll, I did my share of drug dealing and whore mongering, but I had dollars, and if you had dollars, you could live like a king. When the French invaded the Ruhr, prices went up further, but the parties at the Belvedere never slowed down: there was an insane edge to everything, absurd desperation in the air. When winter came, the Oberlins, my landlords, began heating the building with buckets of last week's money like everybody else. Germany's undernourished children died of tuberculosis and war veterans dragged themselves through the streets begging for a bite of stale bread or a ladle of cabbage soup. You could have an entire *Kneipe* dancing naked for a few coins but a billion marks bought you a cigarette. People were sniping from the rooftops out of hunger and desperation. Misery stared us in the face but we danced at the Kleist Casino.

In my sheltered, privileged life in Königstein, we had profited from pain. My new family just happened to survive very well.

In Neubabelsberg, the studio was stockpiling food for the cast and crew. Inside the Grosse Halle, there was only one law, one rule, one thing that had to be done: whatever Fritz Lang wanted.

Fritz Lang. Even before I ever met the miserable son of a bitch, with his monocle and superior airs, I hated him. Hot off *Dr. Mabuse*, Lang had been all over the papers with his marriage to his screenwriter bride, Thea von Harbou. In bad times, a little bit of celebrity goes a long way, and the public was eating up every idiotic rumor about the master and his muse. I had heard things, too: that the suicide of Lang's first wife had been anything but, that he couldn't climax unless he had the taste of blood on his tongue. On set, Fritz and Thea were aloof and unapproachable, like King Gunter and his Queen in the German legend we were filming, a turgid saga without hope or love.

I detested Lang's histrionic style, the ghastly overacting and oppressive angles. In person, he was an insufferable asshole. He bellowed orders and treated people like puppets. He made his actors repeat scenes for twenty, thirty, fifty takes and directed by assigning numbers to gestures and facial expressions. Then he'd count them off while the camera rolled: one, two, turn your head, smile, six, seven, faint, nine, ten. He had nothing but disdain for actors; he was a bully and a bore. And yet I watched him closely, learning as much as I could.

On the day Lang shot Siegfried's arrival in Worms, I was coming down from a three-day bender, having trouble standing up straight in the knight's heavy chain mail and helmet. Holding the shield before me, I stood shaking where Lang had placed us on a tiled floor, lined up symmetrically. By the time we redid the scene for the twentieth time, I was itchy in the ill-fitting costume. I had loosened the strap that held my leg in place. Just when Kriemhild was descending the staircase again, I could feel my leg slip until, with a slight thud, it fell flat on the ground before me.

"Cut!" Lang barked through his bullhorn, his monocle dropping out of his eye. I had ruined the take. "We are hiring cripples now? All I needed was somebody to *stand* there, and you get me a guy who's missing a leg? The warriors of Worms don't suffer from runaway limbs!"

Out of the darkness behind him, Thea von Harbou appeared, cradling her lap dog like a baby. She was always on set, wearing the same green outfit every day. She knitted sweaters and dictated novels to an assistant.

"Fritz," she said, putting a calming hand on his arm. I had witnessed this before, Thea smoothing over Lang's rough edges, calming his fearsome tantrums for the sake of the production. "Everyone's good for something."

With my leg in my hand, I went blank. She was buying me time, giving me an opportunity to speak up for myself, but I didn't know what to say. What *was* I good for? The only job I wanted was Lang's, but if I'd told him that, he would have pulled out his Browning and shot me on the spot. My career would have been over before it started – if Gerhard Gruber, the set designer, hadn't explained that he was having trouble setting up Siegfried's epic battle with the dragon. Gruber had constructed a huge beast, a monster of twenty-five meters that was operated from the inside, but the man who worked the tail complained there wasn't enough room for his legs.

Lang lifted the eyebrow that didn't hold the monocle and grinned.

Siegfried's fight with the *Lindwurm* was a marvel. The contraption was heavy as a tank and took ten men to move. For endless, claustrophobic days, I had to kick my stump, which was attached to the lever that manipulated the dragon's crocodile tail. We moved the creature's eyes, mouth, legs, and tail, we made it breathe fire and smoke, we pumped the blood that gushed from the wound where Paul Richter, the foppish son-of-a-bitch who played Siegfried, pierced the rubber skin with his sword. We damn near suffocated on the fumes. It was the most grueling work I have done in my life. The only way to bear this wretched work was to stay perpetually high, and every morning, I doled out a generous allotment of cocaine for every man inside the monster.

Word got out. One person introduced me to three others, and soon I was providing *Zement* to the entire production. The cinematographer, the camera and lighting crews, and the costume designers bought huge quantities for their departments, and Steffen started coming to the set to make deliveries. I became the best friend of crew and cast. Thea von Harbou sniffed lines and dictated with such speed that white foam formed in the corners of her mouth. She was full of ideas, she was efficient. Thea was the one with talent. As the shooting of the dragon scene dragged on, a peculiar bond formed between the ten of us who made it come alive from within. We were the bones of the beast, it was our blood that circulated through its veins, our breath that fanned the flames from its nostrils. We made the creature move and fight. Through the alchemy of Kino, we became the dragon. The dragon taught me the power of the crew, coming together to make a film like the craftsmen who built cathedrals in the middle ages. Everyone's contribution, every single detail, was essential. Inside the dragon, Herr Dokter, we all understood that.

But Fritz Lang didn't know how to marshal the talent at his disposal. In my version of *Die Nibelungen*, the dragon would have killed that *Arschloch* Siegfried and eaten his entrails, but Lang was too stupid and too proud of his silly script to see. He didn't know how to let an idea flourish. Under his rigid dictatorship everything turned into a grotesque, lifeless pageant. Can you understand why the dragon's preordained fate did not sit well with us? It seemed unfair to stage this tremendous battle and not give the creature a chance. Paul Richter, prancing about in his sexy loincloth—it was a lie the monster we had created could not abide. There wasn't a word spoken, but somehow, we reached a decision nonetheless.

Lang's counting method should have left no room for mistakes—one, two, the dragon's eyes roll while Siegfried jumps left, three, a blast of fire as he strikes, four, five, a whip of the tail, and six, he impales the Lindwurm on his sword. It was during what seemed like the hundredth take of Siegfried jumping from rock to rock and striking at our vulcanized rubber skin that I flung the tail into Paul Richter's leg, a move he wasn't expecting till four or five count more, and delivered a mighty whack that sent him flying backwards into the pond.

All ten of us inside the dragon cheered!

Curses from Lang, laughter from the crew.

A Dokter, so old he must have served under Bismarck, came along swiftly. Richter had suffered a contusion and would be unable to work for a week. The shoot was now delayed, the production bleeding money, and Lang was raging with anger. Gruber, who had saved me the last time Lang wanted my head, fingered me as the one responsible. I swear I saw him reach for the gun he kept inside his vest. But Thea was back at Lang's side, reminding him that I provided the *Zement*. In the throes of hyperinflation, I was the one who kept the production going, and he knew it. Even Paul Richter, that oaf, couldn't hold a grudge when we sent Ute the Mole Girl to visit him in his hospital room. Siegfried recovered quickly.

I had learned something crucial: the dragon beat Siegfried, but that's not what *Die Nibelungen* showed. Lang's movies didn't allow room for the incidental; he imposed his will on every element on the set. He was a liar and a fraud. But I had felt the power of the dragon, had tasted the unfettered potential of cinema to create something true and beautiful and dangerous, and I had to have more.

Die Nibelungen kept shooting into the New Year. To celebrate the end of production—in Hollywood, they call it a wrap party—Ufa turned Grosse Halle into a beer garden, serving up *Bretzel* and Schultheiss to the legions of extras who had all dutifully died for Lang's horrid epic. Later that night, Thea and Fritz hosted a more exclusive affair at their notorious Hohenzollernstrasse apartment. Thea asked me to make sure that cast, studio bigwigs, and investors were properly entertained. Together with Steffen, I supplied bowls of *Zement*, a samovar of opium tea, a hookah packed with Turkish kif, and a dozen Friedrichstadt dancers.

Thea and Fritz had turned their apartment into an exotic museum, stuffed with paintings and art objects, Chinese carpets, Japanese temple flags, sacred vases, Buddhas, shrunken heads, and cabinets filled with trinkets so Lang could brag about his travels. He was a bore, but no matter: we had made it into the inner sanctum, a place I'd only seen in the photo spreads of glossy movie magazines. In the purple library, filled with grimacing South Sea sculptures, I spotted Erich Pommer, the most successful producer in Europe, responsible for *The Cabinet of Dr. Caligari* and all of Lang's successes. Here was the man I needed to impress! Next to a cage with a large blue-and-red parrot, Thea von Harbou, who listened to an animated Rudolf Klein-Rogge, waved me over. Her black Schnauzer shook his tail at me.

"See?" Thea said. "I knew you'd be useful."

Klein-Rogge excused himself to follow Ute the Mole Girl down a corridor.

"Making a movie is like constructing a creature," I told Thea. "The cast is the face, the director the brain, the cinematographer the eyes and the crew the hands. You, *meine sehr geehrte Frau*, provide the heart."

Thea smiled. "It appears that your domain is the nose."

I proffered the tin of cocaine. Two Tauenziengirls in flapper dresses had talked Lang into taking down wooden African masks from their showcases on the library wall, Carl Meyer had procured some bongo drums, and together, they began an obscene tribal dance. A small crowd gathered to watch them. Lang, Pommer, and Richter sucked on cigars and clapped along to the jungle beat. Margarete Schön, who had played Kriemhild, joined the dancers.

I had another sniff and took the risk. "Can I ask you something, Frau von Harbou? Something that has been bothering me about *Die Nibelungen*. If you're going to make a movie in two parts, shouldn't one of them have a happy ending?"

"Don't be a *Dummkopf*," Thea said. "*Die Nibelungen* is a story about inexorable tragedy. The first sin entails the last atonement. There can be no happy ending."

"Sounds gloomy!" Steffen, drawn by the syncopated bongo beat, had come dancing into the room. "You and your tragedy. I can't believe that's what people want. Look around! They want beautiful women and a good time! Why are you trying to depress them with tragedy?"

"My, my." Thea smiled, gesturing for another bump. "Your friend can dance and insult the highest paid movie writer in Europe at the same time. I suppose you have better ideas, my red-faced dervish?"

"I don't," Steffen said. He pointed his thumb in my direction. "But he does. That's why they call him Kino."

"They do?"

I gave Steffen a look—this wasn't how I would have approached it. "Well yes," I admitted. "They do. If anyone gave me the chance, I could do great things. I am full of ideas."

"He has ideas!" A familiar voice barked over the drums, loud enough to make them hesitate and stumble. Lang had noticed me talking to his wife and turned away from the jungle dance. The drumming stopped. Every head turned. "Extras, drug dealers, and pimps have ideas now?" Lang said. He projected as if he were making a toast. "What is this business coming to?"

Erich Pommer let out a belly laugh. He was bleary-eyed and in a jolly mood. "Now, now Fritz! Isn't this the young man who kept your production on schedule? Let him talk. You know I'm always looking for talent in unlikely places. Lubitsch is gone; we need to think quick if we're going to stay ahead of the Americans! This *Schelm* here calls himself Kino and says he has ideas? I want to hear them!" He folded his hands over his belly. "Talk."

Suddenly I was the center of attention, my mind raging from the cocaine. Pommer was calling my bluff. Here was a room full of Ufa-*Bonzen*, producers, actors, directors, Thea, Lang, Richter, Klein-Rogge, even Steffen, waiting for me to deliver on the name I'd given myself. I had nothing, but I knew that there was nothing worse than saying nothing, that I had to say anything at all, and say it with confidence. Everything else would follow if I just took that first step into the void. I looked around the room, my eyes came to rest on a picturesque oil painting of a windmill, and—

"The Tulip Thief," I said.

As simple as that.

"The what?"

It was a title and a promise: *Tulpendiebe*. That word was all I had, but it contained everything that followed. It arrived complete; I just had to unpack it. And that's what I did, right there, start to finish, on the spot, in front of the most powerful people in the Weimar film industry: fields and fields of flowers, the sailor, the Duke, Lilly, the stolen tulip bulb, the burning windmill, the entire story right up to the final shot.

When I was done, there was a moment of uncertain silence before Thea clapped her hands. "Bravo," she said, and her approval gave the rest of the guests permission to show theirs. Lang turned his face into a blank mask, Steffen winked at me, and Pommer nodded, as if to say that *Tulpendiebe* was a movie he wouldn't mind watching—perhaps even producing.

"Very American," he said, slurring the second word. From his mouth, it was a compliment. "Come see me in my office on Monday." Then he dropped his glass of beer and fell backwards into a wooden sculpture with a gigantic erection that Lang claimed he'd traded for a smoked ham with a tribe of cannibals in Papua New Guinea.

There you have it, Herr Dokter: proof. If you have enough faith in the imagination, nothing is impossible. I invented myself as director, and that's what I became. From the moment I stepped into that void and said the word *Tulpendiebe*, everything aligned just right. My wildest dreams were becoming reality, and there were no limits.

Over the course of one golden year, I made my movie, cast a beautiful actress, fell in love, and made her my wife. How could I have known that Penelope was my salvation and my undoing at once, the spark that ignited *Tulpendiebe* and a miserable mistake that would ruin my career?

Oh my Lilly, my Penny! I'd give anything to see her again the way she looked in twenty-seven, when I first laid eyes on her, four beer steins balanced in each arm. Impossible to conceive now, isn't it, Herr Dokter, that the appalling, hysterical *Dreckfotze* who delivered me here was once the Duke's luminous daughter, the most exquisite face on German screens? I wanted to make her immortal, to burn the image of her face overlooking a sea of flowers straight into history, but I can't make Penny into Lilly again anymore than I can grow another leg.

Chapter 8

Pulp Fiction, Barbarella, The Wages of Fear. Uma Thurman, Jane Fonda, Yves Montand: film posters that could've been anywhere, like the faint morning light falling in through the curtains. Wherever she was, it was very early. Mina was gliding awake out of a muddled dream involving palm trees, windmills, and her father spitting insults at her. Wherever she was, it was cold and Mina pulled the thick covers tighter around herself as she tried to retrace the events of the previous day: the bomb threat, the department store, the stranger at the Holocaust memorial. The notebook and Dr. Hanno's flushed cheeks as they read it together on his couch, red wine and more *Döner* –

Oh shit.

This was not her airline-comped room at the Tegel Ramada.

This was Dr. Hanno's bed.

Mina lunged out from under the covers, bare feet on cold hardwood, eyes anxiously searching the room. She found herself wearing black-and-white silk pajamas emblazoned with the likeness of Humphrey Bogart and Lauren Bacall.

Below the chest pocket, it said "You know how to whistle, don't you?"

Dr. Hanno's pajamas. *Oh God, please no.* With one swift motion, Mina pulled the fluffy covers off the bed.

It was empty. She felt for her wedding ring, still on her finger. Good. Whatever had happened, she was sure she hadn't slept with Dr. Hanno.

Relieved, Mina considered lying back down. According to the cheap digital clock on the bedside table, it wasn't seven yet. But her heart was beating fast now; the shock and the cold had woken her up for good. She put on her clothes and stepped out into the living room: large, bright, with wood floors. Judging by what she could see through the tall windows, she was on the fourth of five floors. The room was lined with shelves stacked with books, DVDs, video tapes, and film memorabilia. In a corner, a flat screen TV was stuck on the menu of the *Die Nibelungen* DVD, the heroic theme playing over and over. Had they watched that? Mina couldn't remember. Had she been drinking a lot? Her head felt fine, more or less.

Dr. Hanno was asleep in his clothes on the standard-issue futon that doubled as his couch. On the coffee table in front of him, stacks of papers, books, photocopied pages, and a laptop were crowded together amongst remains of Turkish food, half-empty coffee cups, and beer bottles.

Mina was remembering bits and pieces from the journal: the fire at the Koblitz estate, the amputation, Steffen and the Belvedere, the dragon, Lang's wrap party. And, the last thing she'd read before falling asleep, something about Penny and Lilly that she couldn't quite piece together.

The mysterious man who had snuck up on her at the memorial had told her not to show the journal to Dr. Hanno, but she hadn't been able to hide it from him. She knew how excited he'd be, and she'd been right: "A major discovery!" and so forth. It was a way to make up for losing *Tulpendiebe*, perhaps. Now, on his futon, smiling in his sleep, he looked so young, so innocent. He reminded Mina of a boy she'd slept with a few times in college, Eric Ambrose. Poor, goofy Eric Ambrose.

Mina watched Dr. Hanno's chest rise and fall and thought of Sam. At the hospital, she had watched him sleep for an entire week, but not once had he looked as peaceful and content as Dr. Hanno now. All that tossing and turning, it had driven her crazy. She was glad not to be there, at the hospital.

There had been no word from Sam. Mina had called of course, but it was an impossible hour in New York and the nurse had been curt. She'd said something about a "biphasic pattern," taken down Dr. Hanno's phone number, and hung up without a good-bye.

Then it dawned on Mina that she'd have to fly back today, and her heart sank. Another airport, and back to her plastic chair in the hospital. At least she'd have time to read the rest of the journal on the plane.

Speaking of. Where *was* the damn journal?

Another jolt of fear ran up Mina's spine. She rifled through the mess on the table. Had she managed to receive and promptly lose yet another obscure item from the past? The notebook wasn't on the table. It wasn't under the table. It didn't seem to be on the floor.

She shook Dr. Hanno awake. "The journal. Where is the damn journal?" There was more panic in her voice than she'd expected.

Dr. Hanno groped around for his glasses. "Oh," he mumbled. "Oh. *Es tut mir leid.*"

"What?"

"It's right here." He rolled off the futon, and there it was, under his ass, a standard issue spiral notebook with a yellowed cover. Mina picked it up and leafed through the pages, as if to make sure they were still filled with Kino's jittery handwriting.

"Did you read any further? After I fell asleep?"

Dr. Hanno yawned, rubbed his eyes. "That would have been inappropriate. With your permission, though, I scanned the pages so there's a backup—just in case you should lose it again. This material is invaluable."

Mina wasn't sure she liked the idea of Dr. Hanno keeping a copy of the pages, but she didn't know why. She shrugged it off.

"What time is it?" Dr. Hanno wanted to know.

Mina clutched the journal to her chest. "Time for coffee."

His kitchen was small, and Dr. Hanno worked quickly to set up breakfast—rolls, dark brown bread, a plate with cold cuts, Nutella. Mina was used to a bowl of cereal on most days, unless she somehow woke up early enough to join Sam for oatmeal, or they went out for brunch. The week before had been nothing but doughy hospital bagels with Philadelphia cream cheese.

She went for the Nutella, carefully transporting the gooey hazelnut spread from the jar to her slice of bread. She didn't want to get any on the journal, which she had propped open under the edge of her plate. They'd only gotten about a third into the book before she'd passed out from exhaustion. Without taking her eye off the page, she sank her teeth into the bread.

"This is the part I don't understand," she said between bites, "'My Lilly, my Penny!'? Is he saying my grandmother was in the movie? And what does *'Dreckfotze'* mean?"

Dr. Hanno just drank coffee. He hadn't even gotten out a plate for himself. "It's not a very nice word. It refers to–" was he really blushing? "–a part of the female anatomy–and yes, I do believe your grandmother's maiden name was Penelope Greifenau."

"Are you sure? Oma Penny? That was her in the movie, the blonde girl?"

"You didn't know she was an actress?"

"I had no idea. My God, she was beautiful."

"According to a footnote I found in a Murnau biography, she refused to be interviewed."

"Sounds about right. I was terrified of her as a kid."

Dr. Hanno watched with something like pity. Mina realized that he must have known that it was her grandmother in the movie all along, but he hadn't bothered to tell her. She let the last bite of her Nutella sandwich sink back to the table. "That was her, in the movie. I have to talk to her."

"Right now?"

"Right now."

Dr. Hanno rubbed his hands together, instantly excited.

Mina washed down her last bite with a swig of coffee while Dr. Hanno dialed directory assistance in California. He handed her the phone. Mina hadn't really thought about what to say when a distant voice at the other end cackled "hello."

"Oma Penny? It's Mina, your granddaughter."

A cough. "Detlef's girl?" Another cough, a sound like phlegm. "What do you want?"

"I saw you in the movie—"

"What the hell are you talking about?"

"*Tulpendiebe*. I saw you in *Tulpendiebe* and I want to—"

"Impossible. It's been destroyed for sixty years. All the prints were burned. You're talking crazy."

The theme from *The Godfather* began playing somewhere. It was Dr. Hanno's ringtone, coming from his cell phone on the window sill. He picked up— "*Broddenbuck, am Apparat!*"— and started to talk in rapid German. He sounded agitated. It was hard enough to hear her long distance call, and Mina waved for him to leave the room. He didn't. "*Langsam,*" he said. "*Ich verstehe kein Wort!*"

Mina raised her voice, trying to drown him out. "Oma, I'm telling you. I've seen *Tulpendiebe*. The movie just showed up on my doorstep. I'm in Berlin because of the projector. You were so beautiful with all the flowers. Lilly, the Duke's daughter. I had no idea. Nobody ever told me."

Oma Penny was silent for a second. "What do you mean about the projector?"

"The movie was in a weird format, and they only have it here. I don't—"

Dr. Hanno cupped his hand over his phone and turned to her. "*Doppelnockenverfahren,*" he said.

"Right," Mina said. "*Doppelnockenverfahren.*"

"Who's there with you?" Penny said. "You worthless ditz. Don't talk about this on the phone. Don't call me again, *verstanden*?" She hung up.

Mina cursed.

Dr. Hanno, too, was cursing into his phone: "*Verdammt nochmal! Danke*, Frank."

"She hung up on me," Mina said. Could that gruff voice really have belonged to the same woman who'd played the frail daughter of the Duke?

Dr. Hanno put a hand on her shoulder, startling her. "That'll have to wait," he said. "We have to leave, right now. Get your bags."

"Excuse me?"

But he was already in the living room, picking up books, papers, his laptop, shoving it all into a knapsack. "That was Frank, the projectionist, warning us. Americans came by the museum, asking questions about *Tulpendiebe*. They're on their way here."

"Good," Mina said. "Maybe they know what happened. I want to talk to them."

"No, you don't. Trust me."

"I don't trust you. I want you to tell me what this is about."

Dr. Hanno stopped for a moment. "Frau Koblitz. Please. Powerful interests have a stake in your grandfather's legacy. We have to leave."

"What does that even mean? That's bullshit."

"You seemed to take the bomb threat seriously. These men are dangerous. You've already been robbed once. Do you want to lose the journal, too?"

That struck a nerve. Dr. Hanno thought the bomb threat had been about her, after all. But hadn't the man in the red leather jacket told Mina not to trust him? Who was she to believe? The one thing she knew was that she didn't want to lose the journal. It was the only palpable thing to come out of this mess, and she was determined to bring it back to New York with her.

Dr. Hanno's house phone rang in Mina's hand. She hadn't even been aware that she was still holding it. Without thinking, she picked it up, blurting, "What now?"

"Uh. Baby? It's me. Are you still in Holland? Where are you?"

Sam.

"Oh Sam, thank God, it's you. I'm in Germany, baby. Germany."

"You wrote something about tulips."

Dr. Hanno came in from the bedroom holding Mina's suitcase. He tapped his wrist and twirled a finger to hurry her. Mina didn't care. Sam sounded confused and weary, but she was relieved to hear his voice. "How are you? They said you're getting worse."

"It's awfully hot here," Sam said. "I have bad dreams, and I wake up in the middle of the night and I'm all alone. I don't trust these doctors. They tell me something different every day. Did you hear we bombed a wedding in Iraq? Cluster-bombed the entire village. I saw it on the news. I sweated through all my pajamas. Your father yelled at me. I wish you were here. I miss you."

Dr. Hanno was picking up Mina's things himself now, stuffing them into her suitcase. He made a point of showing the journal to her before he stuck it into her knapsack's front pocket with her passport.

"Oh baby," Mina said. "I'm coming home today, okay? I promise. It's been crazy. This guy at the Holocaust monument handed me Kino's journal. I never knew he was missing a leg, or that Oma Penny was the Duke's daughter. She used to be beautiful. I called her in Los Angeles but she wouldn't talk to me—"

The doorbell rang. Dr. Hanno rushed to the window, stuck his head out, and turned to Mina. "*Scheisse!* We have to go. Now!"

"What?" Mina looked down to the street. Below, three men in suits were waiting by the front door. One of them looked up and pointed her out to the others. The door bell rang again, and again, and again.

"What's going on?" Sam sounded even more confused than before.

Mina sighed. "These guys are here looking for me. Dr. Hanno thinks they're dangerous. He wants us to leave. He's actually sweating he's so nervous."

Dr. Hanno put on his coat, grabbed Mina's parka from the hook, and shook it at her impatiently. "Frau Koblitz, we must go right now. Your grandfather's legacy is at stake."

"Oh," Sam said. "Weird. Maybe it's the same guys who came by here."

"What?"

"After your dad left, these guys in suits came by and asked me questions."

"They came to the hospital? What did they want?"

Dr. Hanno froze.

"They asked about you and the movie," Sam said. "I think they're secret agents."

"What?" Mina said. "Sam, you're delirious."

"*Scheisse*," Dr. Hanno said. "We have to go right now."

"Listen Mina," Sam said. "That Hanno guy is right. Get out of there now. I love you. Go."

"What?" Mina said. "I love you, too." But Sam had already hung up.

Mina looked out the window again just to see the men disappearing into the building. Someone had buzzed them in. Dr. Hanno took the phone from her hand and put it in its wall-mounted cradle.

"Frau Koblitz. They're coming for you."

"Okay." Mina took a breath and slipped into her brand-new parka. The irrational fear she'd felt at the airport was back. Whoever these men were, she didn't want to find out. "Where do we go?"

Dr. Hanno ushered her into the hallway, closed the door quietly behind him, and led them up two flights of stairs. They climbed quickly and quietly; they could hear footsteps coming up from below. They reached a latched metal door marked with a warning. Mina knew what *"Verboten"* meant. Dr. Hanno made eye contact, nodded, and pushed the door open. An alarm rang as they stepped onto a rooftop overlooking the city.

Dawn was coming up pink and sullen. The city was a jumble of construction sites, pre-war buildings with sloping roofs, modern apartments with roof gardens and swimming pools, and the odd landmark in the distance. The golf-ball-on-a-needle shape of the Fernsehturm loomed over the gold-green dome of the New Synagogue. Streets cut through at all angles, forming oddly-shaped blocks and yards. It would have been pretty if they weren't running from a bunch of creeps in suits.

"Quick," Dr. Hanno said, carrying Mina's suitcase across two roofs to a metal ladder bolted to the side of a building. Mina looked over the edge: it went down all the way, six tall pre-war floors, to a cobblestone backyard.

"No way," Mina said. "I'm not climbing down that thing."

"Please," Dr. Hanno said. "I'll take the suitcase."

Over the ringing of the alarm, Mina could hear voices coming from the door they'd opened. A man in a dark suit emerged from the door, followed by two others.

"Come on, *schnell!*" Dr. Hanno disappeared over the edge, awkwardly holding Mina's suitcase between his body and the ladder.

The men were beefy and sported crew cuts. They spotted Mina and Dr. Hanno and began shouting Mina's name. One of them was waving what looked like an oversize manila envelope. When Mina didn't react, they started to run toward her, deftly navigating the rooftop with precise, athletic movements. "Mrs. Koblitz! Wait!"

Who were these men? Did Mina imagine seeing a curly wire in their ears, as if they were communicating with a mission control van waiting for them downstairs? Sam had called them secret agents. She glanced around the other rooftops, half-expecting to see snipers moving into position.

"Fuck," Mina said. "Fuck, fuck, fuck."

Whatever they wanted from her, it couldn't be good.

She swung her leg over the ledge. *Just focus on the ladder,* she told herself. *Don't look down.* This couldn't be worse than the time she went repelling in college. The ladder had held Dr. Hanno. She remembered something about a three point rule—only move one limb at a time? She had no time for that. Rung by rung by rung, she descended, the metal cold against her fingers.

Don't look down, she reminded herself.

There was shouting above. They were closing in.

She had almost caught up with Dr. Hanno when she heard him give a strange sigh. She looked down and saw him let the suitcase slip. It teetered on his hip for a moment as if it were, perhaps, able to defy gravity and support itself, and then tumbled slowly downwards. It took a fearfully long time to hit the ground, and there wasn't much of a sound when it did. Just a dull thud. Mina could see her things—flippers, underwear, flowered sundresses—spill across the cobblestones below.

Suspended between the brightening Berlin sky and the approaching voices above and her honeymoon luggage and the sheepish face of Dr. Hanno below, Mina winced.

"You've got to be fucking kidding me."

Chapter 9

Herr Dokter, you make a living out of the misery of others. The days here are deceptively mild like all California days, but at night, when the sedatives wear off, I hear the screams. I know I'm not alone in here. How many of us do you keep locked up? Don't you know there is no treatment for what ails us? If I was a car you'd stamp me *Totalschaden* and leave it at that. You're a junkyard attendant, warehousing wrecks. I showed people a better world. You're the warden of hell, and I am losing patience. I am trying to get to the point.

When I was led into Erich Pommer's office, my sweaty hands clutching the completed screenplay of *Tulpendiebe*, I had not slept, and I was pale, jittery. I had gone straight from Lang's apartment to the Belvedere, where Steffen's lover Ray kept an Adler typewriter in his study. I brewed coffee, snorted Zement, chewed cigars – whatever it took to turn the story I had spun at the party into a script.

Pommer shook my hand, took the pages from me, and barely looked at them. On his desk, I noticed the famous stack of silver coins he tossed to writers with good ideas. He motioned for me to sit. He wanted to know about my childhood in the Rheinland. He asked what kinds of movies I liked, and I told him Chaplin, Murnau, von Stroheim, Griffith, Dryer. He asked if my leg would be a problem on the set, and I told him that if Lang's dragon hadn't killed me, the director's chair certainly wouldn't. I wanted to tell him about my vision for *Tulpendiebe* but he cut me off with an axe chop of his hand that landed on a piece of paper he proceeded to push across the desk. It was a contract, already prepared. I flipped through the pages but didn't care what it said. It was a movie contract, and that was all I needed to know. I signed it "Kino."

Later, I found out that Decla-Bioskop, Pommer's old company, had just been bought by Ufa and was being phased out as an independent entity. *Tulpendiebe* would be produced under their auspices. Pommer was worried about American predominance in the market and had signed off on some of the most expensive movies in Ufa's history. My historical romance–that's what he called it–would be made on the cheap as a way of diversifying the risk from the mega productions the studio's fate was riding on. Pommer was hedging his bets, and *Tulpendiebe* could be written off if it failed. I committed to a tight budget and was given little control. I was to shoot my movie in four weeks in a Bioskop studio. The ship, the market, the Duke's palace, the tulip fields, even the windmill–everything had to be created inside, on the cheap. We had to use the old Bioskop equipment, which worked with the outdated *Doppelnockenverfahren*. This meant my film couldn't be shown outside of Germany. But of course you wouldn't know the first thing about that, Herr Dokter.

The studio was a dump. Lang was in the Grosse Halle, making *Metropolis*, an even bigger production than *Die Nibelungen*, and Murnau was shooting *Faust*, another special-effects extravaganza, with Emil Jannings as Mephisto. Down the hall, Dr. Fanck was filming interiors for *The Holy Mountain*. I met Luis Trenker and Leni Riefenstahl, who shook her ass in my face. With *Metropolis* already ballooning out of control, nobody cared what we did.

To paint the backdrops, I hired Salvatore Luna, a Mexican painter known for his bold style, one of Steffen's friends. He's famous now, of course, for his extraordinary murals. Extras and costumes were difficult to come by because everybody was marching down the shafts of Lang's futuristic city. I had to fight for every clog and every pantaloon—the costume department was working overtime on *Faust*. The contract also gave me no control over the casting. I didn't meet any of the actors until the first day of shooting. They were fourth-rate talents: Harald Flint, the Czech acrobat who played the sailor, liked to chew tobacco and spit at the painted backdrops. The Duke was an old lecher. My crew consisted of drunks, drop-outs, and halfwits. My cinematographer was an alcoholic with shaky hands.

On the first day of shooting, I gave a rousing speech about cathedrals of light and unfettered potential—but none of them understood. I wanted magic, they wanted paychecks. They wanted to know what cathedrals had to do with tulips. I've never been comfortable with authority, and I found it distasteful to tell people what to do. I didn't want to be like my father, and I'd never direct like Lang, counting out gestures. I wanted to give the actors room, but they saw my openness as weakness, as permission to do as they pleased. I was too young to know what was required of me, and we fell three scenes behind on the first day.

I also found that during my time on *Die Nibelungen*, I had acquired something of a reputation. Everybody kept asking me for drugs, so Steffen and his ever-changing entourage began hanging around the edges of the studio, doling out Zement. Salvatore was addicted to a South American fungus powder that he claimed helped him hallucinate. Soon, half of the cast and crew were hooked, and the cocaine going around was cut with the stuff.

The early rushes were terrible. My worst problem was Sandra König, the mugging fourth-rate diva hired to play Lilly. She was the daughter of a financier Pommer owed a favor, and she was a disaster. *Tulpendiebe* needed an ethereal beauty, afflicted with a mysterious wasting disease, but instead, I had a ruddy-faced broad who couldn't even faint with grace. If the chaos on set didn't do me in, Sandra König was certain to ruin my movie.

Steffen told me not to worry. I am not proud of what happened next, but whatever Steffen's morals, he was a loyal, uncompromising friend. Without warning, Sandra König failed to show up on the set. A letter was discovered in her home that said that she had received a message from God and was leaving on a pilgrimage for the Holy Land. Four weeks later, she telegraphed from Damascus—she had been found locked inside a shipping container filled with specialty foods destined for the Shah of Persia, drunk on Veuve-Cliquot. The last thing she remembered was having a nightcap with a handsome man.

Now I had a new problem on my hands: I had to replace the miserable Sandra König, and fast. Pommer threw a pathetic collection of headshots across his desk and told us to find someone by Monday or the production was finished.

If there was one thing Steffen was better at than anyone in the city, it was finding the right woman for a job, but by

Sunday night, we were desperate. I needed someone who was haughty but also lovely, with an inherent wisdom and a vulnerable innocence. The only girl with a passable face was pregnant. Ute pushed her case relentlessly, but a Lilly with a prominent mole was impossible.

We tried the Romanisches, the Kranzler, Schwannecke, and the Jockey. We tried backstage at the Wintergarten, but the dancers either looked too cheap, too chipper, or too stupid to be Lilly. Steffen was exasperated with me. He had seen dozens of women who seemed fine to him. "Just pick one," he kept telling me. We kept roving through streets, bars, and nightclubs, we even tried the opera and the debutantes at the Schauspielhaus, fruitlessly. My movie was about to be cancelled, but I wouldn't relent. There couldn't be *Tulpendiebe* without the perfect Lilly.

The six-piece brass band was taking a break when we arrived at the Braukeller, a cavernous beer hall where the drunken shouts of a thousand proles were mixed with ripe sweat, cigarette smoke and spilled beer. I saw my Lilly right away, across rows of wooden benches. She clutched six steins to her chest and stood strangely tranquil among the raucous crowd, out of place, beautiful and aloof. She was tall and blonde, with short bangs, a sharply drawn chin, and the large, angular head of a movie star. She stood out like an apparition, and it was obvious that she had no idea where she was going with all that beer in her arms. I had seen Henny Porten, Asta Nielsen, Mary

Pickford. Penelope Greifenau outshone all of them. I had found my Lilly.

Steffen agreed. "Without the glasses, she's perfect. I'll handle it." He sniffed a heap of Zement from his tin.

I didn't take my eyes off her.

"No," I said. This wasn't a word that passed between us in those days, but my relationship to Steffen had begun to change. His faults were becoming obvious to me. I no longer adored him blindly. "I'll do it," I said.

From our bench, we watched the waitress weave through the crowded hall. She nearly spilled the beers two separate times before she unloaded them to a cheering group of Freikorps soldiers. She had already grabbed the next armful before I managed to get her attention. When she laid her eyes on me, my confidence vanished, and my first words to her, my future wife and the mother of my son, were delivered with a blush: "You ought to be in movies." It wasn't a cliché yet.

As if she hadn't heard: "*Was darf's denn sein*? Two beers?"

Close enough to see the moisture in the corners of her lips and the lights reflected in her eyes, I could barely think at all.

"They call me Kino." I stood up and took an awkward bow. "And I want you as the lead in my film."

Steffen shifted uneasily, itching to jump in and save me.

"I have a job," Penelope said.

Without thinking, I put my hand on her arm. "You're above this. Will you come to Neubabelsberg tomorrow?"

She gave me a smile. Her glasses slid down her nose, but she didn't have a free hand to push them up. She sat down at the end of our bench. "My feet are killing me."

A man in the black clothes and wide brimmed black hat of a journeyman shouted for her: "Fräulein!"

Penny ignored them. "Show me the script and I'll think about it."

"The script?" Steffen said, no longer able to keep quiet. "No need to read it. Kino is a genius!"

"It's okay, Steffen." I had the script with me—I always did—and offered it to her. She lifted an elbow and clutched it to her breast.

"*Bier her, Bier her, oder wir fall'n um!*" the journeymen sang, banging their empty steins on the table.

Penelope sat down and leafed through the script, ignoring the calls for more beer with a deep furrow on her lovely forehead. Finally, she slapped the pages down on the table.

"You wrote this?"

Proudly, I nodded.

"It's ludicrous," she said. "You're asking me to play a sick woman who contributes nothing? To pine for a clown of a sailor? This is an insult to the cause of women."

"A liberated woman!" I said. "You are perfect for the role! Lilly is the movie's true center, its conscience, the incorruptible heart of the story!" She continued to frown.

"Don't confuse the notes with the music," Steffen said. "You have to trust Kino!"

"Women don't want to be put on a pedestal. You will never amount to anything if you don't respect your female characters as equals."

"Come, Kino, these insults by a *Kneipentrulla* are beneath you." Steffen made to leave.

But I regarded her carefully. What did she really want? I knew she was beautiful and a terrible waitress. I also knew this was no time to leave.

Steffen took me by the arm. "You can get Asta, or Pola Negri. Let's go."

"Not so hasty," she said. "I listed my objections to the role." She took a deep breath and applied the double negative with precision: "I didn't say I didn't want to do it." She did an absurd little curtsy. "Penelope Greifenau." Steffen clapped his hands. "Hallelujah," he said. "You won't regret this. It'll be great fun."

"Fun?" Penelope said with a frown. "I don't expect to find much fun in it."

Did she know right away, in that soggy beer cellar, that she would be my ruin?

Among the degenerates assigned to *Tulpendiebe*, my new leading lady stood out like a cosmopolitan goddess–sophisticated, earnest, professional. On the first day, she knew the script and understood everyone's motivation, and her dedication to the film changed everything. The entire cast and crew had a crush on her, wanted to impress her. Even Harold Flint shaped up.

After we wrapped the first week with Penelope, she took me aside to tell me she didn't think I was in control of my actors. She told me my style was chaotic. We had filmed scenes in the tulip exchange and I had tried out new gags on the spot.

I told her that shooting was always messy, that I created order later, in the editing room.

"What about the drugs?" she said. She'd seen Flint and Krause smoke a hashish cigarette between setups, down by the loading docks. They had made crude jokes and giggled uncontrollably.

I told her that as long as the actors could still hit their marks, I didn't care what happened between takes. In fact, I

wanted them to do whatever was best for their performance.
I might have suggested she try a little hashish herself. I might
have winked.

Oh my.

She looked at me with a contemptuous mixture of disgust
and anger, a face I have seen many times since.

"You have no discipline," she said, "and you're not
dedicated to this movie."

I thought I hadn't heard right.

"*Verzeihung*? This is *my* movie. I'm dead serious about it."

"Then stop playing around."

"My dear Fräulein Greifenau, 'playing around' is how I
work. Only at play are we open to our full potential! Art is
pleasure! The orgasmic synthesis of ideas!" I was on a roll,
and I quoted Steffen's motto, making it my own: "If it's not
fun, why bother?"

"You're a hedonist!" she spat.

I laughed. "You say it as if it required parades and a flag
and riots in the streets!"

At that moment, Steffen's car pulled up at the studio gate
and honked for me. "You must excuse me," I said. "I must
attend a hedonist meeting, or, as we like to call them,
'parties.' Would you like to join us?"

To my utter surprise, Penelope folded up her wagging
finger and said yes.

On the ride to the Belvedere, she seemed pensive while
Steffen told some story about a friend who had been beaten
by the "brownshirts." I didn't know anything about the
Nazis at the time, but the story didn't surprise me. People
were always getting beaten up in those days—by the
communists, the Freikorps, and apparently, now, by "the
brownshirts." I didn't think about it twice.

I was thinking about Penelope Greifenau.

At Ray's party, Penelope relaxed, drank Steffen's lemon vodka, danced the Lindy, and sat on the pier with me to look at the moon. She told me that she was the daughter of Leo Greifenau, the celebrated physicist who lectured at Humboldt. The old certainties were crumbling in science just like they were in society. After the war, the universities had begun accepting women as students and Penelope enrolled, only to realize upon graduation that there was no future in the academy for women. Things weren't that liberated after all. Her father pulled some strings but the best he could offer her was a position as a secretary.

Penelope took it badly. She threw physics in her parents' faces, left home in a fury, and took the first job she could find. If she couldn't research and lecture, she wanted to embarrass them. The beer hall was humiliating, but she figured a movie was even worse, just the thing to get back at her elitist parents who had spent large sums of money to have their daughter educated at the best schools in Germany and abroad. She had attended the Sorbonne in Paris. To them, acting in a vulgar piece of primitive mass entertainment ranked somewhere below lugging beer steins. "The movies," Leo Greifenau had said to her on more than one occasion, "just toss it all up there on the wall. They require nothing."

Another man might have reacted differently to the insults. But it was a gorgeous night and Penelope was beautiful.

"You're in my movie to get back at your father?"

"Is that a problem?"

I didn't care. It was enough that she was in my film, that she drank with me, laughed, let me sit with her by the lake on a moonlit night. I was hopelessly smitten.

"I ran away too," I said, "from wealth and a family business. My father didn't have any use for the cinema either. He trained me as an accountant, and nothing bores me more than numbers." I told her how I'd given my inheritance away and left our Rheinland estate for the Oberlin's Scheunenviertel-*Hinterhaus*.

"We don't do what's expected of us," I said. "You and I, we don't believe in rules."

"Just the ones I make for myself. You don't seem to worry about consequences."

I shrugged. "Good things happen if you let them."

She gave me a skeptical look. "As a scientific proposition, that's rather weak."

"It's not science, it's aesthetics. It's what I believe."

Her smile said she was attracted to me against her better judgment. If you came close enough, you could watch her think–Penelope had a unique mind, brilliant and complicated, and it showed in her eyes. I could hear the party, laughter and music pouring out of the Belvedere, but I didn't want to join the crowd. I only wanted to spend time with this extraordinary creature.

When I tried to kiss her, she pulled away. Penelope considered a relationship between actress and director unprofessional, and that was that. She might have been the only actress in the history of movies, but she would not sleep with her director. That night at the Belvedere, Ray offered her one of the upstairs guest rooms, and she kept the door locked. I know because I tried.

From then on, I gave up Steffen's girls, Ute and the rest. I sent champagne to Penelope's dressing room, picked the best tulips for her every day after shooting. I *courted* her. I screened rushes for her alone so I could sit next to her in the dark while her face lit up the screen. I projected everything onto her. That is how movie stars work: they make you feel like you've always known them. Penelope became the conduit of all my dreams.

Eating the petals had been Harold Flint's idea. He began to improvise during the scene where the love-stricken sailor breaks into Lilly's bedroom. He might've been stoned. The script required him to climb in from the balcony while Lilly slept and to lay a tulip on her heaving breast. The flower–worth millions of guilders as a bulb–would heal the ailing beauty.

With the cameras rolling, Flint hopped around the set and engaged in all sorts of *Schabernack*. He crawled under the bed, opened every drawer, turned cartwheels. I let him go while Penelope, tired of pretending to sleep, made noises from under the covers. That's when he picked up the flower again, tore off a petal, held it to his lips for a trembling moment, and then chewed and swallowed, like a gourmand tasting a leaf of bitter chocolate. Penelope, who had grown impatient, raised herself, opened her eyes, and laughed.

It was the most innocent, unforced laugh you've ever heard, and even on silent film, the shot conveyed irresistible joy. "Keep on rolling," I shouted, "keep going!" Flint plucked every petal from the tulip and stuffed it in his mouth while Penelope clapped and laughed and cheered him on. When he was done sucking up the last of the stem and dabbed his mouth with his shirt tail, he bowed deep, blew her a kiss, and disappeared the way he had come.

"Cut!"

We all knew the take was perfect: spontaneous and unplanned and true.

"That wasn't supposed to happen," Penelope said to me. I told her she'd been wonderful, and she beamed back. She knew it was true. I was sure, then, that she could love the movies, that she would love me, that all would be well and she'd be mine.

Everyone was in high spirits when we shot the final scene, the windmill amidst a sea of flowers. We'd gone over budget, but in a gesture for which I will always be grateful, Ray put up the money for additional tulips, carpeting the entire studio in bright bloom. Penelope kissed me that night—one single, tantalizing kiss before she pushed me away.

Then I holed up in the editing room. For two months, I was eating, sleeping, and breathing film, hunched over the editing desk between hanging strips of celluloid. With scissors and glue I sped through time, manipulated events at my whim, and shaped the raw images into a tale like a god. I learned to make shots talk to each other and found rhythms and resonance in the fractions of black between the frames.

My whole life culminated in the triumphant night when *Tulpendiebe* opened and I finally made Penelope mine. Salvatore Luna had painted the façade of the Ufa-Palast am Zoo with a mural of beautiful flowers, and the lobby and twin staircases were lined with thousands of glorious tulips in bloom. Murnau was there, and Emil Jannings, Asta Nielsen, Conrad Veidt, Brigitte Helm! My old Scheunenviertel landlords had come out in their best Sunday clothes, and my brother Heinz, who'd moved his business headquarters to Berlin, was there as well.

Tulpendiebe should have been a disaster, but instead it turned out a miracle, not at all what I had set out to do, but stranger and better. Penelope was perfect. Only three years had passed since Steffen had taken me to *Nosferatu*, and here we were, the images I had dreamed up cast against the screen for all to see. I have never been more proud, have never loved every frame of a movie as much as I loved *Tulpendiebe* that night. When the last frame faded, the audience erupted into a thunderstorm of applause. I took my bows, and in that moment, I realized the tulip thief was me.

At the reception, Penelope and I were the center of attention. Thea kissed my cheeks but Fritz was too proud to pay his respects, holding court by the bar. I chatted with a young film critic by the name of Billy Wilder. Two unexpected guests congratulated us: Anna and Leo Greifenau, Penelope's parents.

Penelope couldn't hide her surprise. "Didn't you find it vulgar and glamorous, my beauty objectified and my intellect immaterial?"

"Oh Penelope," the professor said. "I just want you to be happy. And you, young man. Quite lyrical, the story about the tulip. The erratic movements of the market correspond to the movements of the heart, do they not?"

I basked in my success, but all I wanted was to leave with Penelope, more beautiful than ever, stunning in her white silk gown. She was a brand-new movie star, and I was not her director any more. That night, we made love until the sun came up over Friedrichshain.

The newspapers raved, calling *Tulpendiebe* "lucid and full of meaning," while *Metropolis*, that turgid piece of overblown shit, couldn't earn back its budget. A Landei and a cripple, I had transformed myself into Klaus Kino, the Wunderkind of Neubabelsberg, the youngest-ever director in the history of Ufa, a favorite with the critics and the public! I was in love with myself, with Penelope, with the pictures we were making on the screen.

I bought a villa in Charlottenburg and an American cabriolet that we drove across the Alps to Lake Como. Drunk on red wine and mad with the romance of it all, I proposed. Penelope explained to me, at length, that marriage was a tool of the patriarchy—and then, surprising as ever, accepted. We were married that very night, in a musty church in Bellagio with the local fishmonger as witness and a town of strangers celebrating our love.

Penelope Greifenau had become Penelope Koblitz, our vacation had become a honeymoon, and we were as happy together as we'd ever be. We drove on to Venice the next morning.

What happened next cast a dark shadow over our young marriage. At a café just off the Piazza San Marco, we were recognized by a professor from Tübingen, and he and his students joined us for Ramazzotti and soda. They were full of praise for *Tulpendiebe*. Penelope, who pretended she didn't care, loved the attention, and we promised to visit them at the basilica, where they were restoring mosaics. Herr Dokter, have you seen San Marco? Infinite labyrinths cover the floor and every glittering inch of the gilded walls is layered with intricate Byzantine detail, pointing beyond itself, suggesting infinite possibility. I was getting lost in the ornaments of the gem-encrusted altar piece when an infernal sound came growling up through the building. In the left transept, by the chapel of St. Isidor, Penelope and I watched the tall scaffolding on which the professor and his students worked on the ceiling collapse. The wooden frame tore apart under its own weight, sending tools and bodies flying.

When the last echo of the destruction died down, we moved toward the heap, which was still shrouded by a cloud of dust. There were indistinct voices, people crying out in pain, desperate whispers for help. Trapped underneath a large crossbeam, we could make out the smashed face of the professor, distorted into a mask of agony.

Tulpendiebe has been lost for decades, so there is no way you could possibly understand. I realize my current position further undermines my credibility—but try, if you can, to believe me. At *Tulpendiebe*'s climax, the evil tulip notary, played by Otto Gröninger, dies in a conflagration under the collapsing parts of a burning windmill—an extremely difficult shot, one of the best in the movie. There was something deeply moving about his death: at the last possible moment, we discover empathy for the villain, as he, himself, discovers that his fate is bound to all others. It is a moment of pure cinema, Herr Dokter, and one of the most truthful things I ever put on film.

There was no fire in Venice, but what Penelope and I saw in the basilica as we approached the heap of rubble, handkerchiefs pressed to our faces, was precisely what the audience sees at the end of *Tulpendiebe*, down to the framing, the angle, the beams crossed like a game of deadly pickup sticks, and beneath it all, the doomed man's face, not quite dead but aware of the approaching inevitability, his eyes wide to take in the last of what life would show him. There was no mistaking it, Herr Dokter: there was a connection, an undeniable connection, between my film and the professor's agonizing death.

It was dispiriting and horrid, and after the ambulances and the *Carabinieri* arrived, we wandered the streets of Venice till dawn. I'd seen worse back in Königstein where I had witnessed my brother Jupp die, where I watched as Dokters sawed off my limb, but Penelope couldn't stop crying. Our honeymoon was ruined, and we returned to Berlin.

Chapter 10

Dr. Hanno lifted Mina off the last rung of the ladder down to the cobblestone yard just as the first of their pursuers swung his leg over the roof. Mina's arms trembled, with exhaustion or fear, she didn't know. Dr. Hanno was holding her a moment too long, but she didn't mind. She had made it down safely.

Her suitcase hadn't been so lucky. It had smashed in two, and all of Mina's honeymoon clothes – the little red dress, the flippers, the towels they had stolen at the hotel – had gone flying all over the yard. She grabbed what she could and stuffed it into her knapsack. The snorkel mask had cracked. Her favorite dress wouldn't fit.

One by one, the suited men appeared at the edge of the roof and began to climb down. Or rather, they *slid*, moving downwards without actually seeming to move their limbs. They were descending quickly, and they weren't shouting Mina's name anymore. She found herself wishing they did; their silence was more threatening than when they had still bothered to shout.

Mina was still cramming clothes into the knapsack when Dr. Hanno grabbed her by the shoulder. "Frau Koblitz. There is no time." She slung the bag over her shoulder and left the broken suitcase behind. Trailing underwear, they ran through an alleyway lined with locked bicycles and rows of colorful trash cans and out into the street. They found themselves in the middle of a very long block. A few buildings to their right, a streetcar was pulling up to a stop. They were out of breath but kept on running, running. The streetcar driver closed the doors in their faces and pulled away.

"What now?" Mina rested her hands on her knees, trying to catch her breath. Any moment, the men who were chasing them would appear through the alleyway.

"Keep going," Dr. Hanno commanded, leading them down the sidewalk, where to Mina wasn't sure. In front of a wide staircase, a bent old man shook his cane at Mina; she was in his way. She moved aside, and he disappeared through a heavy wooden door. The sign said *"Türkisches Dampfbad."*

"What does that mean?" Mina asked.

"It's a spa."

Mina grabbed Dr. Hanno's elbow and pulled him up the stairs.

They sat next to each other on wooden benches, breathing in hot eucalyptus-scented air, dripping sweat, and trying awkwardly to keep their towels aligned. The spa was a beautifully designed neo-classical bathhouse with vaulted ceilings, tiles with elaborate mosaics covering every surface, and a variety of recessed saunas arranged around a large central pool.

It was also co–ed and all nude.

Dr. Hanno had his towel carefully tied around his waist, but Mina's kept slipping, revealing her breasts. Mina knew how jealous Sam would get if he knew where she was, with this German film professor. He was handsome, almost. She knew she wouldn't mention this part to Sam.

"You could've told me this was all nude."

"You were up the stairs before I could say anything."

"At least they won't follow us in here. They're nothing without their suits."

"I wouldn't be so sure. But I don't think they saw us."

The plan was to hide out until Frank came to pick Mina up and take her to the airport–Tempelhof instead of Tegel, where the men might be waiting for her.

They had found the least hot sauna, a good vantage from which to observe the spa's main room through the glass door. The spa was filled with old naked people. A few were younger and good-looking, but most everybody else seemed well over fifty. Nobody seemed to be the slightest bit embarrassed by the nudity. There was a lot of sagging flesh on display.

"How many of these people do you think were Nazis?" Mina wondered out loud.

"Not all Germans were Nazis," Dr. Hanno said. "It was one thing to be in the party or the SS, but most people were just trying to survive during those years."

"Do you think any of them have seen Kino's movies?"

Dr. Hanno didn't seem to have an answer. Mina felt his awkwardness and decided to give it another twist.

"Maybe he used to come here for bathhouse orgies or something. Do you think this used to be a place for hooking up?"

"Hooking up?"

"Fucking."

It worked: Dr. Hanno blushed. He was sweating hard.

Mina turned to him. "Now, who the hell are these goons, and why are they after me? I don't even have the movie anymore."

"I'm not sure," Dr. Hanno said. "There are a number of possibilities, none of them good. You'd be surprised by the lengths certain parties will go to protect intellectual property."

"*Certain parties?*"

"Powerful corporate interests. The entertainment–industrial complex. No one takes movies as seriously as you Americans."

Mina shook her head. "What do they want from me? That movie just appeared out of nowhere, and it's gone again. I don't know anything."

"In a word, copyright. To them, old ideas are like fossil fuel. These days, everything is a potential franchise, and they treat intellectual property as a non-renewable resource. Ever notice how every new movie these days seems to be a remake or a sequel or a reboot? Plagiarism suits are everywhere. Did you hear about the Eldred Case? Free the Mouse?"

"What mouse?" Mina wiped the sweat off her forehead.

"Mickey Mouse, of course. His copyright would have expired by now, but Disney fought tooth and nail to extend it past the original 70 years. They got what they wanted, but it left thousands of works of art inaccessible to the public domain. It's a disaster for creative production, but for these guys, it's all about control."

"And they want to control *Tulpendiebe*, too?" The heat made it almost impossible to concentrate on Dr. Hanno's impassioned speech. Mina blinked. Sam, she remembered, was having fever dreams.

"They want to control everything. It's how they operate. They want to own history and never let go. If they get their hands on *Tulpendiebe*, it'll disappear forever in some vault."

"But why? No one will watch this movie. It's a hundred years old. Who cares?"

"Frau Koblitz, motion pictures are produced and distributed under severe economic pressures, and they're too expensive to go freely into the world. As a matter of fact, art is never free, not in any sense of the word, and movies least of all."

"Marxism 101, thank you, but you don't have to grow up in the GDR to know this stuff. I watch TV. I went to law school."

"You did?"

Mina nodded. Technically, that was true, but she immediately regretted mentioning it. She would not tell him that she dropped out after half a semester. "I'm going for a dip," she said. She left the sauna for the much cooler main room, found a rack to hang up her towel, and jumped into the cold pool, in full view of the sauna. The water felt ice cold against her skin, waking her up and clearing her head. Swimming naked felt great. She tried to make eye contact with the other bathers, looking for approval for her courage, maybe, but no one seemed to notice.

Back in the sauna, Dr. Hanno hadn't moved. He wore a peculiar face, and Mina wondered if he had a hard-on. Her towel was wet and pointless now, and she didn't even try to cover her breasts any more. For the first time, Mina felt she had an edge over Dr. Hanno. He was looking at his bare feet.

"I still don't get it," Mina said. "If this is about copyright, why not just send me a letter or something? How did they find out about the movie in the first place?"

Dr. Hanno avoided turning his head in Mina's direction now. He cleared his throat. "Maybe the movies have been around for too long for most people to realize this anymore, but your grandfather had it exactly right: the cinema exerts the same pull as dreams. If anything, it is stronger–people pay money to subject themselves to a carefully constructed shared audio-visual experience, a guided trip if you will. That's more than just a high-stakes financial gamble–that's real power, the power to make people dream. Film is the most integrated of the arts, and they have a light side and a dark side. They can be used to liberate, and they can be used for domination. From the beginning, governments have been very interested in the power of the moving pictures."

"You're talking about propaganda," Mina said. "I'm talking about *all* movies. Propaganda is the word we use for the poor examples, the obvious manipulations. The real stuff, the truly potent stuff, doesn't have a special name. We just call it Kino."

"And my grandfather–"

"Your grandfather was an exceptional, uncanny talent. Remember the way he described *Nosferatu*? It altered his consciousness. When he left the theater, he was a changed person."

Finally, Dr. Hanno turned his head to look her in the eye. "Let me ask you something. How did you sleep last night? Strange dreams?"

Mina had, in fact, had odd, vivid dreams of a beach, Sam, and the burning windmill, but she wasn't about to tell Dr. Hanno. "Dreams are private," she said.

"Not anymore," Dr. Hanno said grandly. "Not since the invention of the movie camera. Just because you understand the technology doesn't mean you grasp the essential mystery of it. Kino is nothing to be trifled with, and those who control it now hold no stake in our souls." The sweat was pouring down his face.

"What pisses me off most is that these goons went and hassled Sam. Why would they do that?"

"To get to you."

"He's in the *hospital*. They went into the hospital to ask him about me. My husband."

She was more upset than she knew. Thinking about Sam got her upset.

"I used to be married," Dr. Hanno said.

It took a moment before Mina decided she'd heard right. Dr. Hanno seemed much too young to be divorced; he was handsome and successful enough, but the look on his face told a different story. Mina asked the broadest possible question she could think of: "What happened?"

"I think she expected more from me. Writing about movies wasn't enough. She never saw the point of scholarship or criticism. She got married to a guy who manages a golf club."

Ah, Mina thought. *The movie geekery made her leave.* Mina wondered how she'd get along with Dr. Hanno's ex-wife. She didn't even know, really, what it meant to be a wife yet. On the other side of the sauna's glass door, a naked man emptied a bucket of ice water over his head.

"How long were you married?"

"Would have been two years in June. We just signed the papers three weeks ago. She took all the furniture."

"Oh," Mina said. Just three weeks ago? No wonder Hanno seemed like a zombie at times. "I'm sorry."

"It's okay," Dr. Hanno said. "I think we're both better off this way."

It was one of those phrases that people cling to when there wasn't anything left to do but mourn. Mina could tell he didn't believe it himself but perhaps it was better than nothing. Still, she couldn't help thinking the look of heartbreak on his face now wasn't anything like what she had seen on his face the morning after the film had been stolen.

"She cheated on me from the start," he added.

"I'm sorry." Mina didn't know what else to say. Dr. Hanno was a cuckold. The movies were all that he had left. She couldn't help but feel protective of him. She placed a sympathetic hand on his leg.

Dr. Hanno, misunderstanding the gesture, leaned over to kiss her.

Mina pulled back.

"Oh–," Dr. Hanno said, and at that moment, a strapping spa attendant in shorts and a T-shirt burst in, bearing a bucket of water, a towel, and a sardonic grin: "*Aufguss, die Herrschaften.*"

"What does that mean?" Mina asked, but she could tell from Dr. Hanno's face that it couldn't be good. The spa attendant took a wooden ladle from the bucket and repeatedly, deliberately doused the sauna's coals with water. With a cascade of hissing, the water exploded into clouds of steam. Heat and humidity skyrocketed. Mina closed her eyes and pursed her lips to cool off the burning air in her mouth. She breathed as shallowly as she could. The spa attendant put down the bucket and used a large towel to fan the air in the sauna, creating more and more heat.

Mina thought she was going to die.

The projectionist, Frank, was waiting for them by the curb, engine idling. It had started to rain, a steady freezing downpour. Mina had been too impatient to dry her hair, and she regretted it when she stepped out into the cold Berlin air. Punta Cana, that's where she was supposed to be, by the pool with a stiff Cuba Libre. They ran through the rain to the car. Frank was wearing a leather cap pulled low over his eyes, and he nodded wordlessly when they got in. Mina took the back seat. The rain was a constant drum beat on the roof. She grabbed a handful of wet hair and squeezed water onto the seat. Then she noticed the black Mercedes. "Is that car following us?"

Dr. Hanno eyed the mirrors. "Jawoll. Only one of them in the car. He must have waited where they lost us."

"*Kacke,*" Frank said. It was the first word he'd said. He hit the brakes and took a sharp left down a one-way street. Rain water splashed up on the sidewalk. The Mercedes followed, leaving a few honking cars in its wake.

"Is this now a car chase?" Mina asked, trying to be funny. It came out sounding scared.

"We're not going over the speed limit," Dr. Hanno said, but it was clear he was tense, too. They ran a red light— more honking, squealing tires—but the black Mercedes kept up. The car was close enough now that Mina could recognize the driver as one of the men who had shouted after her on the roof.

They crossed a river by the dome of a large cathedral. The rain was churning the water. There was another red light. Frank tried to swerve around the cars in front of him and get across the intersection, but there wasn't enough room. A busload of tourists—old French people with identical umbrellas—hurried across the street. Behind them, Mina could see the goon getting out of his car. He was wearing gloves and trying to protect what looked like a manila envelope from the rain.

"*Fahr schon,*" Dr. Hanno instructed Frank, "*los!*" But Frank was helpless. He honked once, twice, and revved the engine, but the tourists didn't seem to care.

Dr. Hanno opened his door. "Auf Wiedersehen, Fräulein Koblitz," he said, with a lot of drama. "Be good to your husband. For Kino!" He got out and slammed the door shut. He was immediately drenched with rain, his hair slicked to his forehead. He approached the agent, gesticulating wildly.

"What is he doing?" Mina asked, but it was obvious now: he was blocking the man's way and he, in turn, tried to push Dr. Hanno out of the way, waving wildly towards Mina. His suit was soaked. The men locked in what looked like an embrace. Finally, the light turned green. One last woman pushed a stroller across the intersection. The man made his way around Dr. Hanno. Out of nowhere, an ancient Trabant smashed into the Mercedes. In the confusion, Mina thought she saw someone in a red leather jacket behind the wheel, but it was impossible to tell. As they pulled away, Mina watched Dr. Hanno and the man recede into the distance. She thought she saw Dr. Hanno give her a sad little wave.

The rain had stopped when they made it to Tempelhof Airport. "Good luck, Frau Koblitz," was all the projectionist managed to say. Mina thanked him and he was off. For one panicked moment she looked around for her suitcase before remembering that she had abandoned it, broken, in the backyard. There was no time for an inventory now. Mina slung her backpack over her shoulder and walked through the terminal as if nothing had happened at all. She couldn't help but keep glancing over her shoulder, always expecting another suit. And hadn't she just been at the airport? She was developing a real distaste for flying. Mina was exhausted. The hour in the sauna had knocked her out. Earlier, she had practically jumped off a building. She would read the rest of Kino's journal on the flight, but first she'd sleep.

But there here was one more thing Mina had to do before she could go home. Whatever this was, it wasn't over. At the check-in counter, Mina pulled out her airline voucher and her passport. "Traveling to New York, JFK?" the woman behind the counter confirmed.

"In fact, no," Mina said. "I need a flight to Los Angeles."

Chapter 11

Adolf Hitler became *Reichskanzler* on January thirtieth, nineteen-thirty-three. The Weimar Republic had run out of time, *und das Land der Dichter und Denker* was about to sink into barbarism. I barely paid attention when those criminals took over. I was busy making movies.

The waning years of the republic had been difficult. I followed my "auspiciously poetic debut" (Rheinischer Merkur) with *Land der Gnade*, the story of an expedition to a tribal kingdom in the heart of Africa. Once again, I let pleasure and whim lead me, but this time, nothing came easy. When the stock market crashed, my budgets plummeted as well. Tastes were changing, and *Land der Gnade* didn't do as well as it should have. *Jagd zu den Sternen* was delayed by a ridiculous plagiarism suit, and Pommer ordered endless unnecessary reshoots for *Meine wilden Wanderjahre*.

You could be excused for assuming that history did me in: the war, the Nazis, the next war, the witch hunt that awaited me in America–but I know that I would have persevered if it hadn't been for Penelope. The deaths we witnessed in the basilica had a devastating effect on her. To me, it was just a coincidence that proved that my movies resonated with the world. As tragic as it had been to see the professor die, I couldn't say I was surprised to come face to face with a scene from my movie. Why would that seem any stranger than seeing these images in the first place? It was like a wink from the universe, cruel and horrifying but also reassuring. Penelope, however, couldn't understand it, couldn't fit what had happened into her physicists' brain, and she convinced herself that I was to blame for the professor's death. It poisoned her relationship with my movies, and she began to undermine me.

Beginning with *Land der Gnade,* she tried to wrest control from me, improvising new scenes and demanding co-writing credit. She began drinking in earnest and got used to a bump or two of Zement before her scenes. Who was I to argue? She gave the other actors notes and made impossible demands on set. When I was out of earshot, she abused the crew. She earned a reputation as a diva who was difficult to work with.

Penelope claimed she kept seeing scenes from my movies out in the world—striking workers on Wittenbergplatz facing off with the police as if reenacting the climactic confrontation from *Land der Gnade,* the exact framing of the establishing shot of Saturn from *Jagd zu den Sternen* on a weekend trip to the Baltic Sea. I saw it, too, but it never made any difference to me. It seemed only fitting that these images would appear everywhere, on screen, off screen, in my dreams—and I didn't particularly care about the distinction. But Penelope seemed personally offended, and each time she got angrier, more confused, more shaken. On our way to the premiere of *Der Blaue Engel,* we happened upon the wedding scene from *Meine wilden Wanderjahre,* in front of the Dom, and she begged me to stop making movies.

Can you believe it? I laughed in her face. Because she was upset about a coincidence or two? My art is fueled by bliss, by instinct, and I refused to let fear of the unknown stop me. I was shocked by her lack of faith. The unknown was exactly what I was after. To make the most powerful images possible, I had to give the mystery free reign. If you try to understand it, it disappears.

She would not listen. I swore that I would never stop making movies.

After that, the fighting never ceased. Penelope was still beautiful and witty, and I was too loyal to her to see what was happening. I mistook her for my muse while she systematically undermined me. It was Penny who advised me to turn down the deal with Nebenzal that could have landed me *Pandora's Box*. It was Penny who embarrassed me so miserably at the Adlon during Chaplin's visit. It was Penny who threw my first draft of *Jagd zu den Sternen* out of the window of a speeding train, the pages trailing in the slipstream as if they'd never have to touch the ground. It was Penny who refused to work with the young Rühmann.

Our life at home got much more difficult as well. I had never wanted children—cinema would accept no distraction—and Penelope had agreed. But after her mother died, she asked her father to live with us. I relented, aware right away that it was a mistake. The old man brought a sour smell into the house, shuffling around in his *Filzpartoffeln* and spiking his coffee with Asbach Uralt. When he wasn't bent over his books or the Morgenpost crossword puzzle, he held court in the salon. Former students came and went at all hours, discussing politics, art, science, and metaphysics.

Penelope joined these debates with an ever-rotating group of disciples. Talk was heated, there was the occasional slammed door, and more than a few visitors were banished because of unwelcome political alliances. They had theories about everything. Schnickschnack! What good are theories? There is nothing to understand.

When subatomic particles and Heisenberg's Uncertainty Principle failed to enlighten, they turned to the occult. I don't know who first brought the tarot readers and turban-wearing spiritualists to the house, but soon Penny and Leo engaged in séances and other kinds of mystical hocus-pocus. The talk was all about Aleister Crowley and Hanussen, Madame Blavatsky, black holes, morphic resonance, and the Copenhagen Interpretation. Penny ran her coked-up mouth all night, shoring up her hatred of me and my work.

Meanwhile, my new script was stalled. *Die Piraten von Mulberry Island*, the thrilling and romantic story of daring Captain Darius Silko and his trusty crew, my most ambitious project yet, would be my return to form—if I could only finish it.

Working with Penelope had become a nightmare, but we had signed a five-film deal with Pommer, and the public expected her in my movies. She would play Bonnie, the young bride who is abducted by the pirates and falls in love with Captain Silko. Penelope took up fencing and agreed to take acting lessons in the new style required by sound. Jonas Krugel was cast as the dashing pirate captain. We began shooting on the day of the Reichstag fire: I was so busy it barely registered. Politics didn't concern me, not until a month later, when the NSDAP announced the formation of the *Reichs-Film-Kammer* and invited the elite of Germany's film industry to a meeting at Hotel Kaiserhof. This was March twenty-eight, nineteen-thirty-three. You can look it up in a history book.

When I was a child, my mother hosted an annual Christmas dinner for the local Bonzen. In the last year of the Great War, while the masses went hungry, we ate goose. After dessert, the children were excused from the table, and when I got up, Alexandre Dumas' *The Three Musketeers* slipped out from under my holiday suit. The book fell to the carpet between my mother and Friedensreich Thyssen, the steel magnate. Thyssen—a grotesquely obese man—leaned over with a huff and picked it up. When he saw the title, he frowned, and that was enough: my mother grabbed the book from her guest's hand, slapped me across the face, and tossed it into the fireplace.

"Alexandre Dumas?" she shouted. "*Strengstens verboten!*"

She was right. After Verdun, father had proclaimed all English, French, and Russian books off-limits, the reason *The Three Musketeers* had been hidden under my jacket in the first place. To save face in front of his powerful guests, father ordered all "enemy literature" burned in the morning. I didn't sleep that night.

We were ushered into the courtyard after breakfast. The servants had built a fire. Father made us watch as the *Hofmeister* threw our books into the fire one by one: Dumas, Verne, Ryder-Haggard, Conan Doyle. These stories had meant everything to me.

Herr Dokter, I'm telling you about my parents' bonfire because it's easy, afterwards, for everybody to agree that we didn't know and we didn't understand and we didn't see it coming. Don't believe a word of it. It was obvious that the bastards were up to no good, with their boots and their national revolution. I hated their certitude, their pathological lack of doubt, their complete absence of humor. Even in the early days, when they marched in the streets and sang songs, they looked like Death to me, goose-stepping and staring straight ahead toward some frightful destiny. I hated their torchlight parades, barking speakers, and hero's funerals. Their symmetrical spectacles were *Metropolis* made flesh. My poetic utopias lost out to Lang's nightmare futures. *Die Nibelungen*, dedicated, after all, to the German people, was a tale of blind loyalty that ended in an epic cataclysm. Sound familiar? And who was Adolf Hitler but a real-life Dr. Mabuse?

Yes, we saw them for what they were, but politics always disgusted me. I was bored by the speechifying and the grandstanding. Simple-minded, authoritarian, repressive *Scheissdreck*–that's all politics ever was, from the Kaiser to Hitler to your Mr. McCarthy. They were all the same to me, the Communists and the Nazis, the old Nationalists who wanted the Emperor back, the stiff-necked Republicans, the Social Democrats–all of them corrupt and evil. The mission of my movies was to imagine a life beyond politics.

I was wrong, of course. But it's not *Vergangenheits-bewältigung* you're after, is it? I've been called many things– hack, pimp, wastrel, genius, traitor, sell-out–and most were well deserved. But I was never a Communist, and I was never a Nazi. Did Penny tell you that, too? I never joined the NSDAP. I never made propaganda. All of this was established during my immigration hearings, where I made my case with overwhelming evidence, all of which is, along with transcripts, on file with the INS. My politics are not what's at stake here. I always hated them, even before the ovens. They burned people, and they burned my movies.

Everyone who was anyone was there that night at the Kaiserhof: Albers, Fritsch, Veidt, Jannings, Lorre, Dietrich. The walls were lined with goons in uniforms, and many of the assembled actors, directors, and producers arrived in party uniforms. Lang was wearing one, and he'd pinned on some sort of medal he'd won in World War I. He was in bad shape, pale and haggard. He'd gotten divorced from Thea von Harbou after he found her in bed with an Indian prince by the name of Ayi Tendulakr. The entire city had laughed about it for weeks. His new movie, *Das Testament des Dr. Mabuse*, had been held up by the censors for months, its future uncertain.

Penelope had not received an invitation to the meeting; like Lang, I came alone. Reichspropagandaminister Goebbels, the limping lying crippled sack of shit, came in flanked by stormtroopers, Prince Wilhelm August of Prussia, and Count Wolf Heinrich Helldorf. Some Arschloch from the *Reichsverband der Lichtspieltheaterbesitzer* gave a speech. I didn't listen until Goebbels got up to speak. He moved like one of Lang's actors, with brisk, controlled gestures that might as well have been counted off by a metronome. It was chilling. He called himself "an impassioned devotee of cinematic art" and assured us that he did not want to put boundaries on anyone. I might have sneered if it hadn't been for the SA men. "Tendentious art can also be great art," he said, and then he singled out five movies for praise: Edmund Goulding's *Love*, *Battleship Potemkin*, Trenker's *Rebel*, *Die Nibelungen*, and *Tulpendiebe*. It was incredible: three of these movies were directed by Jews, *Potemkin* glorified the Bolshevik revolution–and *Tulpendiebe*? Goebbels liked my film? How was this possible? How dare he!

But I admit–I was also intrigued. Did Goebbel's taste trump his ideology, or was this just one more blatant attempt at manipulation? But to what end? I needed to know what this meant, for my movies and for my future.

After the speeches, I was introduced. The newly appointed Minister of Culture and Propaganda was hunched over, with a piercing gaze and gaunt cheeks. He regarded my prosthetic leg, barely noticeable to the general public, with a connoisseur's eye. Goebbels knew movies and he knew cripples.

"It's Kino himself," he said to me. I held out my hand, but he flapped his. "*Heil Hitler!*"

I took my hand back.

"Your movies contain the seeds," he said. "They are deeply flawed and yet point the way to a pure, perfect German film art."

"Deeply flawed?"

I must have raised my voice, because the circle of uniformed bootlickers around us tightened instantly.

Goebbels waved them off. "As groundbreaking as your films are, they are marred by imperfections and absurd ideas. Your flawed utopias only hint at the glorious destiny that awaits the German volk. Once you outgrow your ambiguities, I am certain you will become a valuable asset to National Socialist film. One day, your work will live up to the power and ingenuity of the German spirit!"

I was speechless. My films connected with Goebbels because the Nazis, too, wanted to bring about the world of their dreams. Yes, Goebbels recognized my incredible talent. Then again, the Reichspropagandaminister didn't understand a thing. My utopias had nothing to do with perfection because perfection is not something to strive for. All my movies were flawed, and I wouldn't have it any other way. Mapmakers always insert one wrong detail into their maps– a lake that doesn't exist, a county line that stretches a hilltop too far, a misspelled street name. It is a way to identify unauthorized copies, but it's also an opening through which the infinite rushes in: if one thing is wrong, then anything might be wrong. It's the same principle through which a single blank bullet calms the conscience of the entire firing squad.

The missing leg had taught me about flaws early on, about living with limitations. I took it as a sign that I was special, and when I began writing for the movies, I figured that I wanted them to be like my body, unique through their mistakes and missing limbs. Watching a perfect movie is like climbing a smooth wall—there's nowhere for your fingers to grab hold. I was always looking for something broken, a scar, a sign of struggle or damage, something that didn't fit, a crack that would create a space for everything that wasn't perfect.

The world saw later, in black-and-white footage from the liberated camps, the true face of German perfection. A vision of a rigid world without contradiction, where flaws and weaknesses were removed, suffocated, exterminated, and burned. My world would have all the freaks, homos, and Jews in it, and all the gypsies and pimps, Tauntziengirls and Bonzen, too. The innocent were blessed along with the sinners, and that's why everyone gets gold at the end of *Tulpendiebe*. Goebbels was no idiot, but he didn't understand art or truth—he dealt only in death and control.

Horrified, I said my goodbyes and fled from the Kaiserhof.

The next day, I was back on the set, shooting Silko's arrival on fog-shrouded Mulberry Island, when a bunch of SA thugs marched right through the studio gate and ordered the cameras turned off and production shut down, effective immediately by direct order of Hans Weidemann, vice-chairman of the Reichs-Film-Kammer. I was summoned to Weidemann's office, where the self-satisfied bastard explained to me that my film was on hold until the screenplay could be re-evaluated by the censorship office. He recommended changes involving Mulberry Island's anarchic pirate society and the ending. He made it clear that my continued employment in Germany's film industry—and that of my wife—depended on our cooperation. Then he congratulated me on having been singled out for praise at the Kaiserhof by Dr. Goebbels himself. That day, the Ufa board moved to fire every single one of its Jewish employees and anybody who'd ever belonged to the Communist party.

I knew right away we had to leave—even if it meant walking away from the biggest movie of my career. I would not be censored. "It's blackmail," I told Penelope when I got home. We were both drinking from very large snifters of Weinbrand. "It's unacceptable. We will not work for these goons! *Scheiss drauf*," I said, lifting my drink. "To Holly-wood!"

I would have packed up and embarked on the next steamer west right then, but there was one problem: Leo, Penelope's father, the retired, widowed professor, had been stewing in anger and antifascist hatred ever since the Machtergreifung, and he didn't want to hear anything about leaving Germany. When he heard what had happened at Ufa, he worked himself into a state, waving a bottle of beer around by the neck. "It would be a grave mistake to abandon our country in its hour of need!" Already, he'd been beaten for shopping at a Jewish bookstore. He'd come home with a bloody head and his Reklam edition of *Mother Courage* torn to shreds, but the incident only strengthened his resolve. For

Leo, leaving was out of the question, and the next morning, over rolls and soft-boiled eggs, Penelope told me in a calm, quiet voice: "Don't force me to choose between my father and you."

Maybe this is where I went wrong, all those years ago. Maybe that was the moment I made the crucial first compromise, the one sin that entailed the last doom. I can't say for sure, but as always, it was Penelope who pushed me further down the road that led away from my true calling. At the time, it seemed like a reasonable way to buy us time—I thought I could always change things back to the way they were. And so I agreed to the rewrites. I got good and drunk, took the script I'd slaved over, and started changing things around as if I were writing a greeting card. That is why I rewrote *Pirates*: for her and for her stubborn goat of a father. In her infinite generosity, Penelope even helped me! In my original draft, the free pirate nation on Mulberry Island had peacefully co-existed with a tribe of natives for centuries, but we knew Weidemann found this offensive—so we took them out. Deleted the natives, just like that. Then we changed the ending.

The next day, I took the rewrites to the Reichs-Film-Kammer and was briskly informed that Herr Weidemann was in Nürnberg for the *Reichsparteitag*. I left my script on a receptionist's desk and slunk away.

In the weeks after the Kaiserhof meeting, a great exodus began. Marlene and Sternberg were already gone, but now Conrad Veidt, Peter Lorre, Billy Wilder, Joe May, Pasternak, Picator, Reinhardt, Weill, and the Siodmarks left. Pommer's contract was "terminated in view of the impossibility of realizing his productions under present circumstances." He received a special visa from the Ministry of Propaganda, and was escorted to the next train to Paris by ministry officials. Werner Heymann, the director of the Ufa orchestra and composer on all my movies, was offered continued employment if he got baptized. Eric Charell's *Odysseus* film was shitcanned. They all took off. Lang later made up preposterous lies designed to make him look like a hero of the resistance, but the real reason he left was that Thea had humiliated him, and the Film Board had banned *Das Testament des Dr. Mabuse* from exhibition in Germany. The Führer of Cinema! I guarantee you that he came up with that title all by himself! For Lang, it would have taken courage to stay, and he slunk away.

Within the year, most of Germany's best talent had relocated to America. Others fell all over themselves jockeying for the newly available positions. Penelope was drinking too much, she got into shouting matches with her father and sat up in the garden in the middle of the night. I never knew which Penelope I would come home to: the fury who raged and ranted against the Nazis, or the maudlin wreck. All along, I kept making feverish inquiries in America. Pommer put in a good word for me at Metro-Goldwyn-Meyer. Walt Disney was said to have been a fan of *Tulpendiebe*. There was no word from the censorship office about *Pirates;* instead, Weidemann offered me a musical comedy called *Luftschiffwalzer.*

In June, Steffen announced that he was celebrating his grand farewell. He was my oldest friend, but we hadn't seen each other much since he had had fallen out with Penelope during the shoot of *Jagd zu den Sternen*. He'd moved into the Belvedere with Ray and given up pimping for a lifestyle of luxury and a creeping heroin habit. The new regime didn't look kindly upon homosexuals, and Ray left the country as soon as the Nazis took over. Steffen explained that he'd stayed behind to take care of a few loose ends and would now follow Ray to New York–but not without one last blowout at the Belvedere.

We asked Leo to join us for the party, but he preferred to stay at home with his Asbach Uralt and underground leaflets. I've often wondered how different all of our lives would have turned out if the stubborn old man hadn't been so reluctant to have a good time.

When we got to the Wannsee, the villa was already filled with guests and music and food, an extravagant buffet, luxurious wines, even an American band. "How is he paying for all of this?" Penelope wondered. Indeed, the Belvedere had not seen such lavish entertaining since long before the stock markets crashed in twenty-nine.

And yet, the guests–a mix of shady halfworld characters and second-class artists–seemed ill at ease, overly careful about what they said and who they said it to. Nobody danced. During the halcyon days, the Belvedere had been a cauldron of recklessness, but there could be no doubt that the good times were over. In the west wing, where the opium smokers used to congregate, we ran into Ute the Mole Girl, dressed so conventionally I didn't recognize her at first. Awkwardly, she introduced us to her new husband, a dentist.

"You didn't used to believe in marriage," I said. Her husband's hair was parted just like Hitler's, and she mumbled something and pulled him away from us in a hurry.

Out by the pier, Steffen danced to a jazz combo led by one of the last black trumpeters left in Berlin. The sun hadn't set yet but Steffen was zonked out of his mind already, an ivory cigarette holder in one hand, the other buried deep in the pocket of his white dinner jacket. He sang a tune, something by Duke Ellington, while Katja Berber danced naked in honor of her sister, who had been dead for years already. Steffen's good cheer felt desperate, as if he wanted to prove something.

A dour young man who had witnessed the Nazi raid on Dr. Hirschfeld's institute stuffed his face with sausage and pronounced the affair "quite dreadful," but Steffen shushed him."No politics! Tonight, we celebrate!" He blew kisses on Penelope's cheeks and gave me one of his bear hugs.

"To America," I said, and we drank. "I'll miss you," I told him, and it was true.

Steffen's face was as ruddy as always but his eyes looked sadder than ever. I groped for words to cheer him up.

"It's a temporary farewell, right? We'll see each other over there?"

He nodded and tried to light a cigarette but his hand was shaking.

"Soon, all of this will seem like a distant joke," I said.

He laughed at that and gave me a look that made me wish I could go with him. What a team we could have been—a fresh start, a new country, more opportunities than we would have known what to do with. Steffen toasted to friendship and we drank.

Schumann, the winner of that year's six-day bike race, arrived. There was a Polonaise, a French chef presented a cake decorated with a marzipan Statue of Liberty, and Steffen cut it. While we ate our dessert, a brash young man barged in on our conversation, introduced himself as the director of a film I'd never heard of, and broadly congratulated me on *Luftschiffwalzer.*

"What is *Luftschiffwalzer?*" Steffen wanted to know.

Luftschiffwalzer was an operetta about the journeys of the high-spirited musical crew of a zeppelin airship, the film Weidemann had offered me while I waited to hear about the fate of *Pirates,* but that wasn't what I told Steffen. I made a series of halting, half-guilty, half-angry confessions that I hadn't admitted to myself yet. I told him: "We're just holding them off." I told him: "I'm not making *Luftschiffwalzer.*" I told him: "I'm not making *Pirates* either, even if they approve the rewrites." I told him I was sorry. I told him I had no offers from America.

Suddenly, Steffen was frighteningly sober, and he wasn't accepting apologies. He loudly demanded an answer: "Kino, is this true? You rewrote your movie for that pig Goebbels?"

The room went silent. I felt drained, embarrassed, and tired. Everyone was listening now, and it was easiest to answer the question directly. "Yes. I did."

Steffen's red-rimmed eyes offered no solace, no friendship. "I had no choice," I said. "I am Kino."

"You're not my friend," he said. "You have to leave now. Go. Now."

And that was it, simple as that. There was no gushing outburst of Scheunenviertelslang and Romanian gypsy talk, no manic gestures. The very last words Steffen ever said to me were every bit as bitter as his first, at the Wintergarten, had been seductive. He was right, of course. It *was* time to leave. There was nothing left to be said.

Penelope and I took our coats and left the Belvedere for the last time.

I would never see Steffen again.

When we came home that night, we found the house empty. Leo was gone, along with his political pamphlets. A stamped and signed document on the table informed us that he had been detained. The neighbors said they had watched as a Gestapo van arrived and three men in uniform had led Leo down the driveway. *Abgeholt*, that's what it was called: taken away, as if by a terminal disease or God's will.

Penelope swallowed tears, but her face was stern. "Beliefs are not crimes," she said. "We will get him out."

We sat at the kitchen table all night, unable to sleep. At dawn, we went down to Plötzensee prison to find out what Leo was accused of. We spent the day in drab offices decorated with swastikas, taking turns at restless naps on uncomfortable hardwood benches. Finally, we faced yet another brownshirt who adjusted his wire-frame glasses to better read Leo's file with seasoned disdain.

It should not have been a surprise. Leo gave everyone who would listen an earful about the evils of the new government, and for years, he had submitted articles to the communist journal *Vorwärts,* now forbidden. I'd always known that he was risking his life, but he wouldn't listen. He was every bit as stubborn and stupid as his daughter.

A hearing date was set, and the word "*Sippenhaft"* was mentioned, which meant Leo's family could be threatened with investigations as well. We left, dispirited. We knew that Penelope's father could not expect a fair trial. He would be lucky to get tried at all.

There was more bad news waiting for us back at the house: Ute, pale and devastated, was waiting on our front steps. In the early hours of dawn, after the last guests had left the party, Steffen had sent the musicians and the help home, lit the chandeliers, put Whispering Jack Smith on the gramophone, and shot himself up with a lethal overdose of morphine.

He left no note.

Ute explained that he had been lying about Ray and New York—he had been dumped, left behind all alone with instructions to sell the villa and forget their affair. He'd been left to the Nazis and his own diminished devices, and he must have felt that he had nowhere left to turn.

All I wanted at that moment was to take back the rewrites, take back that awful last time I'd seen him. But Steffen had always been savvier than me and I wondered if in killing himself, he had somehow taken control and shown the courage I lacked, and what was I supposed to do now? With my wife's father in a Nazi prison, what options did we have? Herr Dokter, my last true friend was dead, and I was trapped.

With its rightful owner gone, the Belvedere was taken over by the government. Only a few short years after our last sad debauch, high-ranking Nazis met at another lakeside villa, just a little ways up the street, with the same gorgeous views of the sailboats and the lido, the same gentle waves lapping at their pier, and agreed on what they called the Final Solution to the Jewish question in Europe.

Out of desperation, I contacted Thea von Harbou. She had, in fact, joined the Nazi party, but I hoped a fellow filmmaker and great artist might have valuable advice. I was not wrong: Thea liked to think of herself as a patriot, not a fascist. In the end, it was a useless distinction, but at that time, her loyalty wasn't total. She was concerned when I told her what had happened to Penelope's father, and I was glad I'd come to her. I remembered the time my leg had fallen off during *Die Nibelungen* and she saved me from Lang's wrath. Just being in her calming presence made me feel optimistic. I would gladly do whatever Thea suggested.

"Silly Klaus," she said with a wink. "Your worries are only a symptom of your need for drama. You want to be the center of attention, the special case, the outlaw. I am sorry for what happened to your friend, and of course I am also worried about your father-in-law. But do you really think sneaking away like Fritz will help, when you have every opportunity here, in Germany? Why would you run to America and pretend their system isn't ruled by special interests? Who do you think owns Hollywood? You may not agree with Goebbels' politics, but he is a man of discerning taste. The movies are always beholden to somebody–so why not stay home, where truly great things are possible? Accept Weidemann's offer, work for the glory of the German people. It is the only solution."

She poured me a cognac and patted my hand, as if I were one of her beloved lap dogs. What if she was right? At any rate, I felt that I had run out of options. The next day, I called Weidmann's office and accepted his offer to direct *Luftschiffwalzer.*

Don't shake your head at me, Herr Dokter. At the time, it felt like the heroic thing–to hold out hope instead of stealing away like a coward. Hope for Leo, hope for Germany, hope for *Pirates.* Hope for Penelope and myself.

A week later, word came down that my *Pirates* rewrites did not comply with RFK requirements. My older films were banned from public presentation. The verdict claimed that my work was admired "by socialists, communists, faggots, Frenchmen, and negroes." My films were categorized as degenerate art. Under the exhibition ban, all prints were locked away in the Ufa archives. I appealed with the Propagandaminister himself and petitioned Ufa President Hugenberg. I contacted Tobis Film. I even spoke to my brother Heinz about funding me independently, but nothing could be done–the verdict of the Reichs-Film-Kammer was final.

Goebbels' praise for *Tulpendiebe* had been a trap, a lie. He knew enough to recognize my incredible talent, but he wanted to press it into the service of his own dark visions. My movies were to be locked up and hidden from view while I followed orders. I used to write, direct, and edit all my films, but under no circumstances would the nationalized Ufa grant me that freedom. For the next ten years, as the world fell apart, I made idiotic, pandering operetta entertainments ordered up by mass murderers. Instead of constructing cathedrals of light, I built garish tombs.

Luftschiffwalzer, written by a young hotshot from Dotz-heim, was a success with German audiences desperate for escape. Next, they assigned me *Tanz um die Welt*, an insipid singspiel about the world tour of a Bavarian Schuhplattler who picks up local dances on the way and is reconciled with his estranged wife, who also happens to be a dancer.

I can proudly say I never made propaganda about war or destiny, advertisements for death like Leni or Ucicky or Veit Harland. My films were opulently designed and outfitted, and in the beginning, Goebbels made sure I had the budget for lavish productions. I made romantic kitsch designed to numb the masses for a few merciful hours. As much as I hated them, at least they were movies, and they kept me sane. While I churned out fluff, cruelty manifested every-where: *Kristallnacht*, the *Anschluss*, war, fear, suffering, and hatred. Leo remained in prison but we lived handsomely while the world went up in flames.

Penelope refused to take another role. When she wasn't hopelessly pleading her father's case, she retreated into the library while I filmed good Germans waltzing and kissing. Word of American films reached us, but we couldn't see them; even in Germany, my movies were forever second-rate to the big prestige productions, the *Bismarck* movies, *Titanic*, Albers' *Münchhausen*. We waited for Germany to come to its senses.

My brother Heinz brought the news in forty-two: Leo had contracted pneumonia in Bergen-Belsen and died. Penelope was inconsolable, but to me, the news was also a relief. The waiting and the worry were finally over. She would never see her father again—he had disappeared into the camps along with millions of others.

At the time, I was shooting the last scenes of *Matterhorn*, a latter-day mountain movie that was filmed entirely in the studio and was too laughable for even Arnold Fanck. The scripts kept getting worse, and my budgets had been slashed. When I protested, Goebbels offered to send me to Poland as a war reporter. By now, he was busy whipping crowds into a mad frenzy for total war, and he had little respect for movies he now considered overaestheticized and bourgeois.

I had begun to despise my work, and I became an expert at carefully tarnishing shots, sneaking imperfections into the films. It gave me pleasure to subvert them ever so slightly. In the big finale of *Brünette auf dem Kurfürstendamm*, one of the chorus girls has a nose bleed. I was delighted that she made it unnoticed past the censors. I confused street names and purposefully got historical details wrong. It wasn't much, but the flaws inserted a small element of truth into my creations, a chink in the armor, a seed of hope. Eventually, the war would end and I would make films again. *My* films.

After learning of Leo's death, I got more reckless on the set of *Matterhorn*, with absurd line readings, new dialogue, and overuse of the wind machines. There were murmurs of protest from the cast. While Willy Fritsch riffed on what he'd had for breakfast, some dark glances aimed my way left no doubt that I would be denounced if this kept up. Only a few months ago, Herbert Selpin, the director of *Titanic*, had been arrested by the Gestapo in mid-shoot after he openly criticized the script. The following morning, he'd been found dead in his cell, and Werner Klingler finished the movie. It was now obvious to anyone that Goebbels would not hesitate to murder his directors.

Penelope and I drowned our regrets in alcohol. Every night found us schnapps-drunk and morose, every morning hung over and bitter. Something had to happen, and it was Penelope who declared–finally, finally–that the time had come. With her father dead, nothing kept us in Germany. I agreed right away, no matter how difficult it would be.

Lutz Hackauf, once Steffen's man for rough jobs, was now in the refugee business, smuggling people through France and North Africa to America. In exchange for our house and the last of our savings, he furnished us with fake passports and passage on a sleeper train to Paris. I hid our last thousand Reichsmark in a hollowed-out compartment in my leg.

As the steam engine prowled through the night, I felt a surge of freedom that I hadn't felt in years. We were leaving everything behind: the Nazis, the dead father, the war, and the insipid operettas. We'd sold our house and the cars. I would never see Neubabelsberg again–Hollywood lay ahead. Penelope, too, glowed with excitement. We hadn't had sex in years, but on that train, we fucked like young lovers.

We reached the French border at dawn. A contingent of Gestapo officers boarded the train and knocked on every door. I wasn't awake yet when two officers demanded our passports.

They lingered over them for too long.

"Moment mal," the older of the two said, just when he should have handed the papers back. A grin began to spread on his face when it dawned on him that this was a bust he'd brag about for years to come. "I recognize you!" he said, already reaching for Penelope's arm and twisting it behind her back. "Your name isn't Teigmann. I've seen you in the movies!"

We were taken back to Berlin on the back of a truck, handcuffs biting into our wrists, our bright new future a victim of our past, our escape foiled by Penelope's too-memorable face. There was a hearing and we were locked away in Plötzensee prison–separated, awaiting an uncertain fate. I demanded a trial, I demanded a lawyer, I wanted to speak to Thea, to Goebbels, we had friends in high places and didn't they know who I was! But for over a year, there was nothing but the sound the deadbolt made in the door and the guard shaking his beefy head under his Stahlhelm.

The punishment, when it finally came, was worse than death: one cold morning, four SS officers escorted me out of my cell. It was the time of day for executions—I often heard the rifle pops from the back yard—and I was certain I was done for. Starved and sick, I was so weak I could barely walk, and they hit me with the butts of their guns.

Penelope, emaciated and pale, was waiting in the yard. They wouldn't let us talk, and I couldn't read anything in her eyes, still as large and beautiful as always but filled with new depths of suffering I could not fathom. A large, coiled mass of black things snaking out of silver shells filled the center of the courtyard. Penelope's legs were shaking. Then I realized what it was they had dumped onto the cobblestones: a heap of film, carelessly thrown and left to unspool in the morning breeze like so many dangling black curls, flapping over the asphalt, almost light enough to lift up and fly away.

Weidemann, the vice-chairman of the *Reichs-Film-Kammer*, had presided over the delivery of the prints himself. He gave us a curt wave, signed them over, got back in his limousine, and drove away.

It was the saddest sight in the world, my films there on the ground, beyond salvaging, image after image after image unspooling on the cobblestones. Nitrate prints are highly flammable, but that didn't keep the executioners of my life's work from pouring kerosene on for good measure. Just like on the morning during World War I when my father had all enemy literature burned, I clung to hope until the last possible moment while the commander lazily fished a cigarette from a silver case, struck a match to light it, took a deep drag, blew a few smoke rings, and, almost as an afterthought, flicked the match into the amassed celluloid.

The explosion almost knocked us off our weakened feet, and when I close my eyes I can still see the sudden flame, higher than the tallest prison watchtower. What was left after the initial burst burnt quickly and left sticky soot on the faces of everyone there.

I expected them to kill us after the last cinders had turned to ash, but instead, we were shoved on the flatbed of a truck, guarded by two soldiers each. The commander offered us a smoke and handed us a change of clothes, a manila envelope with 200 Marks, passports, and passage through Denmark and from there to America on the steamer Walter Siegfried Steiner. We were to live! Penelope and I would go to America, but Lilly and the sailor, *Tulpendiebe, Land der Gande, Meine wilden Wanderjahre, Jagd zu den Sternen,* even the shit movies I had made on Goebbel's orders, all the images I had dedicated my life to creating, had gone up in the steely morning sky, forever lost. My work and my history, all signs of my genius had been cruelly exterminated before my eyes. We were to live, but I had to go on living in a world where my movies didn't exist.

Ten years after opening its arms to all the other immigrants, America was not kind to us. After months of interrogations, Penelope and I were approved in November, weeks before Pearl Harbor would have made it impossible. In Hollywood, our oldest friends turned their backs on us. We were considered enemy aliens and forced to carry special IDs. There was a curfew, mistrust, suspicion, and outright hostility. The FBI kept tabs on us, and we were asked more than once if we were Nazi spies by the people we used to consider friends. We were treated like outcasts, like traitors. Peter Lorre called me a collaborator. Joe May, that hack, accused me publicly of sidling up to Goebbels. That bastard Lang was allowed to keep on making grim and terrible movies, and we weren't welcome at Salka Viertel's house in Santa Monica where all the émigrés congregated.

Penelope, of course, had changed. The ordeal of the last decade had left her a woman I could barely reconcile with the regal movie star I had fallen in love with. On our transatlantic voyage, in constant fear of torpedoes, mines, and stray allied bombardment, I came to realize that the last remnants of her love and support had vanished, and as if to mark the transformation, she changed her name before we arrived at Ellis Island. Penelope became Penny–quicker, cheaper, meaner. A name well suited to our new life.

I refused to give up. I managed to find work as a writer at RKO. Eventually, I knew, I would find my way back into the business and direct another movie. Penny now openly sabotaged me, and her petty intrigues cost me all sorts of jobs. On the day the Marines landed in South Korea, she surprised me with the news that she was pregnant. Now, when we had nothing, we were going to become parents? I couldn't stand the thought of it.

The boy, Detlef, was never more than a pawn to Penny. It was her who insisted I make commercials when our boy needed an education. Yes, I became a director for television commercials. And why not? I had no honor left. Clean smiles with Colgate! I knew how to do this, show a world where everybody consumes and agrees. It was soulless work, even more mind-numbing and insidious than the operettas. I had managed to slip things past the Nazi censors, but American companies demanded deadly, suffocating perfection.

Eventually, I quit that, too. Instead, I drive a cab. The new automatics are easy enough for aging cripples. At night I criss-cross the streets of Los Angeles, where my old friends still ride white-wheeled limousines to gala premieres. I'm a good cabbie. I like the night shifts, when it's quiet, and between fares, I work on scripts, sketching scenes, polishing dialogue, incorporating snippets from newspaper headlines and overheard conversations in the backseat. Sometimes, I wonder if I could drive fast enough so the passing street lights would flash by at twenty-four frames a second. What kind of world could I see through my dusty windshield then?

I am Kino.

Herr Dokter, I never forget this, even at my lowest. I always knew there'd be another chance, here in America, no matter how much Penny spread lies, smeared my name, and manipulated my old friends into shunning me. If I held on to my imagination, I would make another movie.

And I was right. Two months ago, I picked up a fare at LAX, and when I looked at the man in the rearview mirror, I recognized old Martin Wagner. I could have jumped on top of my hood and danced! It was Marty!

I've driven a few old friends and even more enemies, and lifted their luggage, too, but Marty Wagner and I went back all the way to *Jagd zu den Sternen*, where he was an assistant to the camera man. He has done well for himself since our days in Berlin, very well indeed – he is an executive producer at Paramount, and in my taxi he bragged about working with Stanley on *Spartacus*.

Then came the awkward pause when it was his turn to ask about my life, but I was not asking for pity. I told him that I was working on a new, updated version of *Pirates of Mulberry Island*. I had a copy of it sitting right there next to me on the passenger seat and handed it to him through the divider. He promised to take a look and gave me a nice tip.

Promises come easy in California, and I didn't think about it again. Imagine my surprise when three weeks later, I found a piece of paper in the trash can, between the used coffee filters and the orange rinds. It had been torn to pieces, but I could still make out the Paramount letterhead: "From the desk of Martin Wagner."

Penny had meant to shred the letter but she couldn't even get that much right. I confronted her, and she admitted that she'd been shielding me from inquiries. Marty loved my script! His secretary called but Penny kept her from reaching me, and the letter was his final attempt to set up a meeting. Marty had convinced his bosses that I could do for Paramount what I'd done for Pommer's Bioskop in twenty-seven.

Do you understand what this means, Herr Dokter? They want me back. There's interest in my person from inside the business, from one of the majors. Fate, in its infinite wisdom, has elected to give me one more chance. Since the day the SA marched into my studio and forced me to abandon *The Pirates of Mulberry Island,* I have perfected the script, not only restoring the tragic rewrites we did for Weidemann but making it better, much better. I poured everything I've learned into it. I know now that the true secret to a story's power lies in its architecture. The only difference between tragedy and comedy is where you stop, and I never stopped. The meaning of *Pirates* won't lie in its scenes but in the spaces between them. *The Pirates of Mulberry Island* will be my masterpiece.

And that, Herr Dokter, is why I am here. Hollywood wants me back, and my wife would rather see me rot in your *Klapsmühle* than let me take my proper place in the canvas chair again, with a bullhorn in my hand. That's why she had me committed.

Now, Herr Dokter, can you understand the fury I felt when I found Marty's letter buried in the trash? Penny is attempting to rob me of my reason to live. When she realized she couldn't contain me, she called the police and had me taken away, carried off in handcuffs by thugs in uniforms, just like her father had been taken away, never to return. You and your frocked henchmen did the rest, and now I waste away in your cell while somewhere on the Paramount lot, a producer waits for me. Right now, you see, everything is still at stake. After all these years, there's an offer on the table, my chance to direct *Pirates,* and Penny is trying to keep me from my destiny. Her twisted mind blames me, blames my movies, for everything that went wrong, and that's why she wants to destroy me.

I ask you: which one of us is insane?

Chapter 12

Mina aimed a cherry-red Thunderbird up Pacific Highway. She was filled with wild exhilaration: the sun was setting over the ocean that roared to her left, her hair was whipping her face, and on the radio, Lou Reed sang about Sweet Jane. Mina had come all the way to California, to the far edge of the continent, all by herself. She'd taken the same journey that her grandparents had made by ship and train in 1943, but for her, it was just a long day's flight. The convertible had been a snap decision at LAX.

Mina had reached Sam by phone from the terminal. "Did you get my email? You're not mad, are you?" she'd said, aware right away how disingenuous it sounded.

"I got your email," he said, and that was all Mina needed to hear. Of course he was mad. Finally, he'd gotten mad. "I got your email. You're having a big adventure while I'm rotting in this shitty hospital. Now you're in California. I try to understand you, Mina. I do try."

"Oh I know, baby, it can't be easy. But if you'd seen the movie, if you'd read the journal–"

"Have you heard of dengue shock syndrome? My temperature's been going up again. The doctor says I'll need a platelet transfusion if my blood cell count falls any further. These nurses here, they're the only ones who give a shit. The mortality rate is much higher for people with a second infection, but that doesn't mean I'm not in danger. I could die in here."

"I'll be home soon, I promise."

"You promised before, Mina. This is no good. I want you to come home. I want you here, I need you here, and I hate that I have to ask. I've never seen anyone so stubborn in my life. You're making me feel awful, having to yell at you about this. I defended you against your dad, but now you're in California and I just don't know anymore."

"What is that supposed to mean?"

"It means–I don't know–if you can't even be here for me now, when we just got married and I'm deadly sick, how do you think that makes me feel? Nobody understands, Mina. Everybody I talk to, they all tell me the same thing."

That stung. Who was he talking to? Was he threatening her? "Oh yeah," she said weakly. "And what's that?"

"Mina, you know I love you. I just don't understand why you're not here. I've been so alone–" There was a pause, and then, over the din at baggage claim, she heard a little sound and realized Sam was crying.

"Baby, you'll understand once you see the movie, once you read his journals. You have to trust me. Isn't that what marriage is all about?"

But Sam was done talking. Mina was eager to get off the phone. There was nothing else she could say. She knew he'd understand eventually.

"Here comes my bag," she lied. "I'll call you later tonight, okay? At least we're almost in the same time zone again, right? I love you, baby."

Gently, she hung up on her husband. She wanted to see him, be with him, make him feel better—but not yet, not until she'd met her grandmother and asked about the past, about Kino and Lilly, about Goebbels and *Pirates*. Her grandmother, who'd been a movie star. Besides, she really was in danger. Mysterious goons were after Mina, there'd been a bomb threat, a rooftop chase, and a car crash. Mina faintly understood she was testing something, the limits of their love perhaps, and she didn't know how to turn around now. She couldn't turn around now.

The truth was, finding her grandfather's movie was the most exciting thing that had happened to Mina in a long time. She had panicked, having to take care of Sam like that, when they were supposed to be on their honeymoon. The first day, when his temperature had just begun to rise, she left him in the hotel room with a fresh fruit juice, hitting the beach by herself.

The fight at the wedding reception was a bad omen, but Mina realized that her favorite moment of what was billed as the best day of her life wasn't when she said "I do" or when they leaned in to kiss, pronounced husband and wife. It wasn't when they had sex, hours later in their Caribbean hotel, tired and groggy after the flight. No: the best moment of Mina's wedding day was when she leapt up on the lip of the stage, grabbed the neck of the wedding band's electric guitar, lifted it high over her head, and, in front of all her family and friends and husband of two hours, brought it down hard on a speaker's edge. That crunch and pop, the kickback in her arms and the sudden shocked silence, the electric surge of freedom and courage—that was the part she'd never forget.

More than anything, Mina wanted to keep moving. She switched the car to manual transmission and geared down to pass a station wagon. As she shot past, she could see a father at the wheel, the mother turned in her seat to face children in the back, a toddler in a baby seat and an older girl with pigtails holding a sandwich dripping jelly. One of the girl's eyes was covered with an eye patch, white gauze stuck to her face with band aids. Her other eye looked straight at Mina. With a chill, Mina recognized it as the exact look Lilly gives the sailor at the end of *Tulpendiebe*.

By the time Mina found her grandmother's house, up in the Hollywood hills, it was dusk. She'd been there before, when she was a child, but the two-story Mediterranean house wasn't anywhere near as grand as the mansion of her memories. Mina took the journal out of the glove compartment, stuffed it into her back pocket, and walked up to ring the door bell. When she realized the door was ajar, she gave a half-hearted knock and pushed it open.

For most of her life, Mina's father had been preoccupied with making heaps of money on Wall Street. He talked to his mother only on birthdays and holidays. But the year Mina was ten, a strange invitation arrived: on gold-embroidered stationery covered in thin, spidery handwriting, Penny asked them to come out to California for Christmas.

Here's what Mina remembered from that trip: the musty smell, the pool you could swim in even though it was December, the broken glass on the kitchen floor, and the creepy old woman with matchstick limbs who swung back and forth between morose stupor and howling fury, who threw tantrums unlike anything Mina had witnessed in her parents' polite household. That's where the broken glass came from.

Mina spent most of the holiday in the safety of the pool, and on Christmas day, Detlef moved his family to a hotel on Santa Monica Boulevard. They spent New Year's at Disneyland and Mina had her picture taken with Minnie Mouse. When they got home, Mina told her friends that her grandmother was a horrid old witch, nothing like her other grandmother, the one who brought homemade cookies in Tupperware bins.

Years later, her mother told her what had really happened that week. Penny had run up enormous debts and would have to sell the house unless her son bailed her out. It was a large sum of money even by a successful stock broker's standards, and Mina's parents fought bitterly about it. In the end, Detlef gave in, but they never visited Oma Penny again.

Now Mina looked down a dark, narrow hallway crammed with stacks of old newspapers, broken furniture turned toward the walls, and impressive rows of empty vodka bottles. The smell of stale cigarette smoke hung in the air, and from the far side of the house, she heard the blare of a television. Carefully side-stepping the hurdles, Mina was making her way past an unadorned staircase when she noticed a side table displaying framed photographs. As she turned to take a closer look, her backpack knocked an overflowing ashtray to the floor with a clang. Startled, she took a step back and sent a row of empty two-liter wine jugs rolling across the floor.

A man's voice: "Don, is that you?"

Mina didn't respond.

"Come on in, man. We been waiting for you."

Then she heard footsteps, and before her stood a black man in his sixties wearing jeans and a white t-shirt. He was bald, barefoot, and frowning.

"Who are you?" he asked.

Mina definitely didn't remember any bald black men from her childhood visit.

"Who are you?" she said. "I'm here to see my grandmother, Penelope Greifenau. Is she here?"

He was still frowning. "Chester Burwell. I'm her nurse. I'm afraid this is not a good time. Were we expecting you?"

"It's important that I see her."

Chester hesitated, searching Mina's face.

"It's not Don," he shouted.

A voice answered, hollow and wheezing: "Wo bleibt er denn? Wie lange soll ich denn noch ohne auskommen? *Verdammte Kacke!*"

Chester looked over his shoulder and told Mina to wait. She didn't and followed him down the hall, into a dark, cluttered den where a shriveled old woman sat in an armchair. Heavy curtains were drawn tight and the only light came from an enormous plasma screen showing a black-and-white movie, Gary Cooper in cowboy getup. The coffee table in front of the couch was covered with bottles of whiskey, cans of Diet Coke, pill containers, and pieces of an unfinished jigsaw puzzle. The old woman glared. Mina struggled to reconcile the ravaged face in front of her with the spotless features in *Tulpendiebe*. Could this really be the same person?

"Oma?" she said. "It's Mina. Do you remember me? I'm your granddaughter."

"Please," Chester said, taking Mina by the elbow. "You can't be in here. She's in poor health."

Penny waved a thin arm holding a lit cigarette. "You think just because I'm old I must be senile? I wish I'd lose my

memory every day but when I check, it's still there, all 92
fucking years of it. I know exactly who you are."

She took a long drag.

"Good," Mina said, taken aback. She had wondered if she
was supposed to hug her grandmother, but she would not go
near this woman.

"You're the brat who pissed in my pool and couldn't keep
her hands off my things." She took another drag. "I would've
thought you'd grow up taller than this. What's this outfit
you're wearing, anyway? A turtleneck sweater? This is
Hollywood, girl. *Verkackt nochmal*, whaddaya want already?
Close your mouth, child, it makes you look like a fucking
imbecile. I am watching a movie."

She had almost pushed herself out of her chair. With a
sigh, she fell back into the cushions. She stubbed out her
cigarette and lit another. The flaccid skin that hung from her
spidery arms was nearly translucent, showing red, blue, and
purple veins. On the screen, Gary Cooper put on the sheriff's
star. The movie was *High Noon*. Chester cleared his throat.

"I'm not an imbecile," Mina said. "I came here straight
from Berlin. I need to talk to you."

Penny turned up the volume on the TV. "I have nothing to
say to you. Chester, would you show the little twat to the
door?"

"No," Mina said. She sat down in an empty armchair. "I
won't leave until you answer my questions."

"*Gottverfluchte Scheisse*," Penny cursed. She reached for a
half-empty gallon of Dewars and tried to throw it at Mina,
but Chester caught her arm in the backswing.

"Penny darling," Chester cooed. "You're going to want to
drink that later."

Mina had ducked, but now she froze. What exactly was
her grandmother's relationship to this barefoot bald black

nurse? Penny let Chester take the bottle from her hand and instead grabbed a half-eaten chocolate chip cookie and flung it at Mina. It missed Mina's head and bounced off the bookshelf.

"What's all the shouting? Is there a problem?"

A man with a bushy beard and a white lab coat came through the hallway door. He had a hip bag in one hand, a handgun in the other. He aimed it at everyone in the room before settling on Mina.

"Whoa, whoa, whoa," Chester said. "It's okay. Don. So glad you're here. Put the gun down. This is...Mina, was it? She's family. Put the gun down. There's no problem."

"About time!" Penny snarled.

Don gave Mina a hard nod, shoved the gun back into his lab coat, and removed a number of prescription bottles from his bag. There was also a brown powder in a Ziploc baggie. Chester gave Don a wad of cash held together by a rubber band. Without counting it or saying another word, Don slid the money in his pocket, kissed Penny's hand, shook Chester's, and saw himself to the door.

"Did I just witness a drug deal?" Mina asked.

Penny pointedly ignored her and rubbed her hands together in a parody of glee. "Chester darling, I need a huff, a puff, and a fix. Would you please?" She lit another cigarette and spit on the carpet to her right, where Mina could make out a dark spot. Chester obligingly produced a jade mortar and matching pestle, counted out a handful of pills from one of the bottles, and began to grind them to a powder.

"Thanks for the lovely visit, young Wilhemina," Penny said, "but there's no time for nostalgia–I have drugs to take and movies to watch. Why are you still here?"

"What is all this?" Mina said, picking up the prescription bottles Don had left: Percocet. Xanax. Oxycodone. "I don't think that man was a real *Dokter*, Oma. That could be dangerous, self-medicating like this, mixing and matching?"

"Oh kid, I been doing this for decades, and today you walk in here and tell me it's dangerous? Why the sudden worry, princess?"

Chester delivered the powder to Penny on a silver tray. Through a short plastic straw, she sucked it up her nostrils. Then she looked at Mina. "Wait. Say that again. What did you just call him?"

"I called him a *Dokter*. That's what Kino used to call them, isn't it? He hated them ever since they took his leg off."

"How would you know any of this?" Penny demanded. She was trembling, and Mina realized that she had no idea if Penny always trembled, or if she was in a special trembling state right now.

"I read his journal."

"Pardon?"

"I read the journal that Kino wrote when you had him committed—in 1963, was it?" Mina pulled her grandfather's notebook out of her back pocket and threw it on the cluttered table. "I know you didn't always used to be this way. You were happy once. You were beautiful and famous and in love. I know you were Lilly, I know about the Braukeller, and about *Jagd zu den Sternen*. I know about your father, too, and Goebbels, and the burning of Kino's movies."

Penny was silent. She reached for the straw to do another line but instead knocked the tray off her lap. "*Scheisse*," she said. Chester hurried to set it back on the table and began grinding more pills.

"That *Dokter* was a real pompous ass," Penny said, trying to calm her shaking fingers enough to pull another cigarette from the pack. She smoked a long thin brand Mina didn't recognize. "The nonsense in fashion then was narrative therapy, a combination of creative prompts and pharmaceuticals. I didn't care as long as it kept him out of harm's way. Kino hated the Dokters. Can't blame him for that."

"I saw *Tulpendiebe*," Mina said. "It's not destroyed. I saw it, in Berlin, on a Doppelnocken projector. I saw it. That was you."

Chester put a heavy hand on Mina's shoulder. "Please," he said. "Penny is in frail health, and she can't take any excitement."

"Oh shut your trap, Chester. *Unkraut vergeht nicht!*" She turned her rheumy eyes on Mina. Mina returned the gaze, defiant. "Well fuck me silly," Penny said, reaching for the bottle of Dewars. She unscrewed it and took a deep drink. She offered the bottle, and Mina poured herself a glass.

"Go on," Penny said. Chester shook his head.

"I saw *Tulpendiebe*," Mina said again. "The Dutch town, the tulip craze, the sailor, and Lilly. That first shot of you—you were radiant. You were spectacular."

"Spectacular is right, girl. *Tulpendiebe* was a work of genius!"

Mina took a sip of whiskey. "I need you to tell me," she said.

"Tell you what, princess?"

"What happened after Kino was released." She tapped her finger on the cover of Kino's journal. "You have to tell me everything. Why he killed himself. You used to be famous and in love—how did you end up like this?"

"This will only upset you," Chester interrupted, reaching for Penny's hand.

"Oh, Chester. It's the little princess you should be worried about. She's in for it now. Just look, she wants to know *everything*. She's begging for it!" Penny got a good laugh out of that, a surprisingly sweet, warm laugh that didn't sound like it should emerge from the mangled old body in the arm chair.

"You want to know how I ended up here?" Penny was still shaking with laughter. "Step by fucking step, you twit! Shit happened, like it always does!"

She spit on the carpet again. Mina had to look away. She was revolted by this old woman, but she also wondered how much of it was an act, some kind of attempt to push her away. What was this strange scene she had walked into, and how long had these two been sitting here in the dark, watching old movies, drinking, smoking, taking drugs? How many years? Mina got up and pulled back the heavy curtains that covered the panorama windows, revealing a view of a desolate garden with a patio and a green pool overgrown with yuck. Beyond it, in the haze below, was Los Angeles.

"Poor child. You know nothing. You know less than nothing. You have no idea what Klaus was like." Penny shielded her face from the light, then turned away to light another cigarette. The first was still burning in the ashtray. "He was out of his mind, doped up, at the end of his rope! If you believe the first word of that journal, you're dumber than I thought."

"Hey!" Mina said.

She looked to Chester, but he wasn't going to defend her.

"Hey yourself," Penny said. "You are in my house. Uninvited. I say what I want. You want to know about the man who made those movies? Klaus only loved himself. He drank, he dealt *Zement*, he could never resist a line or a piece of ass or veal at Horcher, he was terrible with money, he was single-minded and stubborn. He was selfish, decadent, self-indulgent, reckless, unpredictable, and cruel. A mega-lomaniac."

"That's what Dad says," Mina broke in. "Decadent and a bad father and a failure."

"Oh, your father? Detlef the Dullard? That's what Klaus and I called him, did you know that? Not when he was around, of course. Jesus, he was a boring child!"

Mina looked down at the rug, at a gob of spit that had not yet been absorbed. Her father was not who she'd come to talk about, and the mention of him made her defensive. She wanted to protect her idea of Kino. A megalomaniac, that was fine. But maybe she didn't want to hear the rest, after all.

"He gave his inheritance to charity," Mina said. "After his parents died and he lost his leg, after the First World War. He didn't want anything to do with the family business and he gave it all away."

"Ha!" Oma clapped her hands together in delight. "He blew his money on coke and whores, and when the inflation hit, it all became worthless! He didn't give his inheritance to charity, he spent it on debauchery, and when it was gone, he sold his company stock to his brother Heinz. Kino was always a fool with money. Sure, he went broke, but he didn't give a penny to the needy." She laughed and laughed.

"Well, how would you know?" Mina said. "I mean, wasn't this before you met him? I'm so bored of hearing about what a failure Kino was. That's what Dad always called him, and that's all I ever heard."

"It's the truth, princess."

Mina shook her head. "Dad was embarrassed by him because he was never around, because his English wasn't very good, because his friends all had more money, because of the Nazi films, because of the suicide..."

"Penny," Chester interrupted. "Perhaps you should-"

"Oh shut it. I'm having a grand old time. Charity! It really is too much. This girl needs an education." She sat laughing to herself, then seemed to remember something. "Chester baby, I believe it's time for my injection."

Chester shifted uneasily. "Do you think that's such a good idea? Perhaps a little oxy instead?"

This time, a look from Penny was all it took, and Chester reached for the Ziploc bag of brown powder, emptied some of it onto a little spoon he took from a leather kit, and heated it over a Zippo. Morphine? Brown heroin? Mina didn't know; Mina didn't want to know. She averted her eyes while Chester cooked up the dope, tied Penny up and prepared the syringe. The anger Mina had felt earlier had given way to sickly pity. Without wasting a movement, Chester sunk the needle into the translucent, saggy flesh of Penny's arm. Oh yes, he was a professional nurse all right.

Penny gave a ghostly sigh and then it was done. When she opened her eyes again, she gave Mina a smile that was almost gentle.

"There's every reason in the world to feel embarrassed by him. Your father is right, of course–Klaus knew no moderation, no boundaries. When I met him, he was an addict and a whoremonger and a glutton, and it only got worse. He spent all his time smoking that opium. Do you want to hear about the venereal diseases your precious grandfather gave me?" She sighed again. Her rheumy eyes filled with tears.

"But that's only half the story. The bastard was also a visionary genius, and he could have been the greatest goddamned filmmaker the world has ever known. His images haunt me to this day. My medication," she pointed to her vein, "it's supposed to make them go away. I watch this shit–" waving her hand at Gary Cooper on the TV screen "– to make them go away. Kino's films never brought anyone anything but pain, death, and suffering, and now you to tell me *Tulpendiebe* still exists? How can I bear that?"

She held out her hand, and Mina leaned forward to take it. Under her breath, the old woman whispered something in German Mina didn't understand. She sucked air in sharply and scratched her scalp. "Every word in that notebook is a lie, princess. I know Klaus blamed the entire twentieth century on me, but his downfall was self-inflicted. He was slyer than he let on. He didn't mind when people underestimated him, thought him a jolly fella from the Rheinland with a taste for Schnapps and an eye for tail. It was real and it was also a façade, a way to hide his ambition until it was time to pounce. Do you really believe the tulip boom just occurred to him out of nowhere? Where do you think that came from? He researched everything. Look it up: Claude MacKey, *On the Susceptibility of Crowds*. That story about writing the script on a three-day coke binge? Bogus! Months of hard work. You wouldn't know it from his piece-of-shit lie-ridden journal, but Klaus had a real German work ethic. He was prepared when he showed up at Lang's party. He was trying much harder than he let anyone know."

Mina shook her head, avoiding Penny's eyes. She felt foolish because she'd believed what she'd read, and now it seemed so obvious that Kino had been exaggerating, working on his own mythology. She should've seen that.

"His cunning served him well at first," Penny said, struggling with the lighter until Chester handed her an already-lit cigarette. It seemed to Mina that she was getting increasingly lost in her story and the drugs, almost unable to stop now that she had begun to talk. "After *Tulpendiebe*, he thought he could get away with anything. But he was too drunk, too careless. He blamed his failures on me. In his journal, did he mention the plagiarism lawsuit that nearly ruined *Jagd zu den Sternen*? Or the costly reshoots after his failed sound experiments? His work grew increasingly erratic and he was developing a reputation at Ufa. It was me who brought in the crowds and filled the theaters, and I was the reason Pommer kept financing his movies. Pabst offered me *Pandora's Box* and I turned him down for Klaus – for *Meine wilden Wanderjahre,* a movie that kept getting postponed."

She didn't speak for a minute. Mina looked for Chester's help but he just glowered at her. Mina poured herself another glass of Dewar's and looked at her grandmother, waiting. Then suddenly, as if she were a toy that had been rewound, Penny continued to talk, her eyes glancing off into the distance somewhere between Mina and the television screen.

"By the thirties, your grandfather spent his days in a drugged-out haze and his nights in bars and brothels and movie theaters. He got into accidents constantly, fell down stairs, crashed through windows, got nearly run over by streetcars. He managed to break his wooden leg regularly, don't ask me how. Those handcrafted numbers were expensive, too. He was banging every starlet between Danzig and Berchtesgaden, *die Drecksau.* He only wrote in the early morning hours, stoned and drunk, getting his dick sucked by some harlot he'd picked up promising her a part in the next project – the one he hadn't even written yet, the one that was half a year behind. Our marriage had become a farce, a front we maintained for the newspapers and box office returns. No matter how much I sacrificed and suffered for his sake, Klaus had lost all interest in me long before."

"He says he loved you," Mina said.

"Ha!" Penny coughed up another mouthful of phlegm, and spit. It was a terrible habit. Mina could not believe that Chester went barefoot in this house.

"Why didn't you leave him?"

"You saw *Tulpendiebe*, yes? You saw the windmill, on fire? You saw the ending, the way the tulip notary dies?"

Mina nodded. "He gets crushed. It's ghastly."

"It really happened. Less than two weeks after the premiere, the exact same thing, right before our eyes."

"I read about that." Mina felt reassured. The journal wasn't all lies. This was something she knew. "You were on your honeymoon, in Venice. My honeymoon was ruined, too—"

She wondered if Penny would ask, ask what had happened to her Caribbean honeymoon. They'd sent her an invitation to the wedding but, as expected, there had been no response. Now Mina wondered if Penny had ever even opened the envelope. It occurred to her that Penny might not know Mina was married at all. Didn't know or didn't care.

"That was just the beginning," Penny went on as if she hadn't heard. "Things in Kino's movies had a tendency to really happen. It was like déjà vu, except that you know it isn't all in your head. It often happened when I was tired, when the light was right and I turned my head just so. I'd recognize the way a group of people were arranged on the street, or lines of dialogue overheard at the butcher. The more I began to notice it, the more I recognized shots, details, angles, and compositions all around me. Once you'd seen Kino's films, these echoes infiltrated the world. Klaus, conceited *Arschloch* that he was, simply shrugged and took credit—he called himself a visionary, and that suited him fine. He didn't understand his power, had no idea how to control it, and he didn't care. His movies set events in motion, I saw that clearly. It was extraordinary. Father and I used to talk about how the new physics might explain the phenomenon, but it only occurred at the edges of subjective perception."

Mina poured herself another whiskey. She felt she was finally getting somewhere. She was also getting drunk. "I don't know," she said. "This doesn't sound very scientific to me. Are you sure it wasn't just the drugs?"

Penny grunted. "No, princess. Movies *are* drugs. And besides, Klaus was the one who was high. Most of the time, he was so careless he didn't even notice when I snuck peculiar bits of dialogue or strange props into our movies just to test my suspicions. Structural variation can create vibrational fields, morphic resonance–well, I had my theories. He was heedless. He didn't care about consequences, didn't care if people died, didn't give a damn about what *happened*. Times were hard and he drank too much, smoked too much kif. He was losing his grip on reality. *Jagd zu den Sternen* flopped, and nobody wanted to work with him. His whims were legend. For *Meine wilden Wanderjahre*, he had the entire ensemble jump into the Wannsee in February–only to cut the scene later. He changed the ending of *Land der Gnade* at the last minute. Some actors never forgave him. His career was riding on *Pirates*, and he might not have made movies for much longer if the Nazis hadn't come along."

"Why did you keep acting for him?"

"Because I wanted to find out how he did it. Kino's movies messed with physical reality, and they were dangerous. I thought I could keep him from doing damage. I thought I could save us both. I was an idiot. There was no saving Kino. He was foolish and out of control. He toyed with a power far beyond his grasp, and little by little, his movies destroyed us both."

Penny closed her eyes again. Mina was afraid that she had passed out and tapped her shoulder gently.

"She does that," Chester said.

Penny slapped Mina's hand.

"Don't interrupt me." She looked at Mina, eyes barely focusing. "Klaus considered himself a conduit. He claimed he knew how to let the images flow through him, arrange themselves to reveal truth, past, present, and future. Oh, he was passionate–that's what had attracted me to him in the first place. But he could have done so much more. He used the movies as a way to ignore everything else, instead of seeing that they were connected to everything around him. He could have changed the world, but Kino only cared about Kino."

Mina came to with a start, disoriented, slowly realizing that she must have fallen asleep in Penny's armchair. It was completely dark outside now, and she had no idea how long she'd been out. She made sure Kino's notebook was still where she'd put it. Across the cluttered coffee table, Chester was helping Penny to another line of white powder, and the TV was turned to the news. Paul Bremer, the new civilian administrator, had arrived in Baghdad.

"Oh," Mina said. She had hoped that her battling layers of jetlag would cancel each other out, but instead, she felt a leaden tiredness. What time was it in New York? In Berlin? In Punta Cana? Had she dreamed up all of those stories her grandmother told her about Kino, or did that really happen? Mina felt that she was slowly losing her grip on reality.

"We are not here as a colonial power," Paul Bremer was telling the cameras. "We are here to turn over power to the Iraqi people as quickly as possible."

"That man is a lying sack of shit," Mina said, almost reflexively. She hadn't had time to think about the situation in Iraq for the last few days, and her anger surprised her.

"Of course he is," Penny said, sucking on another cigarette. "I've heard it all before. They tell you to be scared, they tell you they'll keep you safe, and then they deal death and destruction in the name of God and country. It's always the same."

"You're talking about Hitler."

"I saw the catastrophe coming early on, but Kino was willfully blind. We could have made it out of the country in time. Gone to Hollywood along with everyone else. My father died in a concentration camp, all because Kino wanted to make that damned pirate movie."

That wasn't what Mina had read. This was the worst accusation of them all. "In the journal," Mina said, "Kino claims that your father wanted to stay."

"Did you not hear me? Everything you read is a lie!" With surprising speed, Penny lunged forward and grabbed the journal from the table and tried to rip it along the spine. Mina reached out without thinking, and for a second, the women both pulled at the notebook. Mina was stronger and Penny's fingers slipped. The momentum sent her sliding sideways out of her chair. She crashed into the living room table, knocked over pill bottles and puzzle pieces, and landed on the floor.

"Penny!" Chester shouted.

"Now look at what you've done," Penny said, flailing her arms like an overturned bug. "You attacked me."

"You were going to rip up the journal," Mina said. She felt guilty for fighting with the frail old woman. She noticed blood on her arm—her grandmother had scratched her, trying to take Mina down. Mina smoothed the notebook on her leg. "It's your own fault. This is mine."

"The girl has no manners," Chester said, helping Penny back onto the couch.

"Of course she doesn't. She's a Koblitz. She's as wild as the best of us." Licking the blood off her arm, Mina couldn't help but smile. Her grandmother had given her an actual compliment.

"Don't smile," Penny said. "It's a curse, you'll see. You've got it all ahead of you. Disappointment. Betrayal. Loneliness." She took a moment to arrange herself in her chair, motioned to Chester for another cigarette, took a deep drag. He seemed reluctant to sit back down, rubbed his hands on his pants, and looked around helplessly.

"Chester baby," Penny said, "Are you nervous? Why don't you take one of the blue footballs, and leave us alone for a minute, just Oma and her inquisitive granddaughter? I am passing on stories of the past."

Chester didn't say anything, but he did reach for a pill.

"And you, my dear?"

Mina tilted her head. "Maybe something for my jetlag?"

"Up or down, Mädchen? Your choice."

Mina needed to sleep. She needed to take a bath, wash herself clean of the airplane. But she also wanted to know everything, think everything through to the end, find out all there was to find out. She wanted to keep up with her grandmother. "Up, I guess."

Penny nodded, and Chester popped a prescription bottle, shook out two red pills, and dropped them into Mina's palm.

"Have them with some juice," he said, and pushed a carton Mina's way. She took the pills with a mouthful of cold orange juice.

"Well," Penny said. "Why don't you go for a swim, Chester darling?" She flicked her hand at him, sending him away. Mina did not understand why he needed to leave, what there was left to say that this man couldn't hear, but Chester sighed, got up, geared up to say something to Mina, didn't, and let himself out the sliding door into the garden. Obviously, he was used to this treatment.

"Now," Penny said with weary satisfaction. "The son of a bitch didn't want to leave his precious pirate movie behind. Your Kino. Did he care about the Jews? About his homosexual friend? About what happened to my father? About democracy, the book burnings, the beatings in the street? No! All he could think about were his goddamn pirates! I could see the Nazi threat coming for years, just like anybody with half a brain can see these criminals for what they are." She flicked her hand at the TV, where Donald Rumsfeld lectured reporters about how to fight a war. "It was clear Kino couldn't work for them under any circumstances! But Goebbels kept dangling *Pirates* in front of him even though any fool could have seen that they'd never let him make it. The Nazis thought *Dr. Mabuse* was about them—a movie about a bunch of multi-racial swashbuckling anarchists on a ship would never be acceptable, no matter how much Klaus tried to please them. Thea encouraged him, and even when most of his actors had left the country, he still wanted to believe Goebbels' lies. Here, finally, was all the praise he never got during the Weimar years. Murnau was dead, Lang was gone, everybody was gone! Believe me, girl, Klaus saw what he wanted to see: an opportunity."

Penny spit again. Mina's heart beat faster.

"Then, the Nazis arrested my father. My father, an intellect, a good man, a thinker! Dragged from our house in handcuffs by the SA! It was a horror. For Kino, it was a wonderful excuse—now we'd have to stay in the country. We couldn't leave as long as there was a possibility he might live, and Kino knew Ufa was his best chance. He'd wanted MGM, but the American studios turned him down, and he signed with Goebbels. Don't you believe for a second that it was for my father's sake. What did I expect? That Kino stopped being Kino?"

Mina chewed on her lip. She infinitely preferred the version in the journal.

"The contract was a trap. As soon as he signed, *Pirates* was scrapped and Kino's Weimar movies were banned. Our fate was sealed—I vowed never to act again, but Kino had to do whatever these swine wanted."

"At least those operettas he made were harmless, weren't they?" Mina said. "It wasn't like he made *Triumph of the Will* or anything?"

For a second, Mina thought Penny might jump back out of her seat. "Did you listen to a thing I've been saying? There's no such thing as a harmless movie, princess! A screen doesn't just show things, it also hides them. There was no truth in Kino's operettas! They told splendid lies about gaiety and happiness when the reality was death and fear and destruction and oppression. No, Klaus never glorified the Führer directly, but the absurd champagne-and-ballroom fantasies he was peddling were used to distract the masses from the blood-letting. Is that any less dangerous? Less damnable?"

Mina felt a sting when she realized the truth of what Penny told her. Of course—her grandfather had deluded himself, and he had been guilty, and she, in turn, had let him delude her, and this made her feel guilty, too. She knew Donald Rumsfeld was a scumbag, but she had been taken in by Kino, just like Kino had been taken in by Goebbels. She almost expected Penny to blame her for her father's death in the camps, too.

"He wasn't allowed to cut them himself, so his new films never resonated the way his Weimar films did. They didn't have his rhythm, and they didn't have me. And thank God, the images stopped haunting us. Under the Nazis, his films didn't have room to breathe, but people didn't care—they went to see them again and again anyway. People enjoy being lied to, especially when times are bad. I remember Hitler at the premiere of *Luftschiffwalzer*, flush and rosy-cheeked with destiny, grinning and waving that stiff right hand of his. Kino was a success, but he hated himself for it. And all the while, my father's situation grew more and more desperate. And that's not all."

Penny gave Mina a look that frightened her. "The operettas weren't the worst of it. Did he neglect to mention Dr. Spielmann in his journal? *Die Schwarze Sonne?* Sachsenhausen? Of course he did."

Mina didn't like the sound of this. She'd heard of Sachsenhausen. It was a concentration camp.

"You see, it wasn't just Kino and me who'd seen the echoes, the images that leaked from his films, the way they caused or anticipated events in the real world. Others noticed them, as well—but it wasn't the kind of thing you talked about if you wanted to be taken seriously. Most people managed to convince themselves that it was just coincidence and went on with their days. But I'm sure now that Goebbels had seen it, too—he was a man with a keen sense for cinema and oh, he was on to Kino. Yes, he assigned him to operettas, but they never stopped trying to uncover whatever it was that had given Kino's Weimar movies their unique power."

Mina nodded, too hard. She clenched her hands into fists, extended her fingers, clenched them again. Was she feeling the red pills already? She had not even asked Chester what it was she had taken.

"When they first took power, the Nazis set up a number of secret departments that developed weapons for the coming war. Rockets, nuclear research, psychological warfare, you name it. The experimental program of the Propaganda Ministry's film department was called *Schwarze Sonne*–black sun. In the thirties, Kino got occasional visits at the studio from a shadowy SS officer by the name of Spielmann. He asked Kino to shoot short scenes, with whatever actors were at hand, and he took the undeveloped film with him. We never knew where he took the footage or what he did with it, and we had better things to worry about. Once the war started, Spielmann showed up more frequently, and he took Kino with him for days at a time. I was informed that he was gone on top secret Reich business–that was all. Every time they dropped him off afterwards in a black Mercedes limousine, Kino looked miserable, tired and distraught. He wouldn't talk about where they'd taken him. I always asked if he couldn't find out more about my father, but he just glared at me. He'd sit up all night, drinking. Once or twice I saw him cry, and Kino was not a man who cried. He wouldn't talk to me, and I gave up trying. We were already festering in our own private hells, accusing each other for everything that had gone wrong. Seeing him in his pathetic agony only made me hate him more."

She gazed off into space. Mina didn't speak. She locked eyes with her grandmother, and then Penny roused herself.

"I finally found out what happened when we were debriefed at Camp Evans, when we entered the U.S. *Schwarze Sonne* was a program of secret experiments aimed to isolate and optimize the movies' mind-control properties. Spielmann was a sick bastard, a psychiatrist who dabbled in paranormal research. He wanted to make movies that could turn a crowd into a frenzied mob, cause riots, and drive people insane. He wanted to make movies that could make people kill. Artistic talent, lyricism, it all meant nothing at *Schwarze Sonne*. They wanted to weaponize Kino. They forced prisoners to watch test movies, first at a secret screening room at Castle Wedestein, and, later, in a special section reserved for medical experiments at Sachsenhausen. After the war turned and the Führer became desperate for a *Wunderwaffe*, they projected films into isolation cells on an endless loop until the prisoner lost his mind. They forced their eyes open, drugged them, beat and tortured them, all the while displaying images designed to elicit responses, some harmless, some violent. They starved them and attempted to see if a movie could keep them from eating. They turned prisoners on each other. No matter what the outcome, everybody was executed afterwards, anyway."

"That's terrible," Mina said, and then she didn't know what else to say. Gloom settled over the room. She wasn't sure what to believe—the Black Sun? It sounded like the paranoid delusions of a bitter old junkie, but then again, she'd heard about Dr. Mengele's experiments, so why not this? She felt more conflicted about Kino than ever.

But even if everything Penny had told her was true—that Kino had been seduced by Goebbels, that his movies had helped the Germans to forget about their crimes, that his work had been used to torture prisoners—who was to blame? Wasn't Kino as much a victim as anyone? All he'd ever wanted was to make movies, everyone seemed to agree on that. Something else had crept into Mina's feelings about Kino, some new pride tinged with guilt. He was her grandfather and she didn't want him to be culpable.

"Tell me about 1963," Mina tried. "Tell me why you had him committed, and about his . . . " She let her voice trail off.

"You can say it, girl. His suicide. The fucking *Ladung Schrot* he shot through his genius brains."

Penny leaned over and started to shuffle through the assorted detritus on the table in front of her for another pill.

She swallowed a blue football and two aspirin and chased them with a slug of whiskey. She stared off into the distance. "With these eyes, I watched our movies burn. And you know what I said? Good riddance! Finally, we would go to America and put everything behind us. I wanted to forget and start over. I wanted a family, a normal life. But not Klaus. He was heartbroken but wouldn't admit it. He acted like the world was still waiting for a new movie by Kino! Hopeless idiot. He threw himself into writing new scripts. He hadn't learned a thing. And look what happened! A few years later, Americans were fleeing their country because they were alleged Communists! Nowhere is any better than anywhere else, I learned that the hard way. The movies would only lead to more trouble. There was nothing but pain that way."

She ate one more pill off the table, seemingly at random. Mina wondered if she should stop her. She suddenly wished Chester was still with them.

"Klaus didn't stand a chance," Penny went on. "I watched as he broke his back while Hollywood chewed him up and shit him out in chunks. He claimed he was working, and there were always manuscript pages on his desk, but it was nothing more than a convenient way to avoid his family."

"And then?" Mina prompted.

"Always the same," Penny said. "Even when he sold toothpaste and drove his cab, that pathetic dreamer never quit. He was forever making changes to his beloved pirate screenplay. He scouted locations and acted out scenes by himself between fares. It would have been heartbreaking if my heart hadn't died long ago."

She spit again.

Mina imagined them both in this house, younger versions of Penny and Kino going about their days. She tried to reconcile the things Penny told her with what she'd read in the journal. It seemed like hell to Mina, this life of theirs together. Why had they stayed married? How long had Penny been spitting on the carpet?

Penny took a drink of whiskey straight from the bottle and gave Mina a look that was almost kind. Her voice was huskier, frailer than before. "Kino's films poisoned everything," she said, sounding tired and resigned.

"You had him committed."

"And not just once, girl. Because he was nuts. He beat me with his wooden leg! Don't look so surprised. When that shithead Wagner showed up and asked for a meeting, I shielded Klaus from the phone calls and destroyed the letters from the studio."

"But he was released, he made the movie, and when it flopped, he killed himself?"

"Oh, no. The movie you saw was a travesty. That was not *Pirates*, not the way Klaus intended it. It wasn't even supposed to be called *Pirates of Mulberry Island* anymore. The studio had promised him full control but when they found the movie he was making unacceptable, they took his precious vision away from him, recut the footage, and released a butchered version."

Another swig of whiskey straight from the bottle. Penny's voice was barely a whisper now, and Mina had to lean in close to hear a word she was saying. Her grandmother's pupils were pinpoints.

"It was one defeat too many. After the premiere, he went back into the El Rey theater, made his way behind the linen wall, and stuck a double-barreled shotgun in his mouth. They had to replace the screen because it was splattered with his blood and bits of genius brain. The shot had ripped right through it."

Mina absently chewed on her hand.

"That's all there was to it," Penny said. "I'd seen it coming, I had tried to protect him from himself, but it was all useless in the end. I wasn't able to save either one of us."

Penny's chin came to rest on her chest. Mina had gotten attuned to the rhythm of Penny's little nods, but this time, Penny's head didn't lift again. Mina was just beginning to nod out again herself when Penny suddenly began to shake, her entire body grabbed by some sort of seizure, twitch after violent twitch. Mina took Penny's spasming body by the shoulder, called her name. The tremors didn't stop. Her eyes rolled back in her head, and now her limbs were flailing and foamy spit dripped from her mouth. Her skin felt clammy to Mina's touch.

On the patio, Mina found Chester in a plastic recliner without a cushion, eyes closed and a baseball cap over his bald head.

"Chester, quick," Mina said. "I need your help. Please."

Chapter 13

Hospitals. Mina couldn't seem to get away from them. She was struggling with the espresso machine in the waiting room of the Olympia Medical Center, where Penny had been taken into the ICU. She was in a coma induced by opiate overdose: by law, the police would have to be notified. It was past midnight, and Mina had spent too much time filling out forms she didn't know the answers to. The espresso machine refused to take her crumpled dollar bill.

Over by the yucca plant, Chester sat shaking his leg and stared at a silent TV. After Mina called for his help, he'd gone back into the house, taken Penny's vitals, called an ambulance, put on socks and shoes, and then methodically hidden all evidence of controlled substances.

"Fuck," Mina said.

She smoothed the bill and tried again. The machine dispensed a blackish liquid into a plastic cup. It tasted awful.

"Chester," Mina said. "I know you think this is my fault. I don't know, maybe it is. But I don't know what I could have done differently. There are people after me. Whatever happens to Penny, she did to herself."

Chester said nothing.

"You gave her all those drugs," Mina said. "You're just as much to blame." Mina understood that she felt guilty. She was begging Chester for forgiveness.

But Chester didn't take his eyes off the TV. "If you want to go, that's fine," he finally said. "I'll stay here with Penny. That batty old white woman is my life, sweetheart. I got nothing without her."

Mina stared at him blankly. She had no words of comfort.

"My husband is sick," she offered.

"I see you're taking good care of him."

"He's got good doctors."

"Dokters," Chester sighed, turning back to the TV. He was done with Mina, and it was just as well. Mina nodded and tossed the disgusting coffee into the trash.

Chester handed her a key from his key chain. "There's a guest bedroom upstairs. I'll call you if there's any change. Get some rest. You look like hell."

The unexpected kindness confused Mina. It had been easier to forget about her grandmother's coma when she could be angry at this guy Chester. She could use some sleep, even though the idea of being alone in the house filled her with dread.

"I think I will," Mina said.

Chester didn't respond. Jay Leno was on TV with a juggling midget. Mina blinked. The image did not change. She left the hospital. The moon was almost full.

She had just found her way back to Sunset Boulevard when her cell phone rang. Her father had been alerted to his mother's condition by the hospital. He sounded weary and confused—it was three hours later on the East Coast—and as he talked, his anger started to build. "Tomorrow morning you can explain to me what you're doing in California."

"Why tomorrow morning?" Mina asked, even as the answer dawned on her. Her father was coming in on the red eye. "I expect you to pick me up," he said. "On time."

"I am always on time," Mina said, but they both knew it wasn't true.

After she hung up, Mina realized that she'd missed her turn. She had gotten lost in the L.A. night. If she could find her way to the ocean, she ought to be able to backtrack from there. Was she exhausted or not tired at all? Were the red pills doing anything? She couldn't tell.

She reached the coast and then drove aimlessly along the beach, just to be driving. When she saw the lights of a boardwalk, she pulled into a parking space. There was a Ferris wheel, a carnival, and a pier that stretched out into the dark. Venice Beach.

Mina bought a lemonade at a stand and took it to the pier. It was late. Only a few people milled around, lovers dressed in leather kissed, an old man talked to himself, a stray dog sniffed an overflowing trash can. The sounds of the fair echoed over the water. Bugs buzzed around the fluorescent lights. Mina's feet were damp with sweat in her new boots, boots that had been perfect for Berlin. She watched the traffic up and down the coast, the lights of the city reflecting off the sky in the distance. A moment of peace, just by herself with the roar of the ocean. She hadn't felt anything like it since the cans had arrived . . . what was it now? Only three days ago? It seemed so much longer than that. The lemonade was cold and good.

Had Kino been a debauched fool, a visionary artist, or a Nazi tool? Was her grandmother a backstabbing saboteur or had she tried to save the man from himself? Could all of these things be true at the same time? What kind of twisted love had kept them together? Could movies really have echoes? Would Sam understand any of this? Would he understand her? He'd been so angry on the phone. Her father was angry, too. And Chester. And Dr. Hanno, dejected and naked in the sauna. Mina had disappointed everyone, and she had nothing to show for it.

"Why so sad?"

A man in a light brown dress uniform had come up behind her. He was tall, slender and young, younger than Mina. He wore a white cap. Was that Navy? Was he a sailor? Mina didn't know.

"I'm not sad," she said. "Just tired."

The sailor, if that's what he was, leaned on the railing next to her. "The night's still young," he said. "It'd be a shame to spend it alone."

Oh man, Mina thought. *Horny sailors are the last thing I need right now.* She held up her hand to show off the gold wedding band. She didn't particularly care for rings, didn't like wearing them, but she realized that this one was going to be useful.

Then again, he was handsome, this sailor. Was he on his way to Iraq? Had he just come back? No—something about his eyes told her he hadn't seen war yet.

"She's married!" the sailor said with fake surprise. He leaned in closer. "What kind of husband would leave his beautiful wife alone on a night like this?" He leaned in for a kiss and Mina didn't stop him. Their lips touched, he put his hands on her shoulder blades, pulled her closer, and there was the tongue. His clean-shaven cheeks were smoother than Sam's, and now he had her in a muscular embrace that felt good, too good, and he was already moving one of his hands under her sweater.

Mina thought of Dr. Hanno and the kiss he had attempted in the sauna. She had liked Dr. Hanno, even though he could be insufferable when he talked about the movies. She might have led him on. Mina thought of Sam, how different his hands felt from the sailor's, and ah, here was a genuine twinge of guilt. She had been married for less than two weeks, and here she was, letting herself getting felt up by a stranger. Finally, finally, she pushed the sailor away.

"No, no, no," she said. She meant it to sound decisive but it came out more like a sigh.

"Aww." The sailor gave her a goofy smile. He was not her type but undeniably cute in the moonlight. Mina had never kissed anybody in a uniform before. She gave him a smile and a shrug and turned to walk away. She was grateful when he didn't pursue her.

Mina backtracked up Pacific Highway, but before she got to Penny's house, she stopped at an all-night media emporium and picked up a cheaply packaged DVD of *The Pirates of Mulberry Island*. Back at the house, she carried her suitcase into the empty upstairs bedroom, found a bathroom, and took a long hot shower. She explored the house while she dried her hair, wearing a long T-shirt and flip-flops. The master bedroom was as filthy as the rest of the house: an unmade king-sized, both bedside tables stacked with books, DVD cases, glasses, cups, still more pill bottles, empty boxes of Kleenex, and discarded tissues on the floor. There was a small study with a library of German books, a gigantic walk-in closet filled with old-fashioned evening gowns, and a pantry stocked to the ceiling with canned goods.

Mina knew she needed to sleep. Her father would be there in the morning, angry and full of questions, but she was too wound up. She regretted taking the red pills. She made herself a ham sandwich, poured a glass of her grandmother's Dewar's over crushed ice, and, in the darkened living room, watched *The Pirates of Mulberry Island*.

"Love! Revenge! Adventure!" the box proclaimed. "Swashbuckling!"

The beginning of the film reminded Mina of *Tulpendiebe*: there were images of a port city on a Caribbean island, and a title card announced: "Santa Lupe, Anno 1835." The town was in preparations for a wedding, palm fronds and ribbons, and in the first scene, the audience learns that Bonnie, the beautiful bride, is unhappy because she doesn't love the wealthy merchant her father has arranged for her to marry. Bonnie had obviously been cast for her resemblance to the young Penelope Greifenau. Her husband-to-be is overweight and has a mean temper and a black moustache.

Cut to an imposing pirate ship anchored in a nearby inlet, where Captain Darius Silko and his motley crew of sea dogs are celebrating on the beach, passing rum and grilled meat between them, climbing on trees and roughhousing drunkenly in the turquoise surf.

Mina didn't recognize the actors, but she drew a sharp breath at the first close-up of dashing Captain Silko: he shared a striking resemblance to the clean-shaven sailor she had just kissed on the pier. There he was, in the movie: as if he were winking at her.

Mina found herself liking the movie, and she settled back into the couch. She pulled a blanket over herself and poured more whiskey, happy to be just where she was, watching this movie. Sam had liked watching it when it came on late night cable.

The night before the wedding, under the light of a full moon, the pirates raided St. Lupe. While his men are breaking into the bank, Captain Silko meets Bonnie on a rooftop, where she is contemplating suicide. He knocks her unconscious and orders his men to leave their loot behind and take her instead. "For ransom," he says—but it is obvious that he has fallen in love.

Mina woke up with the credits rolling.

"It does get ridiculous," a familiar voice came out of the dark, heavy with a German accent. "Almost incoherent. They positively butchered the second act."

Mina jumped, knocking her drink, which had been balanced precariously on the cushion next to her, onto the floor, where it joined the dried puddles of Penny's spit. The glass bounced unharmed off the thick rug. In the corner arm chair where Chester had cooked up Penny's injection, the man with the red leather jacket was eating what was left of Mina's ham sandwich.

"I am sorry if I startled you. Tobias Schnark. Remember me? Don't get up."

"Jesus motherfucking Christ," Mina said. She was wearing nothing but a t-shirt and pulled up the blanket to cover herself. "You scared the living shit out of me. What the hell are you doing here? How did you get in here? This can't be your jurisdiction."

"German cultural heritage doesn't know any borders. Granted, my wing of the BKA does not enjoy the best relations with its American counterparts. My department was established without knowledge of the Allied Oversight Committee and later merged with the *Bundesnachrichten-dienst*—after all, many of the items in question had been removed by the Allies themselves, and we could not act until their retrieval became politically expedient."

Mina shook her head. "I don't care. I want you to tell me why you broke into this house. And why I shouldn't call the police right now."

"A little more attention to the details might have helped. Especially when it comes to my instructions."

He took another bite of Mina's sandwich.

"Excuse me?"

"Didn't I warn you about that film professor? You're a little naïve for your age, no? Haven't seen much of the world yet?"

"Look here, I've about had it with all the cloak-and-dagger bullshit. Are you actually wearing gloves?"

"Shhh." Herr Schnark put his gloved finger to his lips and cocked his head as if to listen. And yes: over the drone of the city in the distance, there was the very distinct noise of tires on gravel. Somebody was coming up the driveway.

Mina looked at Schnark. He was already on his feet. Car doors slammed outside.

"Get up. Now. We've got to hide," Schnark said.

Mina didn't particularly trust this guy, but there was no point arguing now. "The backyard?" she said. She didn't know the house very well.

Schnark nodded. "Let's go."

They'd just made it through the sliding door to the back patio when they heard muffled voices from the front of the house. Somebody was already inside. The air had cooled off and Mina wished she was wearing more than an oversized T-shirt.

They rounded the pool, the water thick with algae, and hid behind an overgrown rosebush. The garden was walled-in by hedges, and the only escape routes led through or around the house.

"Down," Schnark commanded, and Mina didn't hesitate. She could see the shine of flashlights teetering on the living room curtains, then someone flipped on a light switch. Shadows of what looked like two men were searching the living room. Then they pulled back the curtain.

Mina recognized them immediately.

"The men who chased me through Berlin!"

Unbelievable.

"They're agents," Schnark whispered. "Quiet, bitte."

Agents. That's what Sam had said. She hadn't believed him.

They could see the two men confer, then they disappeared again. One by one, lights turned on all over the house.

"What are they looking for?" Mina asked, but she already knew: they were looking for her.

"There are two cars parked out front, so they know we're hiding somewhere," Schnark said. "Does this path lead around the house? Let's bolt."

"I'm not dressed," Mina protested.

"But you have the journal, right?"

Oh fuck.

Mina pointed at the house. "It's on the table."

They could see the shadow of one of the men upstairs, searching the master bedroom.

"Gottverdammte Scheisse," Schnark cursed.

From inside his jacket, he pulled out a stubby revolver and lifted it up to his face like James Bond. "Stay here. I'll take care of it. Go start your car." He gave her a grim face, an expression that looked like he'd learned it from the movies.

Mina took the elbow of his raised arm and gently pulled it down. "Are you crazy? You are going to kill someone over that old journal? Put the gun away."

Schnark was shaking his head, but now Mina made the grim face. "I'll take care of this." Before he could stop her, she stepped out behind the rosebush and walked into the living room. "Excuse me!" she hollered. "Men who broke into my grandmother's house? Can I speak to you?"

The men came rumbling down the staircase and Mina's bluster gave way to doubt immediately. In Berlin, Mina had only seen them from a distance. Up close, they looked just as beefy but more alert than she had suspected, with mean eyes and tough jaws. Apparently, they were agents of some sort. They had followed her from Germany to California and broken into her grandmother's house. And if Schnark was right and a gun was the only way to deal with them, it was too late.

"What are you doing here?" Mina repeated. She picked up Penny's phone and waved it at the men. "This is my grandmother's house, and if I don't get an answer immediately, I will call the police."

"I wouldn't do that," the older agent said. "It's really not necessary. We just want to ask you a few questions."

"Is there anyone else here?" the other agent asked. He had a scar across his right cheek that looked like he had gotten knifed a long time ago. He peeked through the curtains into the garden.

That's when Mina's eyes betrayed her. Before she knew what was happening, she'd glanced at the mess on Penny's coffee table for the journal—there it was, next to a heap of puzzle pieces, half obscured by the whiskey jug—but the agent with the scar had noticed her look and seen the spiral notebook.

"Now, what is this?" he said. He wiped a few stray pills off the table and picked up the journal. "Certainly looks interesting."

The other agent turned away from the curtains.

"Mr. K is going to like this."

Watching them leaf through the pages filled with Kino's handwriting made Mina furious. "The journal is mine," she said. "Hand it to me right now."

"I tell you what," the older agent said. "Why don't you come to our office, and we can discuss all of this. It's only a short ride away."

"And if I don't want to?"

"We're not asking. Don't make this any harder than it has to be."

He reached for her elbow, but Mina stepped away and picked up Penny's telephone from the table. She waved the handset like a weapon. "I'm not going anywhere with you. Give me the notebook and leave this property right now."

She dialed 911.

"Hey!" The agent with the scar swiftly swiped the phone from her hands, dropped it on the carpet, and crushed it beneath the heel of his elegant Italian shoe.

Mina had to process this. They had broken her grandmother's phone. Once people started breaking things, the situation could escalate quickly. Where was Schnark? Why was Mina always wrong?

"What do you want?" she said again.

The older agent slid the journal into a black briefcase. "Like I said—we'd like you to come to the office with us." He reached for her arm again, and this time Mina was frightened enough to let him.

"Would you mind if I put on some clothes?"

"Of course." He motioned for the agent with the scar to follow Mina upstairs. She led him to the guest bedroom, where she kept her bag. "Do you mind?" she said and closed the door in his face. She put on the jeans and boots she had bought in Berlin.

"Hurry up," the agent with the scar said through the door.

"One second!" she said. The room's only window opened over the garden—she waved but couldn't see if Schnark was still in the darkness below. The pool, glowing green, was close to the house. If she had to, she could probably—

The agent knocked on the door. "We have to go now."

There was a commotion downstairs—a knock and a crash, glass splintering, a lamp maybe. Mina locked the door. The agent started banging on it immediately. She opened the window. Perhaps the pool wasn't as close as it seemed. There was no safe way to climb down. The banging on the door continued. She couldn't hear any more noise from downstairs. Mina removed the screen from the window and dropped it on the patio.

For a moment there was nothing but silence. Then, a crash that shook the door frame.

Okay, Mina thought. *I can do this.*

She climbed up on the sill, perched for a moment in her new boots and calculated the distance. Another crash against the door, her muscles tensed, and Mina jumped.

Foul water rushed up her nostrils, and the weight of her wet clothes pulled her down. A stroke up, a stroke over, and she heaved herself onto the grass, dripping wet hair in her eyes. She'd done it! Angry yelling from above: the agent had broken into the room and shouted at her from the window.

A hand offered to pull her up. Mina reached for it and came to her feet. It was Schnark. Behind him in the living room, Mina could make out the legs of the older agent, prone on the floor.

Schnark saw her fearful look. "Cocked him," he said, miming with the butt of his revolver. "Got the journal back, too," he said, nodding to the agent's briefcase in his hand. "It's about time you listened to me, wouldn't you agree?"

Mina rolled her eyes at him, but she was flush with excitement from the jump. She'd done that, she'd really done that and gotten away with it. They took the path around the house, Mina's boots splashing with every step. Why did she have to get dressed *before* she jumped? They could hear the other agent rumbling down the staircase.

Three cars in the driveway: Mina's Thunderbird, a rental VW, and a large black SUV.

"I drive," Schnark said. Mina tossed him her keys and he and started up the Thunderbird.

She leapt into the convertible without opening the door. It was a cool move, but she knocked her knee on the glove compartment. The front door opened and Mina could see the agent with the scar silhouetted against the light.

Bang! Bang!

Schnark shot his gun into the air. The agent leapt back into the house. Schnark laughed and took aim at the SUV. He fired three more shots before he popped a tire. They squealed backwards out of the driveway, Schnark rammed the Thunderbird into first gear, and they were gone.

Chapter 14

Shaking with exhilaration, Mina laughed at her own courage. She was dripping dirty pool water all over the car seat. Schnark drove fast, checking the rearview mirrors constantly. Without taking his eyes off the road, he put his gun into the glove compartment and reached for the agent's briefcase, which he'd thrown in the space behind Mina's seat.

"Go ahead. Open it," he said. "The journal's in there."

"Those guys were going to kidnap me," Mina said. She untied her boots and wiggled out of her wet jeans, letting them dry in the warm night air. Her shirt was sticking to her chest. Schnark didn't seem to be interested in checking her out and kept his eyes on the road. She found Kino's notebook in the briefcase's side pocket. "Got it."

Schnark gave her a thumbs-up. "Well done," he said. "The BKA is proud of you."

"Well," Mina said. "I'm not sure if I like the BKA any better than those guys. At least they didn't wave any guns around."

"Yeah." His grim face again. "They were too smart to pull theirs."

"Who are they?"

"From what I have been able to ascertain, they belong to a secret branch overseen by a joint board of the six major film studios and the US government. These are the guys who take care of the studios' dirty work. Mainly, they do paperwork, copyright enforcement, a well-timed leak to the press or the cops, that sort of thing. A little bit of intimidation here and there. Snooping. But they won't shy away from violence, and if it's necessary, they'll take someone out. There have always been rumors. Some people think it goes way back. There's a theory they framed Fatty Arbuckle. Got rid of Marilyn when the time came."

"They're with the government?"

"It's a blurry line these days. As you may know, your Vice President has an inordinate fondness for private contractors, and this administration is desperate to make inroads into liberal Hollywood."

"Are you saying they're like Blackwater?"

Schnark didn't answer. Mina wanted to laugh, tell him that he'd watched too many movies, but her fear had been real. Whoever they were, these men had attempted to kidnap her. She had really jumped out of a window into a swimming pool while they were beating down the door. There'd been gunfire. Mina was past laughing. She realized she'd been reflexively checking the rear view mirror to see if they were being followed.

"What do they want?"

Schnark accelerated up a freeway ramp and settled into an empty lane. It was past midnight and there were only a few cars on the road. "Movies are America's greatest export," he said. "Billions of dollars."

Oh great, Mina thought. *Another lecture*. Didn't Dr. Hanno just give her that speech? "I know, I know," she said. "Propaganda and all that."

Schnark ignored her.

"By and large, the industry controls itself. Hayes had it exactly right: 'The quality of our films is such that censorship is unnecessary.' But that doesn't mean the US government doesn't keep a keen eye on the potential of film."

"They also keep a keen eye on speeding," Mina said, "so you might want to slow down a little. This isn't the Autobahn."

Schnark turned his head to give her a half-smile, but he didn't slow down. "In the sixties, the CIA set up something called MK/PSYNEMA, a secret program dedicated to the possibilities of mind control, propaganda, and psychological warfare. But it goes back further than that. *Why We Fight* couldn't compete with the best of the German films, and the Americans knew it. Have you heard of Operation Overcast?"

Mina hadn't.

"Immediately after V-E day, in a race with the Russians, a special unit of Marines rounded up German scientists: nuclear research, cryptography, aeronautical secrets, as well as mind-control and propaganda experts. The same guys who built the V2 to attack London gave the Americans their space program. Heisenberg and Werner von Braun helped them get to the moon and develop ICBMs, and Riefenstahl helped them built modern Hollywood."

"Leni Riefenstahl?" Mina wasn't sure if he were kidding or not. Then she remembered something. "Oma was telling me about secret Nazi experiments, something called *Schwarze Sonne*?"

Schnark whistled through his teeth and regarded Mina with some kind of newfound respect. "Yes, Dr. Spielmann's unit. A disciple of Goebbels. All Ufa directors were ordered to cooperate with him. Apparently, tests with Kino's material consistently yielded better than random results. They were, in some way no one understood, effective."

"Oma said they did horrible experiments."

Schnark nodded. "I got hold of Kino's immigration files. Lots of blacked-out pages. He told the Americans that the Nazis could never use his movies because his was the art of liberation, beyond anyone's control, but I'm not so sure they believed him."

"Where are we going?" Mina finally thought to ask.

"I'd like to introduce you to someone who has some answers for you."

"Now?"

"Marty never sleeps. I hope you're not tired?"

Mina shrugged. She wasn't tired. She was wide awake.

"I'm fine," she said. "I feel fine."

"Good." Schnark settled back into his seat. "Hey, this is a great car!"

They arrived at an art deco house somewhere in the Valley. It was the only one on its block with the lights still on. Schnark rang the bell, and they were buzzed in. They found their way to the kitchen, where a white-haired man greeted them. He looked like he'd once been handsome but was now old and balding, with a rough grey stubble covering his wrinkled cheeks. He wore black silk pajamas. He'd been doing the crossword puzzle at the kitchen counter and eating soup.

"Hey Marty," Schnark said. "It's late for soup."

"I never sleep. Did you bring my cigars? You must be Wilhelmina. It's such a pleasure. I used to work with your grandfather. Aber *Mädchen*, you're soaked! Do you need dry clothes? I got some duds my ex-wife left behind."

"Please, call me Mina. And yes, I would love dry clothes."
Mina followed Marty to a bedroom with a walk-in closet,
where she picked a pair of slacks and a white shirt, both too
big for her, but they would do for now.

She found Marty and Schnark in a dimly lit study lined
with book shelves, reclining in cushy armchairs, drinking
scotch and smoking cigars. They were talking in hushed
tones when Mina came in.

"Much better," Marty said. "You look like Kate Hepburn."

He offered her a seat, a glass of scotch, and a cigar. Mina
settled into the free armchair and declined both the drink and
the smoke. The men seemed like co-conspirators to her,
accomplices, sharing secrets in the dead of night. Mina
leaned back in her chair, ready for anything. Marty exhaled a
pungent cloud of cigar smoke. "Inspector Schnark tells me
Penelope is in the hospital?"

"She's in a coma. The doctors don't know if she will come
out of it. She was doing an insane amount of drugs."

"Always has, always will," Marty said, but when he
leaned forward, Mina could see his forehead crinkled with
concern. "I am sorry. Is somebody with her?"

"This guy Chester. He's her nurse."

Marty smiled. "I've known some of her Chesters."

Schnark was quietly sitting back in his chair, and for a
moment, Mina thought he might have fallen asleep. Then the
end of his cigar flared up, and she saw that he was watching
her intently.

"I was a kid when Kino hired me as a grip on *Jagd zu den
Sternen.* Did you know that?"

"Back in Germany?"

"I was a huge fan. People said Kino was terrible with plot,
that his dialogue was wooden, his characters two-dimen-
sional."

Mina nodded. Three days ago, she didn't know there was anyone who gave a damn about Kino.

"His movies were adventure stories, and he played fast and loose with facts, but out of the Schmaltz and the melodrama, he distilled indelible moments. If you could see past the imperfections, they were full of strikingly persistent poetic images. Hell, if you watched them enough, you began to love the flaws, too. Genius, I tell you."

He puffed on his cigar. Mina couldn't have said why, but this old man, sitting up in the middle of the night sucking contentedly on a cigar, struck her as the most trustworthy person she'd met in days.

"I worked closely with Kino on the preproduction for *Pirates*, in 1933, but my wife and I left Germany after the *Machtergreifung*."

"While my grandparents stayed."

"Kino claimed it was because of Penelope's father. People here thought he was an opportunist or worse. Either way, what happened to his films was a terrible tragedy."

"You believe that?" Mina asked.

Marty Wagner nodded.

"I was practically a kid when I first met Kino. By the time they finally arrived in Hollywood, I had worked my way up at RKO. My name is on more than thirty pictures. *Cat People. Body Snatchers. Citizen Kane.*"

"You worked on *Citizen Kane?*"

Marty pointed to a framed black-and-white photo on the shelf by the door. "That's me in Xanadu," he said. "Orson took the picture."

Mina sat up straight, in awe of the old man in his silk pajamas. *Citizen Kane* was Sam's favorite movie in the entire world.

"Kino and Penny were too proud to ask for my help when they showed up in this town, and I was hurt when they didn't come to see me. Those years were hard for them. They were shunned. Wilder, Lang, Pommer–no one would talk to them. Then and now, it's a company town, and your grandparents were considered Nazi collaborators. They lived in a tiny apartment in East Hollywood, eking out a living I don't know how. After the war I was in charge of the story department writer's stable. The Ruskies were the new enemies, and the movie business boomed. We needed more writers, and I hired Kino under a pseudonym."

"You helped him," Mina said, nodding to herself. Kino had spoken fondly of Marty.

"Penny wanted him to get a job, anything but the movies, to live anywhere but in Hollywood, but Kino wouldn't quit. I've never seen anyone so stubborn in my life. So I did what I could, but the mimeographed pages always came back from the front office with unequivocal notes: too melodramatic, too absurd, too violent. They were forever complaining about plot holes. 'Plot holes?' he'd shout. 'Miserable accountant souls! Life is filled with plot holes!' But he kept writing. Every Tuesday, he turned in a new draft. When he finally came up with an idea they liked, Penny made sure it went nowhere. I'll never forget the time we were all invited to a party at Marlon Brando's house. She threw a marble ashtray at Orson Welles."

Mina laughed at the thought; she was quietly proud of the old bat. "I can believe that," she said, but Marty shook his head. It wasn't an amusing anecdote to him but a painful memory. It seemed to her that Schnark was shaking his head, too.

"I had no choice but to fire him," Marty said. "After that, I didn't see them for decades, but there were rumors: drugs, suicide attempts, infidelity, you name it. Later, he made TV commercials. Didn't last there, either. By '63, they were nonentities. I'd completely forgotten about old Kino until I stepped into his taxi."

"I read about that in his journal," Mina said, glad to know this part of it was true. "You gave him another chance."

"I was at Paramount at the time, and there had been disaster after disaster. *Cleopatra* almost bankrupted Fox, TV was taking over. We were desperate. We were willing to try anything. Cinerama, 3-D, Smell-O-Vision—why not Kino? There hadn't been a major pirate epic since *The Buccaneer,* and Kino's script was good, a reworked version of the movie Goebbels shut down in 1933. It had melodrama, adventure, wenches in costumes, and it would look splendid in Technicolor. Hell, we'd shoot it in Cinemascope. I saw the potential, but Katz had misgivings from the start. He wanted someone else to direct. I knew what Kino was capable of behind the camera, and I got the go-ahead. The hard part was getting him to sign."

"Because of Penny."

"I'd never seen anything like it. Here I was, offering him the chance of a lifetime, a comeback with a major Hollywood studio, and Penny screened his phone calls and threw my letters in the trash! I mean, sure, we lowballed him on his fee, but money wasn't the problem. Penny was determined that Klaus would never make another movie again. When I finally got through to him, she had him committed and pumped full of downers."

"She thought making the movie would kill him."

"And she was right." Marty gave Mina a long, sad look. "They were both drunks, addicted to God knows what else, and they were smacking each other around. The kid, your father, had been shipped off to some school on the East coast.

I thought she was out of her mind, and I pulled some strings to get him released. Hushed up the whole thing."

"You believed in him," Mina said.

"I did. Now, this was not long after Dr. King's march on Washington, Kennedy was still President, and there was hope in the air. 'I have a dream, too,' Kino would say. I got a thrill being around him again, sharing his enthusiasm. Kino admired those kids in France who were breaking all the rules—so why shouldn't we be able to make a movie that was popular entertainment and art at the same time? Yes, I believed in Kino, all the things he said. Most of it, anyway. *Pirates* should have been his masterpiece."

"But that's not what happened," Mina said.

Marty didn't answer. His cigar had gone out, and it took him several fumbling attempts to relight it. There was no sign that Schnark was even in the room except for the occasional red flare from the end of his cigar.

"We shot on the back lot," Marty finally went on. "I was to keep an eye on Kino. He dried out, showed up on time, and was in control of cast and crew. It was marvelous. I'd seen him do amazing work with far less talent and money. The dailies looked great, and I was sure we had a quality picture on our hands. We were under budget and on schedule when the entire production went to Mexico for the location shoot."

"Did Penny go?"

"Oh no. I made sure of that." Marty grinned to himself but didn't explain. "We took over a remote bay in the Yucatan, with a pristine beach and a town set dressed up as Mulberry Island. The location would really make this picture. *The Buccaneer* was all done on studio sets, and we'd blow it out of the water."

"*Tulpendiebe* was shot on a sound stage."

"Right. I don't know what would have happened if we'd stayed inside, but once we got down there, things quickly spiraled out of control. Kino now commanded the biggest production of his career, and when he found himself on location, he lost his bearings. He was like an addict on a binge."

"And you were there to supervise him?"

"Ach Gott, ja. I was." Marty took off his glasses, rubbed his eyes, scratched his beard. Mina was touched by how embarrassed he looked. "I don't know what I was thinking— the best I can say in my defense was that we were all swept away by Kino's vision. He certainly knew how to rouse the crowd. He gave an impassioned speech about Lang's dragon, about how we had a chance to make something great and lasting. We were all seduced by this man who had been broken and beaten again and again but still believed in his art before anything else—even those of us who had never thought of the movies as art in the first place. In that tropical paradise, all seemed possible, and the crazier Kino acted, the more we wanted to believe that we were making something special. A cathedral of light, that's what he called it, and we all cheered. He stirred something in me that I'd long forgotten. I wanted him to succeed, no matter what."

Mina bit her lip. She wondered if *Pirates* ever stood a chance at all. There must have been a moment when everything still hung in the balance, when things still might have worked out. She knew better than to wish for a different ending to the story. She reminded herself that she already knew how it ended.

"It was disastrous, and I should have seen it coming. I was a fool. Instead of betting a few million on a decent adventure movie, I staked my career on Kino's masterpiece. Within days, Klaus was manic. He'd gone off schedule and off script, rewriting scenes in the middle of the night, presenting his actors with new dialogue each morning. I don't think he slept at all. He was improvising again. There was a new drug making the rounds, something a friend of Cary Grant's had brought down in a little vial. It wasn't like the opium we used to smoke, cushy and cheerful. It was acid, and it made everything more real rather than less. Everybody got high on it. The actors were afraid of their own shadows, hiding behind the set, jumping in the surf naked, dancing all night, banging on drums and drinking tequila. We all felt like we were teetering on the edge of revelation. Kino got rid of his hand-crafted prosthetic leg and strapped on a crude prop peg leg."

Mina couldn't help but laugh at the image. She thought of her own burst of anarchy at her wedding reception, but this was on an entirely different scale. Marty furrowed his brow, and she caught herself. "Please," she said, suppressing another chuckle. "Go on."

Marty hesitated. None of this was funny to him. "People stayed in costume at all times, and even the crew started wearing pirate outfits. The camera always seemed to be on, and we wasted a shameful amount of stock. The budget ballooned, and still, I didn't see what I had to do. 'Trust me, Marty,' Kino would say to me, 'trust me! It's all going to come together in the editing room!' And I wanted to believe him so much, I let the madness go on. Kino was gripped by a vision, and he would not compromise. 'Only at play are we open to our full potential!' he would shout. 'Art is pleasure! If it's not fun, why bother'? I'm lucky nobody died. He even wrote a part for himself and he acted in a few scenes—the ghost of Grapefruit Silko. It was ludicrous."

Marty had talked himself into a state, and Mina squirmed on her stool. It wasn't her fault that her grandfather had been out of control, but somehow she felt complicit. She knew that if she had been there, she wouldn't have stopped Kino either.

"He came into my room one night, woke me from a deep sleep, and told me he changed the title of the movie. Now he wanted to call it *Twenty-Twelve, Or The Hair-Raising Adventures of Captain Darius Silko, Heir of Mulberry Island and Leader of His Legendary Crew of Anti-Corporate Pirates of the Gaia II and Their Friends and Protectors, the Noble Mayan Nation of Xunantanich and Their Spiritual Descendents.*"

Marty paused, waiting for a response. "That'd be hard to fit on a poster," Mina said. Marty nodded, satisfied.

"Maybe he could get away with that shit at Ufa," he said, "but it was career suicide in Hollywood. He dressed up crew members in white robes and gave them roles. He was banging Katz's girlfriend. I didn't wake up until I realized he was preparing to torch the entire set on the last day of shooting. The pirate wedding was supposed to be the film's happy ending, but Kino wanted mayhem instead: a riot, a battle, and a fire that would destroy the buildings. Now, a shoot like that wants to be carefully planned, but Kino just wanted to keep the cameras rolling and see what was going to happen."

"He had a thing for fire."

"I don't care. Lives were at stake. There was no excuse for this. I might've been able to ignore the orgies, the improvised whims, the wasted stock, but when I saw the crew dousing the set in gasoline, something in me snapped. I was done fronting for Kino. I tried talking sense into him but there was no arguing with him. He threatened to have 'the shamans' take care of me. He'd completely lost touch with reality. The whole thing was ridiculous, and yes, I called the front office and let them know that the production had gone off the rails."

Mina couldn't contain her disappointment. "You ratted him out!" Out of the corner of her eye, she saw that Schnark stirred and shook his head.

Marty held her gaze. "I betrayed him, yes. I had given him this opportunity, and then I took it away. Kino had his assistants lock me into a trailer while he set fire to the set. The crew torched everything and Kino filmed his grand finale. It was a miracle no one got hurt. A few hours later, Katz himself arrived by water plane. He found a stoned debauch on the beach, his set destroyed, and his producer locked up. He stopped the production immediately, ordered everybody back to L.A., and demanded to see dailies."

"Wow," Mina said. "Busted."

"Yes, wow. Kino was furious. 'I had my film shut down before, and I will never allow it to happen again, you money-grubbing dilettantes! At least Goebbels had taste!' and so on. In the end, he had no choice but to relent. He realized that screening an unfinished answer print for Katz was his only chance to save his movie. He refused to talk to me, but I was there, two weeks later, when the top brass at Paramount gathered at Katz's mansion to screen the rough cut of *Twenty-Twelve*. Your grandfather was still wearing his goddamn peg leg."

"Penny thought that Kino was at his best in the editing room," Mina said. "She said that's where he worked his magic."

"Maybe. But what he had cobbled together for Katz that day was a three-and-a-half hour long disaster. The picture I had approved was a swashbuckling romance: sea battles and a grand love story and so on. I knew things had gone crazy in Mexico, but I had hoped he'd be able to salvage the footage. What he showed us was entirely different."

"No good?" Mina asked. "None of it?"

"We expected missing scenes and rough editing, that would have been acceptable. But Kino had changed the story. In this version, the handsome pirate captain had turned into a villain. Silko kidnapped Bonnie and took her to his mist-shrouded hideout, and he showed a taste for retribution and violence that certainly wasn't in the original script. There was talk about 'destabilizing the financial system,' and brand-new scenes about a below-deck conspiracy against Silko. Once the Gaia landed on the island, Bonnie was drawn into increasingly tangled pirate council politics, with long discussions about Silko's greed for power and treasure, and what was to be done to defend the constitution of Mulberry Island. It barely resembled the script Kino had handed me in the cab, and it didn't work. My heart sank deeper every time Katz shifted in his seat. It was ponderous and boring. And then it got weirder: on an excursion into the wilderness, Bonnie discovered that the Indians living on the island were descendants of a lost Mayan civilization. They were a tribe of shamans whose prophecies and drug-induced dreams took up a big part of the narrative."

"And that's not what you signed on for," Mina said.

"Damned tootin'. As the movie went on, editing, story-telling, and direction got more and more haphazard. Kino's methods had gotten the better of him. Worst of all, there was no ending. The last half hour barely made sense, a jumbled mess of incoherent scenes intercut with shots from the fire and mayhem he shot that last day, along with scenes he seemed to have swiped from other movies, bits and pieces from assembled newsreels, loose ends he found around the editing room. He even put the Cuban Missile Crisis into the film."

"No shit?" Mina said.

"Language, *Mädchen*," Schnark said. It was the first time he'd spoken since they sat down.

Marty ignored them both. "From what I could gather, Silko's own men attempt to assassinate him during the pirate wedding and Mulberry Cove is burnt to the ground. There was an incomprehensible voice-over by one of the Mayans, and I have no idea what happened to his bride, Bonnie. She disappeared. It was a mess."

Mina wished that she could have seen that movie. Maybe it was the effect of jumping into the pool, or the jetlag, or the lingering effect of the red pills and the coffee, but what Marty described did not sound like the disaster he was making it out to be. She didn't say anything though, and Marty went on.

"Katz was outraged. He stormed out of the screening room before the lights had come back on, cursing like a *Schiffschaukelbremser*. And that was the end of *my* career, too."

"I am sorry," Mina said. Somehow, she felt responsible. "So sorry."

Marty sighed. "Katz took Kino off the picture and fired me. After that night, I never worked in movies again. Thirty years in the industry, over. They had some hack write a new script, reshot a few scenes, and went with the original title. *The Pirates of Mulberry Island* was released in the summer of 1963, and let me tell you, it was a piece of shit."

"The beginning seemed pretty good," Mina said.

"It was shit," Marty repeated. "I'd given Kino a stellar opportunity, and he thanked me by ruining my career. He'd blown it for both of us. Now he'd truly lost everything–even hope."

Mina remembered what Penny had told her about Kino's brains on the movie screen. She was surprised Kino had even gone to the premiere. That they had let him.

"What gets me," Marty continued, "is that he must have known what was going to happen. I don't know why he ruined the movie the way he did, why he stopped caring about success. It wasn't the shotgun blast that killed him, it was the movie–and I gave him the movie. I despised myself."

Mina wasn't sure what to say. Marty had gotten Kino into *Pirates*, let him do as he pleased, and then betrayed him. How different would things have turned out if he hadn't called Katz down to Mexico on the last day of shooting?

Marty was waiting for her to say something, but when she didn't, he made a grimace and went on. "I spent a lot of time replaying Kino's final film in my head–not the botched *Pirates*, but *Twenty-Twelve*, the rough cut he screened for us. I know now that he'd done the only thing he could have. Back behind a camera for the first time in twenty years, he tried to pack everything into this one film, all of his disappointed hopes, his accumulated grief, his wildest ambitions. He turned it into something we weren't ready for, using every trick he had learned, from the expressionists, from the Nazi masters of propaganda, from the commercials, from decades of obsessive viewing. *Twenty-Twelve* contained bits and pieces from earlier stories, scenes pilfered from his other movies, and a strange private mythology. It was reality-warping and prophetic."

"Tell her about the assassination," Schnark said.

Marty gave a sigh. "You want to bring that up?"

"Tell the girl the whole story. That's why we are here."

"In one of the final scenes of the cut Kino screened for us that night, Silko and Bonnie are riding through Mulberry Cove in a horse-drawn carriage. The mutineers send a sharpshooter who tries to pick him off with a musket." He paused. "Do you see?"

Mina shook her head no.

"This was months before Dallas, and it was shot from exactly the same angle as the Zapruder film."

Now Mina understood. "Wait," she said. "You're saying *Twenty-Twelve* predicted the Kennedy assassination? That's just crazy. Besides, in here—" she petted the journal "—he does talk about another murder, in the 1920s, that happened the same way. Somebody was shot in a convertible. It's just a coincidence. Movies can't predict the future."

"You're thinking of Walter Rathenau," Marty said testily. He didn't like being contradicted. "He was killed point blank from another car, and there was a hand grenade."

Schnark leaned forward in his arm chair. "Have you noticed anything since you watched *Tulpendiebe*?" he asked. "Moments of . . . overlap?"

"I haven't had a good night's sleep in I don't know how long," Mina said. "I couldn't tell you what's real and what isn't if my life depended on it."

"Maybe we can agree that movies can be mind-altering," Schnark said, "and Kino was a visionary, one of the greats."

Mina nodded. *Movies like drugs*—who had said that to her? She didn't know what to believe anymore. The Zapruder film? It was all getting more absurd and more intriguing by the minute. She wished Sam could have been there with her, just so she could hear how serious these men were. Dr. Hanno, Penny, they all agreed that there had been something extraordinary about Kino. Mina was surprised by how proud Schnark seemed. She wished she could watch *Tulpendiebe* again.

"Over the years," Marty said, "I've seen snippets of *Twenty-Twelve* everywhere. Your grandfather's last movie anticipated Kubrick, Brakhage, Malick, Lynch. It was a new kind of movie, unfinished, but bigger and truer than anything I'd ever seen. For decades I sat on the suspicion that your grandfather had been on to something marvelous. Cinema promises infinite possibilities, but in reality, it's a factory product. A movie passes through so many hands, and there's so much money at stake, that when you're done you're barely able to remember why you wanted to make it in the first place. Kino tried to stuff something entirely new down our throats. *Twenty-Twelve* was a movie long before its time, and I've come to see its failure as an inconceivable loss."

"I would have liked to see it."

Schnark nodded. "You're not the only one, *Mädchen*. You're not the only one."

Mina rubbed her face and took a deep breath. "Thank you for telling me all of this—it's a tragic story. But none of it explains what happened to me. Where did the print of *Tulpendiebe* in my apartment come from? Who stole it in Berlin? And why are these agents still after me, MPAA, Halliburton, or whatever they are?"

"Well," Marty said, choosing his words with deliberation. "Within certain circles, Kino's work has taken on something of a reputation. There are people in powerful positions who have first-hand knowledge of the *Twenty-Twelve* rough cut, people who would be very curious to see it. Katz's nephew is running Paramount now. They know Kino's films would have changed everything. Unconsciously or not, Hollywood has mined your grandfather's final vision ever since. If *Twenty-Twelve* was released today, it might ruin an industry built on one or two ideas per movie, castrated versions of what's possible. Back then, it could have caused a revolution, mass hysteria, I don't know what."

"You're talking about that PSYOP stuff."

Marty cleared his throat and lowered his voice, as if these things could not be spoken of at normal volume, not even in your own home in the dead of night. "There is a lot of renewed interest in mind-control and psychological warfare. What they call coercive interrogation techniques. Homeland Security is reopening old files. These are people who are intimately familiar with MK/PSYNEMA and the experiments at *Schwarze Sonne,* and they would like nothing better than to pick up that research. These people don't want Kino's work to get out. They want to use it for their own horrible ends, in their own secret prisons."

Mina rubbed her eyes again. The lack of sleep was catching up with her. "But it's all moot because it's lost, right?"

The men exchanged glances again. Marty made a display of checking his watch. "Oh, will you look at that." He stubbed out the end of his cigar. "Would you like some breakfast?"

They moved to the kitchen and turned off the lights—early dawn was falling in through the wall-length windows. Working in tandem, Schnark and Marty set up an impressive German breakfast at the table in Marty's study while Mina watched, not even offering to help: cold cuts, rolls, brown bread, homemade jellies, cheeses hard and soft, soft-boiled eggs, fresh coffee. It was much more elaborate than what she'd had at Dr. Hanno's place, when was it, two days ago? The day before? Mina couldn't tell anymore. Yesterday, it must have been yesterday. Mina was certain of one thing: she was hungry. She reached for a bite of brie. "Where do you fit in?" Mina asked Schnark.

"Don't talk with your mouth full."

Mina shook her head. Something about the way he'd said that reminded Mina of her father–who would be arriving soon, she remembered with a sinking feeling. Who was on a plane right now, furious with her.

"Just answer my question," Mina said, her mouth still full of food. She felt that Schnark was holding something back. Something crucial.

"Well," Schnark said very slowly. "There's a remote chance that–well, *Twenty-Twelve* may have survived. You see, my agency is always scanning the Internet against a series of names and keywords related to our mission. Two weeks ago, we came across an alert about a lot of 'movie memorabilia.' Sketches, storyboards, and a 'canister containing celluloid of uncertain provenance' that went up for auction on eBay. There were photos, including of what were clearly two cans marked MULBERRY ISL. - KINO, with a red border. Marty confirmed that at Paramount, a red border indicated an answer print. Chances are good that this is the director's cut of your grandfather's last movie."

He paused for dramatic effect. "Apparently, John Botha, an assistant editor on the film, was a bit of a pack rat and smuggled this stuff out of the studio. Usually, outtakes, dailies, and answer prints are destroyed, but Botha kept this box and stashed it in his attic. He recently died, and now his daughter is hocking everything."

"What are we doing here, then?" Mina sat up. "You've got to stop them."

Schnark ignored Mina's urgency. "We called Miss Botha and asked her to return the materials to the German people.

She suggested that if the German people were interested in the film, they might want to put up a bid."

"And did you?"

"In fact, I spoke to your father."

"You did?" Mina said. How many lies had this man told her? "Why didn't you tell me until now? What did he say?"

Schnark held out his hand as if to shush Mina.

"He shut us down, your father. He doesn't care about Kino's legacy, cinema, or German cultural heritage. He wanted to know if this had anything to do with that movie you'd been sent, and that's how I found out you were in Berlin."

Mina was processing this. "So who sent me *Tulpendiebe*, then?"

Marty and Schnark looked at each other and shrugged.

"You don't have any idea?" Mina said. "Not a guess? I don't get it. Even now, you don't trust me."

"I trusted you with the journal to help you understand what's at stake," Schnark said. He pointed at her with a piece of *Fleischwurst*. "What matters now is *Twenty-Twelve*. The auction was cancelled two days ago. Irene Botha is not returning my calls, and now, your father is on his way to California."

Mina shook her head. She had lost *Tulpendiebe*. It had been stolen from her hotel room while she was sleeping, but neither of these men seemed to care. They were all about *Twenty-Twelve*, a movie that for practical purposes did not exist—except it did, and it was for sale on eBay.

"You understand that we have to retrieve the print before they do," Marty said.

"I think I get it," Mina said. "It's the little guys against corporate power and government control, right?" She saluted with her fist. "Down with the man!"

But they weren't in the mood for jokes. Mina felt sheepish, always joking around, going too far. Dr. Hanno had not appreciated Mina's sense of humor, either.

"Show Wilhemina the cans," Marty said.

"It's just Mina," Mina said. Her heart was beating fast. What cans?

Schnark left the room and returned with two film canisters that looked exactly like the ones Schnark had described: military green with a red label that said "MULBERRY ISL. - KINO." Schnark sat the canister on the table, and Mina remembered Dr. Hanno's excitement when he first laid eyes on *Tulpendiebe* in her hotel room.

"Go ahead," Schnark said. "Open them."

Mina popped the latches and pulled the loose end of the film strip from the reel. It was wider than *Tulpendiebe* and in color. She held the film up into the light. "That's a pirate all right."

"Yes," Schnark said. "With Marty's expertise, we created reasonably realistic-looking facsimiles of the cans Botha is selling, and we put a *Pirates* release print in there. I don't think anybody could tell the difference at first glance."

"You want to switch this for the real thing. Is that what you want to do?"

Schnark put his hand on her arm. "There is a good chance that your father is coming here for the film. The auction has been taken down, and Mrs. Botha is not answering my phone calls. We may not have much time. Should the opportunity arise, you call me, and we will arrange an exchange."

"You want me to help you steal *Twenty-Twelve*?"

"Find out what your father knows. Can you do that?"

"Of course," Mina said. "But I don't think he cares about the movies." These men acted as if Kino meant nothing to her, as if this wasn't her legacy, too. Seeing the facsimile cans here in front of her, holding the celluloid in her hands, all Mina could think about was how badly she wanted to see her grandfather's tripped-out rough cut. How much she hoped it still existed.

The sun had begun to creep up over the ridge of the hills outside of Marty's window, and it was time for Mina to pick up her father.

Chapter 15

"A convertible?" Detlef asked, instead of a greeting. Mina's father was wearing his customary suit and carrying no luggage except for his leather carry-on bag. He looked overtired, and he was rubbing his face irritably. "And what is that you're wearing? Mina, I am going to have a heart attack by the time this is over."

"Dad," Mina said. "Hi."

She had given Schnark a ride to the airport so he could rent another car, but they hadn't talked much and Mina welcomed the chance to sort through the layers of stories she'd been told. She still didn't know what to make of any of it, but she felt worse than ever for losing *Tulpendiebe*, Kino's first movie. If there was a chance to save his last, the original cut of *Twenty-Twelve*, then she would do whatever was necessary. Marty Wagner's slacks and shirt were just one more reminder of how far she'd already come, to Berlin, into its saunas and over its rooftops, out on the Venice Beach pier and into the depths of her grandmother's murky pool, when all along, she should have stayed in Sam's hospital room. Schnark had taken the fake cans with him and reminded Mina to call as soon as she found out anything about the *Twenty-Twelve* answer print. Then she'd whipped back to arrivals to pick up her father, who was waiting by the curb.

"You'd think your husband doesn't work for a living," Detlef said. "A convertible. The way you spend his money. Your mother and I discussed how much you've wasted on airfare alone. You look ridiculous."

"You're repeating yourself, Dad," Mina said. "Get in already, I can't stay parked here."

Mina was nervous. Nervous and angry. She hadn't seen her father since her catastrophic wedding reception, and she dimly recognized that her anger with him was actually with herself. Seeing her father was an unwelcome reminder that New York was still there, waiting. She'd have to go back and face the consequences of what she had done. She hadn't tried to reach Sam since their last call. Mina had told herself it would be easier to talk to him in person once all of this was behind her. On the other hand, of course, Sam could call *her.* He was not too sick to operate a telephone. If he felt like talking to her, he had her number. Why hadn't he tried to reach her?

Mina popped the trunk for her father. "It's tiny," he pointed out, appalled. "This car won't even fit my bag!"

A uniformed man signaled Mina to move the car.

"Just put it in the back seat, Dad."

"My God, Mina," Detlef said. "What kind of mess have you gotten yourself into this time?"

"We have to go, Dad."

Detlef did as Mina said, a small victory, and got into the car. He waved his hand, imperious. "Take me to the hospital first."

Good, Mina thought. The longer they could stay away from Oma's house, the better. She pulled into traffic. She wanted to ask if he'd talked to Sam, but it would provide her father with one more opportunity to criticize her.

At the hospital, Detlef insisted that Mina wait in the hallway while he talked to the doctors about Penny's condition. Ignoring her father, who was interrogating a nurse down the corridor, she slipped into Penny's room. Chester was asleep by the window, in the same kind of uncomfortable plastic chair that Mina had sat in at NYU hospital, in Sam's room. Mina was surprised at the fondness she felt for this bald black man who fed her grandmother illegal drugs. He had stayed all night with Penny, who lay unconscious, surrounded by a web of wires, controls, displays, drips, and catheters. She looked so fragile Mina barely dared to breathe.

She stood by the bed and watched Penny in silence until her father barged into the room, in the middle of a business call. "Tell Miriam to fax it by noon," he said and snapped his cell shut. Chester grunted in his sleep but didn't wake up.

"Why didn't you ever tell me she was an actress?" Mina asked her father.

Detlef didn't miss a beat."What good would that have done?"

"You haven't told me anything. I didn't know I shared the name of a man who burned his son's books and manufactured mustard gas! I didn't know my other great-grandfather was killed by the Nazis. It's my history, too."

Her father was not a man who laughed a lot, a man who rarely even smiled. Now he sneered, the ugliest face in his repertoire.

"Oh, you believe the stories? You don't think those might be convenient fabrications? Koblitz & Söhne was just a paint factory, and Wilhelm Koblitz was a good man. Father had him burn different books every time he told the story about the bonfire. And don't get me started on the Nazis. I have heard enough lies about those years to last me a lifetime."

Chester stirred in his seat, waking slowly to Detlef's tirade.

"Don't you get it, Mina? Your grandfather was a liar and a coward. He didn't leave the country when Hitler took over. What does that say about him? He was a drunk, in and out of mental hospitals for as long as I can remember."

"I didn't say he was a good father," Mina said. "It's just—"

"They were terrible parents. I grew up hearing them say 'Let's kill ourselves.' They talked about suicide as if it were a big joke. Mom would put her knife down at breakfast and ask him, 'How about today? Do we want to kill ourselves today?'"

"That's awful," Mina murmured. She could believe it, could hear Penny saying those words.

"I believed her. Every day, I came home from school worried I'd find them dead. That was my childhood. It was like growing up the child of Holocaust survivors, except that they were on the wrong side. And finally, when all seemed lost, your grandfather got plastered one last time and stuck a barrel down his throat. I was at boarding school, glad to be as far away from them as possible. Mom sent a telegram telling me not to bother coming home, and believe me, I didn't."

"You should have gone," Chester broke in, rubbing his eyes. "She's your mother. She was suffering. You're her only son."

"Excuse me. I am talking to my daughter. Who exactly are you?"

"My name is Chester Burwell. I am Mrs. Koblitz's personal nurse." He stood up, but Detlef didn't shake his hand.

"I just talked to her nurse," Detlef said. "The nurses here wear uniforms."

"Chester and Oma live together, Dad. He takes care of her. Be nice."

The men glared at each other.

Oma Penny's machines pinged into the silence.

"I want you to explain to me exactly what happened at the house, before she collapsed." Detlef looked from Chester to Mina and back.

Mina nodded. "Yes, Dad. Of course. I will."

"The doctors believe that she could be in this state permanently. If she doesn't improve soon, we have to transfer her to a nursing home."

"You can't do that," Chester said.

"Oh yes," Detlef said. "I can. It's the only sensible course of action."

"You never worried about taking care of her before," Chester said.

"The doctors say there were controlled substances involved. If any of this is true, you might be in for some very serious trouble, Mr. Burwell."

"I'm not going anywhere. I'm staying here with my Penny."

"Do as you please," Detlef said. "But my daughter and I are flying back to New York tonight. And now, we have some business to attend to."

Mina was still thinking about the possibility that Penny would never wake up again, and it took her a moment to process what her father had said. "We are? We do?"

And without so much as another glance at Chester or his comatose mother, Detlef took Mina by the arm and led her out of the room.

"Drive. I'll tell you where to go. We've had too many shenanigans and this is where it ends."

"Where are we going?"

"You'll see."

"I'd like to know."

"Don't push it, Mina."

"I'm not pushing anything. I'm asking a question."

There was no answer. Her father gave her directions, and she grudgingly complied. They seemed to be headed downtown. The sun had begun to heat up the day. Detlef got out of his suit jacket. Mina was sweating in Marty's cotton shirt. She realized that except for the short nap during *Pirates*, she hadn't slept all night, hadn't slept since the airplane. All of a sudden, going home to New York didn't seem like the worst thing. She wanted to rest, go out for dinner with Sam, relax. Eat pizza, drink a glass of wine, breathe. Wear her own clothes.

"Pull up here."

They had reached a sprawling adobe-style building with a clock tower surrounded by palm trees and a parking lot. A church? A mall? No—there was a sign over the arched entrance: a train station. Mina found a spot and moved to get out of the car, but her father put a hand on her leg.

"You can call Sam while I take care of this."

"What are we doing here?"

"Wait in the car and call your sick husband."

"I don't appreciate your telling me what to do."

Detlef shook his head. "You are always fighting me. Mina, the boy's heart is broken." He held out his hand to stop Mina's protests. "I am going in here by myself, so use the time to call him. Tell him you'll be home tomorrow."

Had he said heartbroken? Did he say tomorrow? Mina watched her father cross the parking lot and disappear into the station. She massaged her shoulders and temples and tried to work up the courage to dial Sam's number. There was no answer when she did. She tried the hospital.

"Ah, the runaway bride," the nurse said. "We've been hoping you would call."

"Can I talk to my husband, please?"

"That's what we'd like to talk to you about. Your husband checked himself out this morning, against our urgent recommendation. Dengue fever at this stage can cause permanent brain damage when left untreated. We were hoping that you might be able to talk some sense into him."

Was that a migraine headache Mina felt coming on, or was she in the middle of a nightmare? Had the nurse really said the words "permanent brain damage?" Why would Sam check himself out of the hospital? He wasn't the kind of person to disregard doctor's orders. She tried his cell again but there was still no answer.

"Sam," she said to the voice mail box. "Hey you. You're not in the hospital. What the fuck? Where did you go? I love you, you know that. This is almost over and I'm coming home. Call me, okay, call me, because I am worried."

Mina closed her cell phone. "Damn you," she said in the direction of the train station. What was her father doing here? Where could Sam have gone? Mina watched an overweight woman struggling with a luggage cart. She rubbed her temples some more and decided not to tell her father what the nurse had said.

Against our urgent recommendation.

Permanent brain damage.

Mina was hot, uncomfortable, anxious. She was overtired. She was trying to be good, trying to do what her father said, but she could not stay in the car any longer. She got out and made her way inside the train station.

The place was much cooler than the parking lot, and it was gorgeous. Leather armchairs lined the main hall and chandeliers hung from a tiled, cavernous ceiling, bathing everything in a warm, almost sepia-toned light. It made train travel seem a lot more appealing than the cold, white airport terminals she had been hurrying through for the past week. But it was also as crowded as any airport, and it took Mina some long minutes to find her father in a second large hall. He was waiting by an information booth, flipping distractedly through an issue of *Premiere Magazine*.

Mina hesitated for a moment, watching her father from across the hall. Since when did her Dad read movie magazines? He thought nothing was more frivolous. As Mina watched, a middle-aged woman in a sundress approached him, pointed at the magazine, and shook his hand. What was going on?

"Dad?" Mina said, striding across the crowded room.

The woman twitched and gave Mina a skittish look.

"It's okay," Detlef told the woman. "This is my daughter. Didn't I tell you to stay in the car?"

"You were gone a long time."

"I am so sorry," the woman said. The skin on her face was taut in a way that made Mina think of plastic surgery. She looked pale and harried. "That's my fault. I got caught on the

Santa Monica freeway." She introduced herself as Irene Botha. She kept fiddling nervously with the strap of her yellow handbag.

"You wanted to meet here," Detlef said.

"Yes. Thank you. I've had *visitors*, and this seemed safer. Follow me."

Botha, of course, was the name Schnark had mentioned. This was the daughter of the man who had just died, the assistant editor of *Twenty-Twelve*. Her father hadn't come to California for his daughter or his comatose mother. He was here for Kino's last movie.

Irene Botha led them down the hallway into a side arm of the building, where rows of metal lockers stood beneath tall stained glass windows. To one side, workers on scaffolding were restoring tiles on the vaulted ceiling. Mina blinked, recognizing something she couldn't quite place. Irene Botha produced a key, matched the numbers on the lockers, and found the one she was looking for.

"The material is all here."

"Thank you." Detlef had an envelope ready. "This is a check for the agreed-upon sum."

"Good." Irene Botha glanced anxiously over her shoulders and handed him the key. While she investigated the check, Detlef struggled with the locker door.

"Did you say you had visitors?" Mina asked. "What do you mean?"

Detlef gave her a furious look. She wasn't supposed to speak. She was supposed to be waiting in the car.

Irene Botha turned to Mina. Drops of sweat were running down her temple. "Men came by the house and threatened me with lawsuits if I didn't take the auction down immediately. They implied other consequences. They offered money, but I didn't trust them. I told them they needed to talk to my husband. They watched the house, so I had the police chase them off and decided to bring everything here. I don't need any trouble. I just want to be rid of this stuff."

"So do we." Detlef finally got the locker open. Inside, there was a plastic crate holding two cans of film and a thick manila file folder. Detlef picked up a can: *Twenty-Twelve*. Mina withheld a gasp. Her father was holding *Twenty-Twelve*. This was what he'd come for. The canister looked remarkably like Marty's imitation. Schnark's plan might just work, if Mina could reach him to arrange the switch.

A loud bang echoed through the building. One of the men working on the ceiling had dropped a tool from the scaffolding and nearly lost his balance trying to catch it. The entire structure swayed; it suddenly seemed fragile, ready to collapse at any moment. Mina felt something like déjà vu. She scanned the entrances to the hallway for men in suits— she was suddenly certain that the agents would show up any moment.

"We've got to get out of here," she said, pulling her father by the elbow.

Irene Botha glanced over her shoulders anxiously. "That's fine with me. Pleasure meeting you both." She grasped her handbag, turned, and disappeared into the crowd.

Detlef threw his issue of *Premiere* magazine into a nearby trashcan and lifted the crate holding *Twenty-Twelve*. "This way," he said, directing them to the closest exit.

"No," Mina said. "Not past the scaffolding."

He ignored her and kept walking.

"Dammit, Dad, you've got to listen to me for once."

Detlef threw up his arms. "Fine. Which way?"

Mina pointed in the opposite direction, back past the information counter where she'd found him waiting for Irene Botha. Detlef shrugged and gave in. They walked so fast they were practically running. Mina stayed behind her father. She clandestinely flipped open her phone and speed-dialed Schnark's number. They had the movie. They had *Twenty-Twelve*. She couldn't believe it. But Schnark wasn't picking up. Instead, she got a generic robot voice repeating the number she had dialed.

The moment they turned the corner into the main hall, a rumbling welled up behind them, a terrible roaring, screaming, crashing noise that echoed around the building's vaulted ceilings. People stopped and turned. Detlef gave Mina a quizzical look, but she kept pulling him on toward the exit.

"Just keep going, Dad."

The convertible's trunk wouldn't fit the crate with the movie cans, and Detlef crammed it into back seat next to his carry-on. He tapped on the dashboard while Mina hit redial one more time. Where was Schnark? Why didn't anybody ever pick up?

"Come on, Mina, we've got another appointment."

Mina put the phone away and turned around in the driver's seat to inspect the cans. "Just a minute."

"Mina, leave that old junk. We're in a hurry. You can look at it later. Right now, you want to get back on 101 and head north." He checked his watch, dialed a number on his phone, and confirmed a two o'clock appointment with a Mr. Katz.

"You're kidding me," Mina said. "We're going to see Katz? At Paramount? That's the guy who ruined Opa's movie."

"His nephew, actually."

"We just found the answer print of *Twenty-Twelve*, and we're taking it to Paramount?"

"We're just having a little chat to see what they can offer."

"'What they can offer?'"

Mina's father lowered his voice, a register he reserved for real anger. "You think I want this junk? I'm his son, this is my property, and we're selling it. Now drive." He flipped on the radio and scanned through the static until he found Frank Sinatra, doing "Coming In on a Wing and a Prayer." Mina got on the freeway. Next exit, Hollywood.

Mina felt dizzy. "No," she said. "No, no, no. This is what you came for? To pick this up and hock it? You didn't come for me or your mother, you came just to get rid of this movie? You're here to make a deal?" She spit the last word like a curse.

He shrugged. "I am a man who makes deals, yes."

"Don't you even want to see the movie?"

"Why would I want to do that? There was a mention of low six figures. That's a lot of money for doing nothing."

"It's not for nothing. It's for a lifetime of work and you're hocking it like so much crap."

"It *is* crap, crap that will pay for the new kitchen your mother has been wanting for a long time now. What do you know about the value of anything? You never learned anything useful in your life. If you play your cards right, you'll get a share of the money. You can pay off your loans and keep playing Bohemian without driving your husband into bankruptcy. How would you like that?"

A truck honked when Mina tried to change lanes. She had the sinking feeling that events were getting away from her for good. Schnark had been right about the film, but he had underestimated her father's brutal efficiency. There wouldn't be time to exchange the cans; the studio couldn't be far now. Mina would have to save *Twenty-Twelve* from the vaults. Without it, she'd never know if any of the things they were saying about Kino were true. Without it, Sam would never understand why she had to go to Berlin, to California.

Mina didn't expect *Twenty-Twelve* to change the world, but maybe it could save her marriage. Sam had left the hospital, defying doctor's orders. Why the hell would he leave the hospital? Was this how it all ended? Had her grandfather's work blipped back into brief existence on her doorstep and some random attic just to be swallowed up again by an entertainment conglomerate, or worse, some secret government program run by Dick Cheney? Where was Dr. Hanno now? Where was Inspector Schnark?

"We need gas," Mina said, tapping at the gauge. There was still a quarter tank left, but she knew her father never let it get to the red. Anything to gain a little time.

They got off the freeway and stopped at a gas station. While her father filled the tank, Mina tried to call Schnark one more time, but it just kept ringing. They drove on. Detlef was done talking, and Mina had nothing left to say. She felt defeated. She went down Melrose Avenue much slower than she needed to, and then her father told her to turn right on a street that led up to the Paramount gate. Mina had seen it before, in the movies. It looked taller to her than the Brandenburg Gate. A uniformed guard was waiting by the booth. Her father had led her straight to the people who had been chasing her all week.

This was it. Mina had run out of time, run out of options. She knew that without the film, the world would seem diminished. If she delivered *Twenty-Twelve* to Katz, one avenue of possibility, some unnamed potential, would be gone forever. She drove past the turnoff.

"Hey!" Detlef snapped. "Damn it, Mina. How could you miss that?"

"We're not going."

"What do you mean, we're not going? Turn around."

"No," she said and pulled the car over onto the shoulder. She had no idea what she was doing. She hoped something would come to her, anything to save *Twenty-Twelve.* An SUV sped by, leaning on the horn. The California sun was burning down on them in full force now. Mina felt a wet spot on her back where she had sweated through Marty's shirt. Her throat was dry. She turned off the car.

"Mina," her father commanded. "Stop playing around. We're late for Katz. Take us to the studio. This is not the time to throw a childish fit." He got out of the car, opened Mina's door, and told her to get out. He pulled on her arm. "For god's sake, Mina, get a grip on yourself. It's only a movie!"

"That's where you're wrong, Dad."

Mina leaned over and opened the glove compartment. Next to the rental car papers and some chewing gum a previous customer must have left was Inspector Schnark's stub-nosed revolver. Its weight felt good in Mina's hand. Had Schnark fired five or six shots? She couldn't be sure that there were any bullets left, but that didn't matter now.

She leveled the gun at her father.

"It's more than just a movie," she said.

Chapter 16

Subject: I Feel Like a Huge Asshole
From: mina.koblitz@gmail.com
To: samiam@eclecticarts.com
Date: Wednesday, May 14, 2003

Sam, where the fuck are you? Why aren't you answering your phone? Maybe you'll check your email at least. You always check your email.

Listen, baby. I feel wretched about everything. I don't even understand what happened, and I don't understand where you could have gone. They told me you checked out of the hospital. Why would you do that? You're still sick, and they said it could lead to permanent brain damage. Are you ok? For all I know, you're lying on the street somewhere in your hospital gown, without identification, hallucinating. Please call me. Why haven't you called?

I know this whole thing has been a fucking joke, but I had to do it—try and find out about my grandfather's movies. If you'd just call me, I could explain it to you, and then you can forgive me and we can have our life back, ok? Why won't you call? I know you were angry at me for going to Germany, for coming to California, but I needed to do this. We're married, Sam. You can't just run away like that and disappear.

I don't think I've ever felt like such a failure. I've had my hands on two of Kino's movies, I watched one of them, and now they're both gone. My grandmother is in a coma, that guy Schnark disappeared, and I pulled a gun on my father. He was about to sell Kino's last movie to Paramount, and I tried to stop him.

But I couldn't shoot my father. He knew it and I knew it. He took the gun out of my hand, slapped me across the face, and carried the film through the studio gate on foot, by himself, while I waited in the sun, holding my cheek and weeping. Dad sold everything. Not just the stuff he'd gotten from Botha's daughter, but all of grandfather's work in perpetuity, along with all related materials, storyboards, screenplay drafts, costume sketches, all filmed stock, negatives, and prints of previous rough cuts. All of Kino's ideas, everything he'd ever made, he signed over to them, and then he gave them *Twenty-Twelve.* Before anyone could watch it. Gone, deep into some fucking studio vault. We buried him twice, Sam.

Oh, and get this: the German police busted Dr. Hanno with *Tulpendiebe.* They found him and that weasely projectionist at the film museum in the middle of the night, digitizing the film and burning DVDs. It was Dr. Hanno who robbed me after all. That lying sniveling German piece of shit! Now that print, wherever it came from, is being sent back to Paramount, too. I almost wish he hadn't been caught. I still don't know who left the movie in our apartment in the first place. Or why.

If I could take it all back, I would. We were supposed to be on our honeymoon, still. It's not my fault you got the Dengue fever. I love you. It might not seem that way to you, but I do. I know what I'm supposed to do now. I'm supposed to come home and be your good wife and wait until you reappear.

But Sam, here's the thing... the thought of our apartment kills me. All those unopened wedding gifts, all of your things. Our bed. I don't think I can take it, being there by myself. As long as Oma Penny's in a coma, until I know you're back and I know that you forgive me, I'm going to stay here in California. Please call me already, baby. I'm worried sick about you.

M.

Chapter 17

Mina visited her grandmother every day, alternating shifts with Chester. She sat in the chair by the door and watched Penny's chest rise and fall, listening to the ping of the life support machines and the soothing chatter of the nurses in the hall. Penny looked surprisingly peaceful. In a coma, she was much easier to like, to love, even.

For the first week or two, Mina found it comforting to write long emails to Sam. She detailed every little thing that she had done–what she ate for dinner, what Penny's doctor said, the new clothes she had bought–hoping that he might be checking his email, wherever he was.

She also wrote to Sam's parents, but their response was cryptic and to the point: "We are sure Sam will get in touch with you in due time." Did that mean they knew where he was? Did it mean they weren't worried? Clearly, they were angry with her. Mina tried calling, but they wouldn't pick up and didn't return her calls. She called Eclectic Arts and found out that Sam had gone on indefinite leave, "to travel." She asked where he'd gone and when they expected him back, but they didn't have an answer for her.

"He's just fucking with me," Mina told her unconscious grandmother, to see if she could believe the words if she heard them spoken out loud. "He's hiding somewhere, trying to show me what it feels like. He'll be back." Sam adored her. He had *courted* her.

He'd also sounded so disappointed with her the last time they talked. He'd said, "I just don't know anymore." That's what he'd said. Had that been an ultimatum? She'd rushed right past it, so eager to see Penny. Didn't she deserve another chance?

She saw him in her dreams, in strange places she didn't recognize, sometimes happy, sometimes furious, spitting anger so harsh that it woke her up and left her wondering for minutes where she was. She had dreams about *Twenty-Twelve*, about the tulip notary, about the sauna and the train station, Penny and her drug dealer, the murky pool, water rushing up her nostrils. In the mornings, she tried to remember every detail, hoping, perhaps, for a hint of where Sam might have gone.

Her father had presented her with an exhaustive, self-righteous list of failures: she was a disappointment as daughter, student, and wife. He'd made Mina feel awful, but he also didn't seem to mind that she was staying in Oma's house. It made it easier for him to leave if Mina kept an eye on his mother's condition. It was a relief for Mina when he flew back to New York and she hadn't spoken to him since.

She arranged to get her grandmother's pool cleaned, and she grew comfortable around Chester. "You can stay here as long as you like," he'd told her. He cooked meals for them, huge pots of gumbo and red beans and rice, food from New Orleans, where he was born. "Your Oma," he said, "she doesn't like to eat. Just pills and alcohol. I tried to feed her but you saw how she could be." Mina knew she was supposed to make conversation with Chester, take interest in his life, but she didn't. She ate his food and let him clean up after her as if she were a child.

She spent a lot of time walking on the beach by herself, swimming laps in the pool and watching movies on the big TV. She often stopped by the DVD store and picked up anything that remotely reminded her of Kino. She couldn't help thinking about what had gone into making these movies, whose ideas had been stolen, whose dreams were being altered, and whose lives had been ruined in the process. Why had *Tulpendiebe* appeared on her doorstep? Why had Schnark vanished when she'd had *Twenty-Twelve* in her back seat? Mina didn't ever expect to make sense of it. Dr. Hanno had stolen one movie from her, her father had taken the other, and her husband was gone. Mina was recuperating, as if from a bad illness.

In her grandfather's study, Mina found old photos and newspaper clippings, including Fritz Lang's obituary, a fawning profile of Billy Wilder, logs of Kino's cab fares, and an old Leica camera. On a whim, she took the camera to the hospital and took portraits of her comatose grandmother. The old woman was so pale, blue veins showed through the translucent skin of her face. Her mouth hung open a little too wide, revealing yellowed teeth; there were tubes stuck into her nostrils. But something about the angle and the shape of her cheekbones and the light on her forehead reminded Mina of images of another Penny, in another sick bed, taken almost seventy years earlier. Mina still couldn't make sense of how Lilly with the porcelain skin and the saucer eyes had become this acerbic junkie widow who'd be lucky if she ever woke up again.

Mina hated that word, widow, but she couldn't deny that she had become something of a widow herself. There was no telling what kind of harm a man with lasting brain damage could do to himself in New York City. There were a million ways to die: passing out on a subway platform and falling under the train, stepping in front of a speeding taxi, plummeting into the East River. Mina did not want to be a widow. She had barely been a wife.

She kept hoping for Sam to call, for Oma to recover, for someone or something to show up and make sense of what had happened. She got a tan without trying.

When the phone finally rang, Mina couldn't place the tentative male voice that spoke through the distant crackle. For one brief moment she allowed herself to think that it was Sam.

"Frau Koblitz? If you have a minute, I would like to talk to you."

It was Dr. Hanno. Mina's chest filled with righteous anger. How did that treacherous thief find the nerve to call her?

"Wilhelmina?" he said.

"You? You lied to me. You broke into my hotel room. You stole my movie. I hope you're in prison. Are you in prison?"

"I had to pay a fine. Listen, Frau Koblitz, I did not enjoy doing what I did, and I am calling to apologize to you." It took him a long time to get the last sentence out, as if he were struggling with the words. Mina got even angrier.

"Well, I hope they fined you silly. I hope they drive you into bankruptcy. You stole my movie. What the hell were you thinking?"

"What I did, I had to do." Now there was something different stirring in Dr. Hanno's voice. He was getting annoyed. "You didn't like the movie, didn't understand its genius nor its importance. You were going to let the studio take it away. I did it for K–"

Mina cut him off. "Are you not paying attention? The studio took the film anyway. It's back in their vault, along with *Twenty-Twelve* and any other scrap of his they could find, and there isn't a thing that you or I could do about that. So, robbing me was pointless. You didn't have to lie to me. It didn't make a difference. I thought you liked me. Why did you lie to me?"

If she was honest with herself, Mina had to admit that she strangely respected Dr. Hanno for stealing the movie. Yes, he'd been busted, but she had delivered *Twenty-Twelve* directly into the hands of the enemy. At least he'd tried.

"I didn't mean to upset you–"

"Dr. Hanno, my husband is gone, along with everything else. My life's a mess." Even as she said the words, Mina wondered why it didn't feel that way. She was on the patio by the pool, munching on a grilled cheese sandwich Chester had made.

"Please. You must believe me. I am calling to say I'm sorry. I am sorry for what I did. It's just–I'd like you to understand why I had to try to save the movie. I knew what would happen, I saw it coming, and I tried to stop it. Do you understand that? I am sorry about your husband."

Mina blinked a tear away. Either Dr. Hanno was quite an actor, or he really meant it. Then she remembered that she had been certain he was innocent the morning after the robbery.

"Well, I appreciate it, Dr. Hanno, but I should go now."

"Of course, of course." He sounded relieved to be able to get off the phone, too. Except: "There's one more thing."

"What's that?"

"This man Schnark. Can you tell me more about him?"

Ah, Mina thought, her anger welling back. This call wasn't about the apology at all.

"Why?"

"There's something–I don't know how to put this. Do you remember how he introduced himself to you?"

"He said he was inspector of a special branch of the federal government, something about cultural crimes."

"There is no such thing."

"Well, he said it was a secret branch."

"Frau Koblitz, trust me: there is no such thing. When was the last time you talked to him?"

"Not since the morning my father arrived in L.A. He never answered his phone. I had *Twenty-Twelve* and didn't know what to do about it. He simply disappeared."

"Do you have his phone number? Could you please give it to me?"

"It's useless," Mina said. "He doesn't pick up. I've tried."

"Please?"

Fine. What did she care? Mina was going to be late for her visit at the hospital. She gave Dr. Hanno the number.

"If you get in touch with him," she said, "will you let me know?"

"Of course. And Frau Koblitz? I hope to see you again one day. Goodbye now."

"Auf Wiedersehen, Dr. Hanno."

Chapter 18

And then one day, after Mina had been in California for almost three months and President Bush had just told the insurgents to bring it on, two things happened.

First, a certified letter arrived after breakfast. It was addressed to her, at Penny's address, with her full name on the envelope: Wilhelmina Koblitz, c/o Penelope Koblitz. Inside, there were forms emblazoned with official seals. Supreme Court of the State of New York. Dissolution. Settlement. Financial Affidavit. Mina had to leaf through the pages three times before she figured out that these were divorce papers.

She went back into the living room, where she'd been eating cereal and watching *The Third Man*. The form was already counter-signed on the line with Sam's name. Location and date indicated Zanzibar, Tanzania, two weeks earlier.

Mina felt dizzy, and she wasn't sure which word she understood less: divorce or Tanzania. She inspected Sam's signature closely. Something about it seemed wrong to her. Zanzibar? What the hell was Sam doing in Africa?

She called Sam's parents, and this time, they answered. Sam's mother curtly told her to sign the papers and send them back. Yes, Sam was in Tanzania. He had transferred the lease to the apartment to them, and Mina had two weeks to get her stuff before they tossed it.

"Didn't Sam have anything to say to me?" Mina asked. She always thought that Sam might have loved her more than she'd loved him, but he'd also been her best friend.

"I'm sorry," Sam's mother said. She sounded like she meant it. "I guess you kids weren't ready for this."

"But—" Mina said.

Sam's mother cut her off. "Good luck, Mina. If Sam wanted to talk to you, he'd talk to you."

"Goodbye," Mina said and sat for a long time and stared at the papers. What did it mean if she signed her name on this line? That she had never loved Sam? That it had all been a mistake? And why on earth did he sneak out like that, without even talking to her? Didn't she deserve that much? Zanzibar!

Then, for a moment, she allowed herself to think that it was all for the best. She'd been let off easy. Maybe Sam's mother had been right. If they'd stayed married, the same exact thing might have happened in slow motion, Mina drifting away and throwing herself into whatever adventure offered itself while Sam's love eroded over the years until, eventually, she'd be left with the same forms to sign. How different would Kino and Penny's lives have been if they hadn't stayed together? Their marriage had outlasted terrible times but it certainly didn't bring them happiness. There weren't any guarantees, ever. Maybe Sam hadn't been too sure about Mina either, wondering all along if he was doing the right thing. Now he was traveling. He was in Africa and Mina was in California.

Yes, she nodded to herself, maybe it was for the better, even though she already missed him. Sam used to be the only one who'd understand her. That's what she was signing away—but no, she corrected herself, no, she'd given that up already. It was her fault, Mina realized, it had been her fault all along. She'd gone to Berlin, she'd toyed with Dr. Hanno in the sauna, she'd kissed the sailor on the pier. She had no one to blame but herself, and she would miss Sam terribly. When she finally felt the tears come, Mina signed quickly, folded the papers along their creases, and stuffed them in the prepared envelope, addressed to the Supreme Court of the State of New York. There, all done, with the stroke of a pen: she was an ex-wife. She wouldn't cry for long. She found a blue pill in Oma Penny's cabinet that would help with that.

Later that same day, during Mina's shift at the hospital, Penny opened her eyes, blinked, coughed, and slowly focused on Mina. "Where's Chester?" she said.

"Oma," Mina said. "You're awake."

Penny spat, half of it landing on a catheter and dripping down in a gooey streak. "Of course I am awake," she said. "Where is Chester? Why am I in a hospital? Get me Chester."

"He's back at the house," Mina said. "We'll get you back there as soon as we can and take care of you, okay?" She wiped the spittle from her grandmother's mouth, thrilled to see the old bat awake, already up to her shenanigans again.

The doctors were stunned at Penny's recovery. They were cautiously optimistic about her condition. Chester was ecstatic. Penny would need time in the hospital to recover, and before long, she got used to seeing Mina every day. It seemed, Mina thought, as if Penny even looked forward to her visits. Mina took more photos, too, and Penny enjoyed the attention. She had once been a movie star, after all.

Sometimes they watched TV, but when there was nothing on that Oma Penny liked, Mina would ask questions about her life. She learned that Penny couldn't stand Kino's friend Steffen, and that it was true that she had thrown a marble ashtray at Orson Welles. "The fat bastard had it coming." Penny shrugged.

Mina also learned that Kino had left a note before he splattered his brains all over the screen at the El Ray theater.

"A note?"

"Yes, princess, a suicide note. It's common practice among the suicidal. You don't know about that?"

"What did it say?"

"It was a lousy note, really. Pathetic."

Along with excitement, Mina felt a pang of sorrow; Sam hadn't left her with anything but divorce papers. He'd gone to Africa and left her behind without so much as a farewell.

"Do you still have it?"

Penny shrugged. "Threw it out a long time ago. But I still remember what it said." She made a grimace. The thought of it seemed to disgust her.

"Okay," Mina said. "Would you please tell me?"

"*This is the Constitution of Mulberry Island: Anything is Still Possible.* It was written on a kind of parchment, probably a prop or something, with quill and ink."

"That's it?"

"That's it. Signed, Kino. I ask you: what kind of thing is that to write on a suicide note? He was a dumbfuck and a romantic to the last. Down to his bitter grave! Did you know that on the night he offed himself, he wore a pirate outfit and that ridiculous wooden peg leg?"

Chapter 19

Finally, Mina was wearing the exactly right clothes. Short denim skirt, hat, sandals, a tank top. She felt good and looked good, which somehow mattered, even when pushing Penny's wheelchair through the lobby of her Santa Monica nursing home. Mina carried Kino's old Leica over her shoulder; Penny was rifling through a stack of black and white prints, all of her, from an earlier photo shoot.

"That one's not bad," Mina said.

"Ach," Penny said. "Like a corpse!"

At first, Mina barely recognized the man standing in her way, holding a bouquet of roses, and when he didn't move, she whacked him in the leg with Penny's chair. She'd learned quickly that pushing a wheelchair gave her the right of way in all instances, and she expected people to move. But this man here, he just stood there, obstinate, with his roses. Then she realized it was Inspector Schnark, minus the red leather coat, just in badly cut jeans and a tucked-in polo shirt. The look on his face had been contrite, but now he was wincing in pain. Penny's wheelchair was heavy, and Mina had hit him in the shin head-on.

He collected himself quickly. "Frau Koblitz," he said, addressing Penny, kneeling to her level, and offering her the flowers.

"What," Mina interrupted him. "No tulips?" She took the flowers from Schnark's hand and passed them on to a passing teenage girl who was sullenly following her parents through the lobby. "Ooh," the girl lit up, "thank you!"

"I need to talk to you both," Schnark said, ever so slightly slurring his words.

"Have you been drinking?" Mina asked.

"I have something for you. Please?"

Mina snapped. "Where the hell were you? I had *Twenty-Twelve* in the car and you didn't pick up your damn phone."

"I can explain—"

"I had the movie!"

Penny reached for Mina's hand. "I know this man," she said. She spit over the side of wheelchair, aiming at a potted plant. "He came to my house, years and years ago, asking questions. I didn't like you then. Go away. *Hörst Du nicht? Verpiss Dich!*"

"He told me he was an inspector for a spy agency that doesn't exist," Mina said.

"He said he wanted to interview me for a book," Penny said, "but it was all lies. He's an imposter. Let's go, girl. Go." Penny reached for her wheels herself and aimed her chair at Schnark again. This time, he got out of the way, but stumbled and almost fell. Mina used the opening to push Penny past him and through the nursing home's sliding exit doors. A path lined with benches led past a fountain toward the beach promenade. Detlef hadn't called or come to visit his mother, but at least he was paying for a classy nursing home.

"Wait up, please!" Schnark was having trouble keeping up with them. He was fumbling with the top of a silver flask and stopped for a furtive swig. Mina had been right—he'd been drinking. Over her shoulder, she said, "Maybe it's time for the truth, Schnark."

"That's why I'm here," he said, catching up. He was out of breath and one of his shoes was untied. "I am so sorry I lied."

Mina stopped pushing and turned to him.

"Did you know that my husband left me? I got divorced over all of this." The words sounded false to Mina, but her anger was real.

"I didn't know that. I am sorry." He stopped to lean on a garbage can and catch his breath. "You got me good, with that chair. My name isn't Schnark. It's Jupp. Jupp Koblitz."

Penny strained in her seat to turn around and get another look at him. "You're Heinz's son?" She spit again, this time into the bushes. "Let's keep going, princess. We don't want anything to do with this man."

"Wait," Mina said. "Your father was Kino's brother Heinz? You're my father's cousin?"

"No," Schnark—or Jupp—said. "I'm not."

"Named for Kino's younger brother," Penny said. "Jupp died in the estate fire. Heinz made it out without a scratch, and I bet he figured the least he could do was name his son after him."

Mina looked at the man she'd first noticed at Tegel airport, after the bomb scare. Now he was here, drunk, claiming he was family. She didn't know what to think.

"Heinz was always the one who made out fine when others suffered," Penny said. "Always the better business-man, too, even back in twenty-three, twenty-four. When Kino ran out of money, Heinz bought his shares in Koblitz & Söhne for dollars. Kino was living the high life while Heinz consolidated control over the family business. He moved the company to Berlin because that's where the real money was.

He made political connections that guaranteed him a handsome share of Germany's rearmament."

"You mean Heinz was a Nazi?"

"Long before it was fashionable." Penny pointed at the flask Jupp was sipping from anxiously. "What do you have there?"

"Asbach Uralt," he said.

"I'll have a nip."

The man whose real name appeared to be Jupp Koblitz handed Penny the flask. "Not here," Mina sighed, looking around for nurses who might object. She pushed Penny toward the beach boardwalk. It was the nicest place for an old person's home Mina could have imagined—except for all the old people. Penny took a deep swig.

"Keep talking, Oma," Mina said, worried the alcohol might put her out.

"Heinz showed up to the premiere of *Jagd zu den Sternen* in uniform," she said, "and that was in nineteen-thirty. He claimed he had nothing against the Jews—he was supporting Hitler strictly for business reasons. Ha! His wealth was second only to Stinnes. But the greedy son of a bitch was always jealous of Klaus and his starlets. His wife Cornelia was a frigid bore, and Heinz was smitten with our world. He made a pass at me once—I never told Kino. He kept showing up at film parties and the restaurants that mattered. Everywhere he went, he threw money around, introducing himself as Kino's brother."

On the oceanfront, bikers, skaters, and rollerbladers oozing health zipped by in the golden late afternoon light, dodging old people with walkers and wheelchairs. There was a fresh breeze. A swarm of surfers was bopping in the water, waiting for a wave. Jupp sighed and massaged his temples.

"After my father was arrested," Penny went on, "we relied on Heinz and his connections for news. He loved it, the power. The son of a bitch made us suffer and wait and beg and grovel. It was Heinz who finally brought news that my father had been killed, in Bergen-Belsen."

"That man was not my father," Jupp said, with barely contained anger. "You're right, I was named for Kino's younger brother, and yes, I grew up thinking Heinz and Cornelia Koblitz were my parents. But that man was not my father."

Penny shifted uneasily in her wheelchair. "I don't want to hear any more of this. Take me back upstairs, princess. Oma needs her medication."

Jupp ignored her. "It's true that I grew up believing I was his son. Heinz did well for himself after the war. Denazified Germany needed leaders, and he became one of the stewards of the *Wirtschaftswunder*. He groomed me to take over Koblitz & Söhne, but I rebelled against him for as long as I can remember. I was barely eighteen when I left town, lived in communes, traveled, got married. I owned a bar in West-Berlin and didn't hear from my family until Heinz died, in 1989."

He took another drink. "After Cornelia's death—what did you call her? A frigid bore?—Heinz remarried and had three more children. When he died, he split the company and his wealth between them, and I inherited the key to a safe deposit box. Guess what I found?"

"Princess, please? You know what the Dokters said about my blood pressure. This man is lying."

Mina shook her head. "I want to hear this. What did you find—*Tulpendiebe?*"

"Not just *Tulpendiebe*. In the climate-controlled vault of the bank, Heinz had kept prints of all of Kino's films, twelve altogether. There was also a birth certificate stamped *Streng Geheim* that showed I wasn't born in a hospital." From a small leather backpack, he took a yellowed document in a protective plastic sleeve. "The Nazis kept immaculate records. Here, it indicates I was born at Plötzensee Prison." He took one more deep drink. "And Penelope, it says that you're my mother."

With a screech, Penny propelled herself out of the wheelchair and lunged at Jupp, trying to get a hold of the document. The two of them tumbled to the ground, struggling.

"Help!" Jupp yelled. "Get her off me!"

Mina took the document from Jupp's hand and held it out of reach. "Stop it," she said. "Stop fighting." People were beginning to point and stare, and after a few more moments of frenzied grappling, Mina managed to separate the two. She helped Penny back up. The wheelchair had fallen over, and Mina pulled Penny onto a bench overlooking the ocean. Jupp sat down next to her, breathing heavily. Mina thought he was awfully out of shape for a detective, only to remind herself that of course, he was no detective. He was–her uncle?

"My God," Jupp said, rubbing a long red scratch on his arm. "You know how to fight." He passed the flask back to Penny before Mina could say anything. Mina righted the wheelchair, sat in it, and wheeled up next to them. "This is amazing," she said, studying the swastika-adorned document. "This says you had him on June 9, 1943. It doesn't mention the father."

Penny's eyes were aimed somewhere above the horizon, and she began to choke with tears. Nobody spoke. Finally, she cleared her throat. "Oh, the melodrama," she said. "It's like a scene from *Meine wilden Wanderjahre*. Klaus would've been proud."

Mina found a prescription bottle in the wheelchair's side pocket, shook out two pills, and handed them to her grandmother, who downed them gratefully.

After a long pause, Penny began to speak.

"I got pregnant the night we tried to leave Germany, on the sleeper train to France. We thought we were leaving everything behind, but they recognized us and we were arrested. Isolationshaft, you know what that means? I didn't see another soul the entire time. I had the baby in prison, starved, desolate. There were bombs the night you were born. They drugged me and showed me a dead baby. They told me it was stillborn, the umbilical cord around his neck like a noose. I knew they were lying. I screamed and screamed. They just gave me an injection and locked me up again."

Penny paused, looking sideways at Jupp.

"I don't know how many days or weeks I spent in a haze of grief and hatred. Finally, Heinz came into my cell to tell me he had secured our release–provided we left the country and never returned. He told me it was our only chance."

"He sent you and Kino away," Jupp said, "but he kept me as his own. Cornelia couldn't have children."

"How could Heinz get away with this?" Mina's head swung back and forth between Jupp and Penny. Her family.

"In 1943, people had more pressing concerns than following other people's pregnancies, and dead babies were easy to come by," Penny said. Jupp was staring out over the ocean, as if he weren't listening at all.

"He took Jupp, and he kept the movies, too."

Penny made a throaty noise as if she were about to hock up a mouthful of spit, but then she just sighed. "Letting us live, that was the cruelest punishment of all." She began to sob.

Mina had watched Penny's drug-induced seizure and spent weeks staring at her in a coma, but this, here, was the most vulnerable she'd seen her, weaker even than as the Duke's moribund daughter. Of all her accumulated grief and dark secrets, this was the one she'd guarded more than anything. Mina wondered if Penny's frail body felt any different now that they knew. Jupp put his arm around Penny but she pushed him away. "You were never mine. You belonged to that Nazi swine who took you away. You were born in a cell and I never held you, not once. I was never your mother!"

Mina put a hand on Penny's shoulder, hoping to calm her down. She could not imagine what it must have been like, pregnant and alone in a Nazi prison, and to lose the child.

"Why didn't you tell me sooner?" Mina asked Jupp.

"The time wasn't right. Heinz died just after the Wall came down, and my wife was divorcing me. My life was a mess, and I wanted nothing to do with this past. I got as far away from it as I could—Morocco, Corfu, India. During a rave in Goa, I finally realized that I couldn't keep on running. I returned home and found a *Doppelnocken* projector."

"You have seen all the movies?"

"My father's films became my burden and my only pleasure. I learned how to store them and watched them over and over again. I found something comforting in them, and I made them my home. They were all I needed."

"You didn't want to find your real family?"

"Oh, I tried. I came to your house in Connecticut, pretending to be a biographer. Detlef could barely contain his scorn, and he refused to be interviewed. I knew I had nothing in common with him, my angry little brother. I remember you, too, coming home on a bicycle just after he shut the door in my face. I wished I could have told you who I was."

"I don't remember that," Mina said. She was rocking herself back and forth in the wheelchair.

Penny stabbed her finger in Jupp's chest. "You're a coward, just like Kino. Just like Detlef. That's what the three of you have in common."

"You threw me out, too," Jupp told her. "Screaming your head off before I could get a word out. Of course I didn't come back. I swiped my father's journal from the study, and I found Marty, who told me about *Twenty-Twelve.*"

Mina waved for the flask, took it from Jupp, and had a drink herself. The cognac burned in her throat.

"So you sent me *Tulpendiebe.* Why?"

"Kino's movies taught me that timing is everything. When your wedding announcement turned up in the *New York Times* the same week the Botha auction went online, I suddenly knew what to do. Coincidences are the world's way of winking at you."

"I'm in the phone book."

"You came to Berlin because of *Tulpendiebe.* It showed you cared. Your heart was in the right place. That's why I trusted you with the journal."

Mina felt a familiar anger rise in her throat. "If you were testing me, you fucked up good. I screwed up all around. I let that prick Dr. Hanno steal *Tulpendiebe* out from under my nose, remember? I took *Twenty-Twelve* straight back to Paramount. You're an idiot."

Something else occurred to her, something that made her even angrier. "What about the bomb threat, that day at Tegel? Who was that?"

Jupp avoided her eyes, nervously unscrewing and rescrewing the top of his flask. He took another sip.

"You're fucking kidding me, right? That was *you?*"

"You left in such a hurry. I hadn't had a chance to—"

Mina cut him off. "I don't want to hear any more. You're nuts. You could have just sent me an email and explained things. Maybe then we didn't have to lose the movies, and I didn't have to lose Sam." Her voice trailed off. She was determined not to cry in front of them. She reminded herself she was much too angry to cry. If only it hadn't all been such a waste.

Jupp put the flask to his lips again, but it was finally empty. He was looking out over the beach, still avoiding Mina's eyes.

"Well," Penny said, shaking her head. "I've had enough fun for today. Take me back to my room, princess."

Mina got up, glaring at Jupp. "Of course, Oma. We're done here."

The sun was low over the horizon, casting long shadows on the boardwalk. Jupp cleared his throat. "The convertible was a stroke of genius."

"What do you mean?" There was a glimmer of something in Jupp's eyes that got Mina interested in spite of herself.

"You must have known I followed you from the airport to the train station, right?"

Mina shook her head. It hadn't occurred to her.

"Your trunk was too tiny for the cans and you left them on the back seat. Remember you stopped for gas, your father went inside to pay, and you tried to call me? It gave me just enough time to swap the film."

"You switched the cans and I didn't notice? You're saying I pulled a gun on my father over a fake?"

"You did it for Kino. Just like I knew you would. It was noble. We did it, Mina."

"You son of a bitch."

"Exactly," Penny said.

Mina was still processing this. "You manipulated me and—wait. You have *Twenty-Twelve?*"

"Well." Jupp grimaced. "For a professional, Botha did a terrible job storing the film. I spent the last three weeks in

Berlin, with your friend Dr. Broddenbuck. We've been able to salvage only fragments."

"You saw Dr. Hanno?"

"He happens to be a very talented digital restorator. His DVD transfer of *Tulpendiebe* is outstanding. He hid a digital master from Katz's goons, and we transferred the other movies on museum equipment. Most of the films look great, but *Twenty-Twelve* is in bad shape. It just sat in the humidity of Botha's attic and rotted away."

"And good riddance," Penny said. "Come on, Mina, it's getting cold."

The sun was indeed setting. Mina transferred Penny back into the wheelchair. From his backpack, Jupp produced a black metal box and a small silver chain with a key.

"This key opens the film vault in Frankfurt," he said, "and this is a hard drive with digital transfers of the movies. Everything we have is on here. I want you to have it. I can't be alone with them any longer. It's what Kino would have wanted."

Mina took the key and the hard drive. "*Tulpendiebe* and *Twenty-Twelve* are on here?"

"What's left of it, yes—as well as his other films."

"Oh." Mina didn't know what to say. All of this running around, and now she just got Kino's movies handed to her? All she could manage was "Thank you."

"Thank you?" Penny hissed. "Girl, have you not learned a single thing? Don't you understand Kino will cause you nothing but grief and pain?"

"Oma," Mina said. "Don't you think they've already done their damage? I lost Sam over these movies. The least I can do now is watch them, no?"

Penny turned away from both of them, as far as her wheelchair would permit.

"I'll trade you one cranky woman," Mina said, letting go of the handles. "Take her back upstairs, will you?"

Penny protested. "Don't leave me alone with this liar!"

"Come on," Mina said. "I bet you like him a lot better than your other son – the one who hasn't called you once since you've woken up?"

Penny spit and gave Jupp a sideways glance. "Do you have any more Asbach?"

Mina squeezed the hard drive into her bag and gave Jupp a hug. He reeked of cognac. "If you like, come by the house for dinner tonight. Chester's cooking."

Jupp gave her a grateful nod. Mina watched as her uncle wheeled his mother away.

Chapter 20

Mina lost no time hooking up the portable hard drive. Neatly labeled folders contained digital masters of all of Kino's films, the Weimar and Third Reich ones as well as *Twenty-Twelve*, and Mina resolved to watch them in chronological order, starting with *Tulpendiebe*.

This time, she saw the film differently. Parts that had seemed ridiculous and slow to her were now imbued with accidental poetry and optimism. There was love in the way the camera gazed on sick Lilly's pallid face, eyes wide with innocence of everything they were yet to see. Mina sat up all night in the upstairs study, at Kino's wooden desk, looking out over the pulsating grid of Los Angeles' lights. Hollywood was out there, but she had something even better.

Mina watched all of Kino's Weimar output that same night, transported to Jupiter, the jolly vineyards of the Rheingau, and *Land der Gnade's* utopian jungle village. Every movie captured Mina's imagination more than the one before, and Penny, so young and beautiful and talented, was riveting. That she never acted again and her performances went unseen seemed, to Mina, every bit as tragic as Kino's thwarted ambition.

The next day, Chester went to visit Penny, and Jupp, who'd spent the night in one of the spare bedrooms, joined him, apprehensive and hung-over. Mina returned to the study to watch the rest of her grandfather's movies. *Luftschiffwalzer* and the other operettas struck her as limp, forced, with a busy surface that pretended to entertain but betrayed a terrible sadness underneath. For all their countryside picnics and glittering balls, the actors looked as if they were suffocating in their evening gowns and Prussian uniforms.

Mina was glad when she finally made it through *Tanz in den Wolken,* the last of the Third Reich films, and opened the folder containing *Twenty-Twelve.* Unlike the other films, there wasn't one large master file, but a numbered collection of shorter clips that Jupp and Dr. Hanno had salvaged from Botha's reels, a few of them five or six minutes long, but most around the minute mark and some even shorter. Instead of cueing up the fragments in order, she opened them at random, shuffling through them, grasped by the urgent need to know what, exactly, was left of Kino's last movie.

She recognized a few moments from the studio release version of *Pirates,* sometimes with added lines of dialogue or shot from a different angle, cut in a more jarring, haphazard way that made it seem as if they were part of a different narrative altogether. Other scenes, from the back lot set and filmed on location in Mexico, were entirely new to Mina. There were bits that belonged to a subplot about a mutiny, and there was talk about an ancient prophecy. Many of the scenes had a raw beauty that Mina hadn't seen in the cheesy material that was used for the recut release version. Some of them appeared to be outtakes. Mina also found scanned pdf files of a modified screenplay draft. She recognized her grandfather's jagged scrawl on the marked-up pages.

But the more Mina clicked, the more she realized that she had less than half of the film, in discolored pieces, jumbled and scattered. The thought that she would never get to see *Twenty-Twelve* whole made her feel defeated.

What was it the studios had been so afraid of? Was it something that had been lost, cut, rotted away in Botha's attic? Mina didn't expect to find out, and she began to understand what Kino had said about his films: they were beyond anyone's control.

What interested her now was only the film itself, the images on the screen in front of her. She couldn't get enough of them. She was thrilled to discover footage of the set fire Marty had described, the riot in Mulberry Cove, slightly overexposed images of Darius Silko and his bride Bonnie riding in a carriage, men in robes praying and chanting, and news footage of President Kennedy, giving Castro his ultimatum.

Mina also found a short clip of a man in his sixties, standing in the surf at night, illuminated by a row of tiki torches, the waves lapping at his ankles. He was wearing torn pants and a frilly purple blouse, his face covered in stubble and his gray hair long and dirty. He was waving a cutlass and speaking directly into the camera. One of his legs was covered by a thigh-high leather boot; the other was a simple peg leg, so thin that it had to be real. With a jolt, Mina realized that she was looking at Kino.

With an unmistakable German accent, he declared: "On the eve of Mulberry Feast, the ghost of Grapefruit Silko, legendary captain of the Gaia, Schrecken der Sieben Weltmeere, dead for a hundred years, appears in the waves to convey a message of hope and love to his heirs."

Mina leaned in closer. Kino rubbed his face and scratched his stubbly beard. He was hamming it up. "The volcano that looms over Mulberry Island leads down to the absolute unchanging core of the world," he said. "Remember: no matter what, Mulberry Island remains. Anything is still possible." Someone, possibly Marty, mumbled something off-camera, and Kino waved them off angrily. "Cut!" he shouted, and the screen went black.

Mina rewound the clip and hit play again. She stared at her deranged grandfather, in awe of what he had tried to do.

Word from the doctors was that Penny would be able to return home soon. Chester and Jupp were becoming unlikely friends. They claimed the back patio for after-dinner cognac and told stories of their respective lives—which was fine with Mina, who stayed up late every night, rereading Kino's journal and rewatching his films. She began toying with video editing software and learned how to burn the files onto DVDs. The films looked terrific on the large screen downstairs. She researched video codecs and file sharing protocols and downloaded open source transcoding software. After some false starts and wasted hours, she managed to compress Jupp's digital masters into high-quality divx files and seeded them on thepiratebay.com, one of the hub bit torrent trackers operating out of Sweden.

When Mina hit upload on the last file, she poured herself a Dewar's and watched the progress bar creep upwards as the first leechers jumped on the torrent and began downloading Kino's movies. Katz and his goons would be up in arms—and if Jupp and Marty had been right, even the government would take notice. It was risky, but once the movies were out there, nobody could ever lock them away again.

Mina had become a pirate.

The next day, a film critic in London blogged about the lost German films that had appeared on the Swedish tracker, and a number of movie sites picked up on the story, reblogged, aggregated, and propagated it. Downloads surged. Full-length versions became available for streaming and in mobile formats. When the sites hosting the movies were threatened by cease and desist letters, the torrents disappeared briefly, only to pop up again on other trackers.

Initially, *Jagd zu den Sternen* and *Tulpendiebe* were the most popular. A meme developed around the sailor's eating of the tulips, and film students in Chicago reenacted the scene on YouTube. Mash-up clips appeared and were, in turn, blogged about. But over time, more and more people kept returning to the zipped archive containing the surviving fragments of *Twenty-Twelve.* An online community began clustering around the film's husk, recutting scenes according to their own theories, mashing up the footage with found bits and reenactments that were meant to fill narrative holes, redubbing dialogue that didn't fit their version, voting on their favorites, and doing it all over again. Most of the fan-made videos lacked finesse, some were filmed in backyards, basements, and dorm rooms, some were animated, and some were brilliant. *Twenty-Twelve* had escaped into the wild, a constantly procreating mutant film that belonged to everyone.

Mina understood that her grandfather's final film had always been an invitation to be altered, a film that chafed at all constraints and was right at home in a distributed network where it could grow into an ecology of stories, a coral reef of ideas that multiplied and morphed into a common repository of dreams and desires until, perhaps, one day they might align perfectly–and then, Mina wondered, what would we see?

Every night, Mina sat alone in Kino's study, assembling the images in her own way, combining the snippets on the hard drive with footage from the Internet. She found pleasure in the structuring, teasing out shifting meanings and new narrative possibilities, searching for the hidden rhythm that governed the events on screen. She knew that if she worked hard enough and put the right scenes in just the right order, she would arrive somewhere, and *Twenty-Twelve* would find its ending. Sometimes, near the edges of the frame, Mina thought she caught sideways glimpses of Sam.

ABOUT THE AUTHOR

Jürgen Fauth is a writer, film critic, and co-founder of the literary community Fictionaut. His short stories have been published in a number of journals including *Chiron Review*, *La Petite Zine*, and *Berkeley Review*. He is a long-time film critic for About.com and has written for *Huffington Post*, *New York Newsday*, and *Flavorpill*. A native of Wiesbaden, Germany, he lives in Astoria, N.Y., with his wife, the writer Marcy Dermansky, and their daughter, Nina.